The Book Of DeMao

By: Charae Lewis

The Book of DeMao

Published by It's Timeless Publications

"Thankful for my papa, nigga taught me how to get it. Gotta make sure my brothers is eating I'ma split it."

-Bryson Tiller

ONE

Camara sat next to her bay window, exhaling smoke from her nose. Her body was riddled with rage as she looked into the inky night sky. Her eyes roved down to the screen on her phone and noticed it was five minutes after three o'clock in the morning. She had been calling her husband, Kiyan, for over an hour and he had yet to return her calls. Camara wished that this wasn't a weekly routine. She wished she didn't have to stay up, wondering if and when Kiyan would come home, but somehow, this had turned into a jaded, weekly ritual that she'd grown weary of.

"I swear I'm sick of his shit," she muttered before taking another pull from her blunt.

Camara had never been a smoker, but these days, she'd welcomed any vice to help soothe her frazzled nerves. She and Kiyan's marriage had been on the rocks for a while now, and she had run out of options for them to get back on the right track. Long gone were the days of marital bliss and fulfillment. She once looked at her husband with pure adoration. Now that had been replaced with resentment and detestation.

Camara's thoughts were suddenly halted when she heard the alarm beep. She quickly put out the blunt and stood to her feet. Her hands were planted on her hips as her heart rate sprinted to a rapid tempo. Camara was prepared for a fight; she was ready to confront her husband of four years for his terrible behavior.

Seconds later, Kiyan entered the bedroom with bloodshot red eyes, alerting her that he too had been smoking. He was handsome with toffee-colored skin, almond-shaped eyes, and full lips. His thick, kinky hair had grown into a small 'fro, accompanied by a kempt beard. He stood at six feet even with an athletic frame that used to drive Camara insane. But now, not so much.

Kiyan smirked at Camara, prompting her anger to spread like a wildfire.

"Why you smoking in the bedroom?" he asked, taking off his jacket.

The nerve!

Camara stared at him, wondering why he couldn't get it right. Their relationship had started off rocky, but after she bore their first child, he swore that he would do better. Now here they were back at the starting point of their union, and she was completely fed up.

"Why the hell are you just now coming home?" she seethed, not bothering to hide how upset she was.

Kiyan dismissively waved his hand and ambled into their walk-in closet. Camara quickly followed after him.

"So you're not going to answer me?" she hissed.

He offered her an uninterested expression before saying, "I was at the bar with Dinero and Big. Now leave me the fuck alone."

"The fucking bar closes at two o'clock, so why the hell are you just now getting home? Do you think this shit is acceptable?"

"Yeah, it is," he shot smugly.

Camara was appalled as she jerked her head back. It seemed as though Kiyan was becoming more disrespectful by the day.

"Oh, so, I can come home after three o'clock in the morning too? If so, just say the word."

Kiyan shrugged. "Shit, if you want to. I really don't give a fuck what you do," he responded casually.

"That's the difference between me and you. I respect you, but you continue to give me your ass to kiss. Since when has it been okay for a married man to come home whenever he feels like it?"

"Cam, you don't give me a curfew. Shit, actually I can do whatever the fuck I wanna do. I'm a grown-ass man, and I don't need another mama telling me when and what time to come home."

Camara chuckled bitterly. "You're really fucked up in the head if you think as a married man you can do whatever you want."

Kiyan smirked. "Why you wanna argue with me?"

"Why the fuck you keep disrespecting me?" she countered.

He rubbed his hands down his face. "This is why I hate coming home. You're a fuckin' nag. All you do is complain and quite frankly, I don't want to hear that shit. I give you everything you want, and you're still not happy. That's some crazy shit to me."

Kiyan’s words stung, but Camara refused to display how hurt she was. He wouldn’t care anyway because somehow, he had become unaffected by her sadness.

“Well, I wouldn’t complain if you did what you were supposed to do as a husband and a father. You leave me to do everything while you carry your ass on like you don't have a family. The only thing you do is pay the bills and give me a fucking headache. If you think you're a fucking joy to be around, you're sadly mistaken.”

“Can you get out? I at least want to take a shower in peace without hearing your bitchy ass.”

Camara grabbed the cologne bottle that was sitting on the dresser and hurled it at his head. Kiyan ducked just in time for it to hit the wall.

“Aye, if that shit would've hit me, I would've whooped your ass,” he threatened.

“Fuck you,” she spat before stomping back to the bed.

Camara snatched her phone off the nightstand and walked out the room. She headed down to the guest room and decided to sleep there. Kiyan had no regards for her or her feelings, and that left her with a feeling of dejection.

As Camara laid down and covered her legs with a comforter, tears slid from her eyes. She had spent many nights crying and wondering when things were going to get better. She had prayed, fasted, and hoped for her marriage to improve, but the fact was her union was deteriorating right before her eyes, and she didn't know how long she would be able to hold on before she completely threw in the towel.

***

Keece kissed Paris' collarbone before he trailed his lips up to her neck. She squirmed and giggled from his touch as he pulled down her panties.

"Keece," she whined. "You know the kids will be knocking soon."

"This ain't gon' take long," he whispered, pecking her lips. "Just be quiet."

Paris bit her bottom lip and nodded. Keece successfully pulled her thong off and slid his boxers down. He positioned his penis at her opening, but before he could slide in, there was a knock at their bedroom door.

"Fuck," he groaned.

"I told you," she said laughing.

"Who is that?" Keece yelled.

"It's me. I want some cereal," requested their three-year-old son, Deuce.

"Go ask Kya to make you some," Keece demanded.

When the couple didn't hear a reply, they got back to their original task. Keece plunged into Paris' wetness while sucking on her bottom lip. She opened her legs more to provide better access.

"You feel so good," he mumbled in her ear before licking it.

"Mmm, you're gonna make me yell out," she murmured.

"Don't," he ordered, pinning her legs back. "I have to get this nut out, and I don't need the kids to think I'm in here killin' you."

Paris tittered before grabbing his face and devouring his lips. Keece was deep into her center, feeling like his orgasm would approach at any second. He picked up the pace and began to hammer her. He was on the verge of cumming but before he could release, there was another knock at the door.

"What the fuck?" he grumbled. "Who is it?" he yelled out.

"It's Parker. Someone is at the door."

Keece rolled his eyes before pulling out of Paris. She poked her lip out and then smiled.

"Ain't shit funny, Paris," he quipped, pulling his boxers over his glazed manhood.

"I'm not laughing," she chortled.

Keece stomped toward the door and snatched it open. His five-year-old daughter stood wearing her pink nightgown and furry slippers.

"Someone's at the door, Daddy," she said once more.

"A'ight," he replied, marching down the staircase.

Keece advanced toward the front door and opened it. His visage immediately contorted into a grimace once he stared at his daughter's mother, Riley. They had dated for years before Keece went to jail, and she cheated on him. When he was released, he found out that Riley hid their daughter, Kya, from him for two years. Ever since her betrayal, Keece lost all respect he had for Riley. It also didn't help that she was a half-assed mother as well.

"Why you at my door?" he clipped.

Riley shifted her weight to her left leg as she peered at Keece timidly. "I wanted to get Kya for a couple days."

"Yo' ass was supposed to get her two days ago," he reminded her.

"I know, but I was out of town at this hair show and couldn't catch a flight back in time."

Always got a fuckin' excuse.

Riley typically put her career and personal agendas before Kya, and Keece loathed it because he and Paris always had to clean up her mess.

"Let me see if she wanna go with you, and don't show up at my house without calling first."

"I called Paris' phone, but she never answered."

Keece closed the door in her face and walked to the kitchen where Kya was sitting at the island eating cereal.

"Kya, do you wanna go with your mama?" he asked, leaning on the counter.

Her eyes seem to light up instantly. "Yes, I do."

"A'ight, she's at the door. Go brush your teeth and get dressed."

Kya jumped from her seat and raced upstairs. He hated how Kya was always excited to be with Riley, but she never showed the commitment in being consistent with her motherly duties.

"Daddy, Kya going with her other mama?" Deuce asked with his mouth full of cereal.

Keece smirked at the miniature version of himself. Deuce was his junior that he had prayed relentlessly for. He was so proud to have a son after being in a house full of girls.

"Yeah, why? Are you gonna miss her?"

Deuce smiled. "Yeah."

"That's what's up."

After five minutes, Kya came back down, holding her overnight bag. "I'm ready, Daddy."

"Do you have your phone?"

"Yes."

Keece nodded and followed her to the front door. Kya opened it and jumped into her mother's arms. He would've appreciated the gesture if Riley didn't try to play Kya all the time.

"Hey, baby," Riley gushed.

"Have her back here on Monday," he ordered.

Riley nodded. "Okay."

"Bye, Kya. Call me later, a'ight?"

Kya ran toward Keece and hugged his waist. "Bye, Daddy."

He kissed her cheek. "Don't forget to call me."

"I will. Bye."

Keece watched as Riley and Kya got in the car before he closed the door. He checked on Parker and Deuce before going upstairs to finish what he and Paris started. When he entered the bedroom, he was surprised to see that she wasn't in bed. The door from their en suite opened, and Paris came out wrapped in a towel.

"Where you going?" Keece questioned.

"I have to go get my hair and nails done."

"Come on, baby," he groaned. "I need you to handle this." He pointed to his private area.

Paris giggled. "I can't honey. I'm already running late for my hair appointment, and this is the second time I had to reschedule this week. I can't miss this."

Keece shook his head, not liking how he had to walk around with blue balls until Paris came back home.

"Damn, Paris, I won't take long. My nut is sitting at the tip of my dick."

She chuckled, walking up to him. She kissed his lips, causing his manhood to grow even harder.

"I got you, baby. As soon as I leave the shop, I'm coming straight home to take care of you."

"Fine," he grumbled.

"Who was that at the door?"

Keece plopped down on the bed. "Riley's trifling ass."

"Oh, she finally showed up to get Kya. I saw that she called me, but my phone was on silent."

"Yeah, she came. I wish I didn't have a baby with her ass. She really be fuckin' Kya over."

"I know," Paris agreed, "but Kya loves her mama so we kind of have to deal with it. All we can do is continue to pick up the pieces whenever Riley drops the ball."

"Or she can disappear." Keece grinned.

Paris gave him a knowing look. "Keece, no. Don't do that."

As badly as he wanted to get rid of Riley, he would never take her away from Kya even though she wasn't shit. The most he had done was get full custody of Kya.

"I'm just playing," he said even though he had toyed with the idea of making Riley disappear permanently before.

"Good."

Paris went inside their walk-in closet to get dressed. Keece grabbed his phone and replied to a few text messages. He made plans to go see his father, Dom, soon since he had been asking him to come by.

"Maybe I'll take the kids to go see him," he muttered out loud.

After ten minutes, Paris entered the bedroom wearing an olive-toned Ivy Park bodysuit with the matching leggings. Her toes were propped in some clear sandals and her jet black tresses were bone straight with a part down the middle.

After five years of marriage, Keece was still strongly attracted to Paris. Her slanted eyes always pulled him under a spell. Her glowing skin was the shade of peanut butter. Paris' face was completed with a small nose, high cheekbones and lips so big Keece couldn't help but to suck on them.

"Aye, come straight home."

Paris grabbed her purse, walked over to him, and pecked his lips. "I promise to come straight to you."

Keece watched her walk out before he got up to take a shower. While Paris was gone, he planned to take Parker and Deuce to see Dom.

***

Diar smiled as she gazed at the screen while FaceTiming her fiancé, Case. He was telling her about his day of tattooing and while she was trying to be a listening ear, the only thing she wanted to hear was when he was coming home. His thick curls were covered with a Brewers snapback. She marveled at his sienna skin that was free from any blemishes. Case's deep-set eyes displayed how tired he was with bushy eyebrows posing over them. Diar stared at his bow-shaped lips that were encompassed by a perfectly lined goatee. After years of being together, Diar was still captivated by his charming presence.

"You listening to me?" he quizzed.

"No," she grinned. "I'm actually admiring how fine you are."

He blushed a bit. "Stop gassin' me up."

"You know you're sexy as hell. When are you coming home?"

"I told you already; on Monday."

Diar sighed dramatically as she rolled her eyes. Case was a well-known tattoo artist who traveled often. Ever since he appeared on Inked Magazine, his clientele had skyrocketed. Diar was beyond proud of him and the career he'd built for himself, but she missed her man terribly.

"Why do we have to go through this almost every week?" he asked.

"Because I want you home. I need you to stop traveling so much so you can be here with me. And yes, I'm being selfish as hell."

He chuckled. "Stop being a brat."

"I'm not," she countered. "I just want you home. I'm tired of sharing you with everybody. I get so jealous when I see you out having fun without me."

"Diar, chill out. I'm going to have a break soon."

"When?" she spat. "Are you even going to show up for our wedding?"

Case shrugged. "Maybe."

Diar glared at him before smacking her lips. "You know what? I'm about to hang up on your ass."

"Alright, alright, alright," he said all in one breath and then laughed. "I'm just fucking with yo' sensitive ass."

"That's not funny to me. One of my biggest fears is being left at the altar."

Case smirked. "I would never do that to you. I can't wait to be your husband so you can get on my nerves even worse."

She chortled. "I ain't that bad."

He twisted his lips. "That's what you think."

"Whatever. Well, let me go. I have to go meet my mom at some shop for flowers. I'll talk to you later, baby."

"A'ight."

Diar ended the call and went into the bathroom to curl her hair. In just three months, she would be Mrs. Case DeMao. Their journey together had been one for the books, but after spending three years together, they were finally ready to make it official.

Once her hair was styled to her liking, Diar grabbed her purse and slid her feet into some slides before she walked out the door. She got inside her truck and headed to the flower shop. When Diar arrived, she spotted her mother's car right away so she parked next to her. She stepped out and walked inside the place that was filled with an array of flowers. Her mother, Tina, was standing by the register, so she approached her.

"Hey, Mama," Diar greeted her.

Tina spun around with a smile on her face. "Hey, sweetie. I'm trying to get you a deal on these Gardenia flowers for the wedding."

Diar chuckled. "You're always trying to get a deal, Mama."

"I don't pay nothing at full price. Plus the owner knows me so I think she'll work with me."

Diar took a seat in a chair and released a deep sigh. Between her job and the wedding, she hadn't had much time to unwind and take a break.

"You tired, sweetie?" Tina asked.

Diar tipped her head. “Yes, I actually can’t wait for this wedding to be over.”

“Well, you're the one who wanted a huge wedding. You could’ve gone to Jamaica or something to get married.”

“No, me and Case wanted a wedding.”

“Speaking of Case, where is he?”

“He’s in Vegas. He was booked for a tattoo thingy for the weekend.”

“He’s been busy a lot lately,” Tina noted. “How are you handling it?”

Diar peered at her mother with a small simper. “Truthfully, I hate it. He’s never home, and when he is, he’s still busy. I don't want to keep complaining to him because I know this is the career he wanted. Plus, I would never want him to feel bad about working.”

Lately, Diar had been feeling like she wasn’t Case’s main priority. He had become so busy with his work that she sometimes felt like she was last on his list. She knew it wasn’t intentional, but she still missed being with him.

“Do you think he will slow down after the wedding?”

Diar shrugged. “I hope so, but I doubt it. I don't see him slowing down anytime soon.”

Tina rubbed her shoulder. “Distance makes the heart grow fonder, so don't be so down.”

Diar sighed as she pondered her mother’s words. It was easier for Tina to say don't be down when she wasn’t the one going to sleep by herself at night. Diar wanted Case home more often and despite her trying to be mature about the distance, she didn't know how long she would be able to deal with Case's schedule.

TWO

Asia sat on her knees as she watched Dinero sleep peacefully. He laid on his back, snoring lightly as his pecs rose and fell. She glanced over at her four-year-old daughter, Mila, and put her index finger to her lips. Mila smiled sneakily before covering her mouth with her little hands. Asia's eyes landed back on Dinero as a faint smirk graced her face.

"Dinero!" she bellowed.

His eyes fluttered open as his body jumped. He glowered at Asia as Mila's giggles sounded through the room.

"Oh, baby, did I scare you?" Asia feigned concern. "I didn't mean to."

"Why the fuck you playing?" he groaned with reddened eyes.

"Because it's after one o'clock in the afternoon, and it's time to get up. I'm about to put a stop to you hanging with Kiyan because you seem to think it's okay to come home whenever you want," she ranted.

Dinero smacked his lips as he turned over. His tattooed back was now facing Asia.

"You ain't gon' do shit, now get out."

"Daddy, you said you were taking me to the movies today," Mila reminded him.

"I said tomorrow."

"No, you said Saturday," Mila countered.

"Today is Friday," he lied.

Asia chortled. "Stop trying to play my baby. She's knows it's Saturday."

Dinero groaned and covered his face with a pillow. "Damn, y'all getting on my nerves today. A nigga can't sleep in for shit."

"I let you sleep in but it's time to get up. Besides, I need to talk to you about something."

"Daddy, are we going?" Mila questioned.

"Yeah, go get dressed," he replied begrudgingly.

"Yay!" Mila ran out the room with glee.

Asia took the pillow from his head. "Dinero, I need to talk to you."

Without saying a word, he got up from the bed and marched to the bathroom. Asia followed after him and watched him lift the toilet seat to take a piss.

"So, you know my grandma has lived in the Philippines, but she recently lost her house due to a bad storm. I want her to move here with us, so she won't have to struggle anymore. Plus, she's getting older, and I just want to be there for her."

Dinero was still quiet as he flushed the toilet. He then stepped over to the sink and grabbed his toothbrush. Asia stared at him as he turned the faucet on. His long dreads hung in the middle of his back. His penny-toned skin was blemished with a couple scars on his arms. He possessed tattoos that adorned the upper half of his toned physique. Dinero peered at her through the mirror with his deep-set eyes. His handsome mug was completed with a straight nose, darkened full lips, and a thick beard.

"Did you hear me?" Asia asked.

"Send her some money to get her shit fixed 'cause she ain't coming here," he declared before inserting the toothbrush in his mouth.

Asia's jaw descended. "Why not?"

Dinero scrubbed his teeth as Asia waited in disbelief for his response. After minutes of silence, he spit in the sink.

"We don't have no room for her."

She sucked her teeth. "Dinero stop playing. We have plenty of room."

He smirked and then rinsed his mouth out with water. He grabbed a towel and wiped his lips. "Why you won't send her ass to Big and Aimee's house? That's Aimee's grandma too, shit."

"Because they already have a full house with all the kids. Besides, we have the space. There are three extra bedrooms in this house."

"And they all 'bout to be occupied. I'm making another man cave, a room for Nero, and shit, the last room is gon' be storage or some shit."

"Really Dinero? You're making a room for a damn dog."

He smirked. "Yeah, my lil' nigga needs his own space."

"Dinero stop being an asshole. She can go in the room downstairs near the kitchen."

He walked out of the bathroom, prompting Asia to follow after him.

"I'll think about it," he hissed. "You always trying to be Mother Teresa and shit. Her old ass bet' not get on my nerves, or she's going straight to the nursing home."

Asia smiled brightly. "Thank you, baby. My grandma is so sweet. You won't even know she's here."

He waved his hand as he plopped down on the bed. "I ain't trying to hear all that shit. Just make sure she stays out of my way."

Seconds later, Mila returned wearing a fluffy rainbow skirt, rain boots and a denim jacket. Her hair was styled in braids with beads at the end.

"I'm ready Daddy."

Dinero glanced at her and immediately frowned. "Girl if you don't go take that Dolly Parton-ass dress off."

Asia cackled. "Dinero stop. I think she looks cute."

"I like this, Daddy," Mila defended.

He shook his head. "I don't like that fluffy ass skirt."

"She looks like a little girl, so stop complaining. She actually did good picking out her own outfit. Stop being so damn mean."

Dinero snorted, grabbing his phone. "Whatever."

"Mila, did you brush your teeth?" Asia asked.

"Uh…I'll come right back," she said then ran out the room.

"She was about to be all at the movies breath hot as fuck," Dinero fussed.

Asia chuckled as she stood and walked over to him. She climbed on the bed and straddled him. She leaned down and kissed his lips softly. His hands immediately found her ass and began to caress it gently.

"When you come back from the movies, I'll have something wet waiting for you," she purred in his ear and then kissed it.

"Give it to me now," he requested in his usual impatient fashion.

"No," she pecked his cheek. "When you get back."

"Well, then get your ass off me."

Asia tittered as she stood. "I'm going to get some editing done while you two are gone. I'll be upstairs."

Asia traveled to their third floor where she had converted it into her office and closet. She did some of her photography duties there. She was so relieved that Dinero had agreed to allow her grandmother to move in. Asia as well as Aimee wanted to take care of her, and they weren't able to do that with her being in the Philippines. This was her maternal grandmother, and they both felt like they would be honoring their late mother by making sure their grandmother was completely taken care of.

***

Big descended the stairs and entered the kitchen where his wife, Aimee, was cooking breakfast. His children, Zaria, DJ, and two-year-old twins, Devyn and Dylan, were seated at the table waiting anxiously for their plates. Big stepped behind Aimee and kissed her cheek. She squirmed at his touch and turned around to face him.

"Where are you going?" she asked, noticing that he was dressed.

"I'm going to take my mama to her dialysis appointment. I'll probably sit with her too."

"Has she adjusted yet?"

Big shook his head. His mother, Elle, had been on dialysis for one month, and she was still having a hard time getting used to it. Usually after her appointments, it caused her to become fatigued, and she couldn't do much except lay down.

"Nah, she hates it, but she don't have no choice but to do it."

"I wish I could go, but I have to drop DJ off at his karate classes and then take Zaria to gymnastics. I don't want to bring the twins up there because they'll probably mess up the clinic," Aimee joked.

Big eyed his twin girls as they both tried to escape their high chairs. "Man get off my twins. They ain't that bad."

"Well, take them with you then," she challenged.

He snickered. "Nah, I'm straight."

She pushed him playfully. "Exactly. That's what I thought."

He kissed her lips sensually. "I'll be back later."

"Bye, baby."

Big walked over to the table and kissed all of his kids. "DJ, I'm going to come to your next practice, okay?"

DJ nodded. "Okay."

"I'll see y'all later."

Big walked to the garage and hopped in his truck. He always had to mentally prepare his mind to see Elle because she had been so down since she'd started dialysis. When they were notified by her physician that her kidneys were shutting down, Big became fearful. He felt like he had just gotten his mother back after years of her battling an alcohol addiction. Elle had been sober for almost five years, and she seemed to be loving life, up until now.

After a fifteen minute ride, Big pulled up to Elle's house. He got out the car and used his key to let himself inside. The smell of cinnamon hit his senses as he ambled into the kitchen. Elle stood over the island, sipping on some piping hot coffee.

"What's up, Ma?" he greeted with a kiss to the cheek. "You ready to go?"

"Yeah," she groaned. "Not like I have a choice."

Big peered into her big brown eyes with a sympathetic expression. Her salt and pepper hair was slicked into a sleek ponytail. Her dark brown skin was complimented by the berry-toned lipstick she wore.

"Cheer up, Ma. You'll be a'ight, plus I'm gonna sit with you."

She smiled. “You're so sweet, Dakaden, but you don't have to. I know you have a lot to do.”

“I made sure everything was straight so I can be with you today.”

Elle sighed. “I can’t wait until I get a transplant. I don't know how long I can go through this. I'm so tired afterward and my muscles cramp so bad that I can barely stand. Not to mention, the nausea and vomiting. It’s really the worse.”

“Why you won’t let me give you a kidney?” he queried.

“No, honey. You need both of your kidneys. What if your kids need one in the future?”

Big chuckled. “Ma, you thinking too much. My kids gon’ be good. Don't speak that on them.”

“I'm not. I just don't want to take one of your kidneys. Even Danica offered but I just can’t take from my kids. I've put you guys through enough already.”

Elle often felt guilty of her alcoholism because she wasn’t able to raise her children. Big never held it against her and still treated her with love because she was his mother.

He wrapped his arm around her shoulder. “Stop talking like that. Me and Danica ain't thinking about your past. Right now, we’re concerned about your health, a’ight?”

She nodded. “Okay. Let’s go so we won’t be late.”

Big grabbed her bag of books while Elle grabbed her purse. The two walked out of the house and got inside the truck.

He said a silent prayer hoping that the side effects wouldn't be too severe, because he didn't want to see her in any discomfort today.

***

Keece studied his father, Dom, as he winced while holding his shoulder. Dom didn't look like his usual vibrant self. His silky fade had grown out a bit and his goatee could use a shape up. Dom's face had been balled up ever since Keece had arrived with Parker and Deuce, who were sitting in the living room watching Teen Titans.

"You good, Pops?" Keece quizzed.

Dom rubbed his shoulder. "Hell nah. My shoulder and jaw has been hurting for days."

"Why you won't go to the doctor?"

Dom snorted. "So they can kill me? Fuck that. I hate hospitals, and if I'm ever unconscious or in a coma, pull the fuckin' plug."

Keece chortled because his father had always been against going to the doctor.

"So you're going to sit in pain and complain about it rather than go get some medicine?"

"Man please," Dom waved his hand dismissively. "That medicine they're prescribing is killing people. Shit, the side effects are worse than the got-damn symptoms. I'll pass."

Keece shook his head at his father's pig-headed ways. "Stubborn ass old man."

"Whatever. How ya' mama doing?" Dom asked, changing the subject.

"She's good. I think she's in New Orleans with Carlos this week."

Dom chuckled. "She still hates me?"

Keece smirked. "You know that won't change. It's always gon' be fuck you."

Keece and Dom burst into a fit of laughter. Rochelle would forever despise Dom for keeping her from her sons when they were growing up.

"I deserve it though," Dom muttered. "I'm glad you came over because I've been thinking about some shit."

Keece's brows furrowed. "Like what?"

"When I die, I need you to become the official leader of this family."

Keece sat in silence, pondering his father's statement. Dom rarely talked about death and Keece was wondering if something was going on that he wasn't aware of.

"When you die?" Keece hissed. "You know something that I don't."

Dom smirked. "Nah, lil' nigga I'm just telling you what I want to happen when I die. You know I'm not going to live forever, right?"

"Yeah, I know that, but I just hate talking about that kind of shit."

"Well, you can't escape death, Keece. That shit is going to happen whether you talk about it or not."

Keece nodded without a verbal response.

"Now like I was saying, I want you to be the head of this family. You've always been a leader and made great decisions when it came to the family business. I know that Kiyan is the oldest out of you all, but you've always displayed a certain matureness that he didn't have."

Keece had been the decision maker when it came to their construction company and drug empire. When Dom stepped down, he appointed Keece to replace him and so far, he had been doing a great job.

"I also need you to look after Case and Dinero when I go. They're the youngest, and I need to know they're good."

Keece shifted uncomfortably in his seat because the conversation was becoming quite eerie. He almost felt like Dom was speaking his death up and it wasn't sitting well with him.

"Pops, you sure you're good?"

Dom laughed and then winced quickly. "I just told you…yes. I wanna make sure you know what I expect of you when I go."

Keece nodded, still not feeling their chat. "A'ight…now what were you saying about Case and Dinero?"

"I want you to always look after them, especially Case because he's the youngest. And with Dinero, he's a wild card, and

I need you to keep him in check. I would hate for him to do something crazy and land in jail or get himself killed."

"Now why do you think Dinero would listen to me? He doesn't listen to anybody except you."

Dom sat back in his seat. "He looks up to you. I know you don't think so, but he does."

Keece smacked his lips. "Man, that nigga stay trying to buck up on me."

Dom chuckled. "He bucks up on everybody. It's not just you, son."

Keece sighed, folding his arms over his chest. "Anything else you require because I really want to change the subject."

"That's it for now. How's Paris, and where is Kya?"

"Paris is cool, and Kya went with Riley for the weekend."

"Has she been consistent?" Dom questioned, referring to Riley.

Keece offered a knowing look. "She shows up when she wants to. I really can't stand that bitch."

Dom snickered. "Maybe you should've strapped up."

"Yeah, but then I wouldn't have Kya."

"At least Kya has Paris when Riley doesn't show up."

"Yeah, that's true."

Interrupting their discussion was Dom's live-in girlfriend, Olivia. She was thirty-three, which was the same age as Kiyan. Her youthful face was adorned by oval-shaped eyes, small nose and heart-shaped lips. Her hair was styled in a blonde pixie cut which complimented her khaki-toned skin.

"Oh, hey Keece. I saw the kids, and I just knew Dom was babysitting," she joked.

Keece chuckled. "You know he thinks he's too good to watch his grandkids."

Dom twisted his mouth. "I'm not that kind of grandpa. I'd rather give them some money or candy and send them on their way."

"You ain't right, Pops," Keece joked as he stood. "I'm 'bout to bounce. I'll get up with you later."

The two men shook hands and gave each other a hug.

Keece then turned to Olivia. "See you later, Liv."

"Bye, Keece."

He walked to the living room where the children were watching TV. "Come on y'all."

Parker and Deuce hopped up and met Keece by the front door.

"Daddy, can we go get ice cream?" Parker asked with hopeful eyes.

"Yeah, we can do that."

Parker and Deuce cheered as they ran to Keece's car. He smirked at their giddiness and pulled his phone out of his pocket. He sent Paris a text before he got inside the car.

Keece: Don't forget to come straight home after your appt. I need you bad.

THREE

Camara sifted through the various styles of earrings in search for some gold hoops. When she found them, she sat them in the packaging box and sealed it with some tape. Camara had been an entrepreneur for over three years now, and she enjoyed it fully. Leaving her full-time job as a paralegal was a task she had been fearful of, but after stepping out on faith, she was content with her decision.

Camara's online jewelry boutique *Classique* had become so successful that she decided to rent some space in Asia's photography studio instead of work inside of her house. Over the weekend, she'd had a huge sale that resulted in over six thousand orders. So, she and her five employees were working diligently to get everything packaged and ready for the post office.

"It's a good thing that sale went well because we now have room for our new inventory," said, Tae who was her employee.

"Yeah, I know," Camara agreed. "I'm so grateful for our online following. It also helped when Asia and Aimee posted from their IG page because they have over a million followers."

"It pays to have sisters with a big following," Tae joked.

Camara laughed. "I know right."

Interrupting their laughter was Camara's phone buzzing on the table. She glanced at the screen and noticed that the school her daughters, Milan and Kamryn, attended were calling so she quickly answered.

"Hello?"

"Hi, can I speak to the parent or guardian of Milan DeMao?"

Camara's heart rate accelerated a bit. "Yes, this is her mother."

"Hi, this is the nurse, and Milan has a temperature of 100.2. She's very fatigued, and I was wondering if you would be able to pick her up. There's a virus going around the school we're trying to stop it from spreading."

"Of course, um… I'll be there as soon as possible."

"Okay. Thank you."

Camara ended the call and stepped out into the hallway. She dialed Kiyan's number and waited anxiously for him to answer.

"Yeah," he answered dryly.

"Hey, the school just called and said that Milan has a fever. Do you think you can pick her up?"

"Why you can't do it?" he quipped.

Camara inhaled a deep breath to keep herself from getting annoyed. "Because I'm working, Kiyan. I have over six thousand orders to pack and mail out. I really can't step away right now."

"Well, I'm busy so you gon' have to take a break and go get her yourself."

She pressed her lips together as she rolled her orbs. "What the fuck are you busy doing that you can't go get your sick daughter from school? Damn, can you just help me out for once?"

"I'm doing shit, Camara!" he barked. "Plus, I ain't even on that side of town. That lil' boutique can wait so go get her."

"So I'm supposed to stop fulfilling my orders to go get Milan while you run the fucking streets? You never help me out when it comes to the girls."

"What the fuck are you talking about? I pay all the bills and support all y'all expensive-ass needs."

"Do you think that's all it takes to be a good husband and father? You paying the bills don't mean shit for someone who can do it herself," she quipped.

"Man, go get Milan. I'm done talking to you."

When Kiyan hung up on her, Camara looked at the phone in disbelief. He was becoming more disrespectful by the day, and she didn't know how long she could tolerate his blatant disregard for her.

Asia emerged from her office with Mila running closely behind her.

"What's wrong?" Asia asked with crinkled brows.

Camara swayed her head, releasing a deep sigh. "I'm so tired of Kiyan."

"What did he do?"

"Milan is sick with a fever, and I asked him to pick her up. Of course, he says he can't, and I have so much work to do that I really can't leave the girls to package everything themselves. I swear I feel like a single parent."

"Aww," Asia poked her bottom lip out. "Don't be stressed. I'll go pick her up for you, and she can lay down in the lounge area. I'll even stop at CVS to get her some medicine."

Camara breathed a sigh of relief. "Are you sure? I don't want to take you from your work."

Asia waved her hand. "I'm done with my appointments for the day. Besides, I was going to get something to eat for me and Mila so picking up Milan is no problem. Right, boo?" Asia asked Mila.

"Right, mommy."

Camara smirked. "Thank you, even though you shouldn't be the one doing it. I really appreciate it."

"No problem. It takes a village girl. I'll be back."

Camara watched Asia and Mila stroll down the hallway. Although Asia had saved the day, she was still bothered that her husband didn't even try to come to her rescue. She couldn't say this wasn't a routine with Kiyan. He often left her alone to handle the responsibilities of parenting their two daughters. He thought because he paid all the bills that he was exempt from being an active father. Running a lucrative business while parenting the girls and taking care of the house was weighing Camara down physically and mentally. She felt like if she had to do everything on her own, then there was no point in continuing to be with Kiyan. He was unfortunately adding nothing to her life.

***

Diar lay on her side getting some of the best sleep she had in a while. The fan was blowing on high and the room was pitch black. The fluffy covers were up to her neck until she suddenly felt her body exposed to the cool air. She awoke suddenly, trying to adjust her eyes in the darkness. When the weight of the bed shifted, Diar attempted to get up, but her arms were pinned down.

"What the fuck?!" she yelled.

"It's me, baby," Case laughed.

She smacked her lips and relaxed her tensed body. "You play too damn much. Why would you scare me like that?"

"My bad. I just wanted to fuck with you."

Diar couldn't see his face, but the enticing scent of his cologne seeped into her nostrils. Despite her being frightened seconds ago, she was elated that Case was finally home and in her presence.

"You missed me?" he questioned in a sexy, husky tone.

"You know I did. I didn't know you were coming home tonight. You told me Monday."

"I lied 'cause I wanted to surprise you."

Case kissed Diar's lips with so much passion that her nipples ached profusely. Her body was warming up to a temperature she couldn't contain, and the only person that could handle her was Case. She had craved everything about him while he was away. His touch was electrifying; his fragrance was alluring as he slipped his tongue inside her mouth.

"Baby," she moaned. "I missed you so much."

"I missed you too. Now turn around."

Diar joyfully obliged and turned around. Her size eighteen frame was positioned with her chest pressed evenly on the mattress and her ass in the air. Case lifted her nightgown and rubbed her bare ass. Diar licked her lips in anticipation as she listened to him fumble with his belt buckle.

Within seconds, Case was sliding his thick member into her wet tunnel. Her body shuddered as he stroked her with ease. He gripped her waist as Diar rotated her hips.

"Why you so wet baby?" he asked, picking up the pace.

"Because…I missed you."

"I see your pussy did too."

Case thrusted into her with force as the sounds of her moist center filled the room. Diar's teeth were sinking deeply into her bottom lip as she gripped the sheets.

"Let go, Diar. I know you trying to hold it."

Her breathing increased as well as his strokes. He was right; she was trying to hold on to her orgasm because she was enjoying the way his dick massaged her insides.

"Come on, baby. Let me see that cream."

Upon his request, Diar's walls pulsated as her essence coated his dick. Her legs were vibrating uncontrollably while Case pumped in and out of her.

"Case…shit," she groaned as pleasure ripped through her frame.

Case abruptly pulled out. "Turn around."

Slowly, Diar flipped over and laid on her back. He placed her thick legs in the crook of his arms and entered her pussy.

"You love me baby?"

"You know I do," she moaned.

Case plunged into her wetness at rapid speed, prompting her legs to shake once again.

"Oh my...god. You're fucking me so good, baby."

Case kneeled down and devoured her lips hungrily. She cupped his face with both of her hands and welcomed his tongue inside her mouth. After more powerful thrusts, Case released his juices inside her.

"Fuck," he grunted.

Rapid breathing filled the room as Case pulled out and laid next to her. Diar was feeling so relaxed now that he had given her the release she'd desperately needed. She turned over and wrapped her arm around his torso.

"How long you staying home?" she asked.

He chuckled. "Damn, Diar, can I come down from my nut."

She tittered. "My bad."

"I don't have any events or sessions out of town for a while. Is that cool?"

She beamed. "Yes, I hate when you go out of town. I be so lonely without you."

"I know, but I gotta make money for us."

Diar loved when he referred to them as us. Case took pride in taking care of Diar, and she truly appreciated him.

"You still wanna marry me?" he asked with humor laced in his tone.

Diar smacked his chest. "Why would you ask me something so stupid? You know I wanna marry you."

"I had to make sure you didn't change your mind."

"I'm never changing my mind when it comes to you. You know that."

Case graced her forehead with a kiss before lifting his upper body. "Let's get in the shower," he suggested before getting out of the bed.

Diar followed him to the bathroom and showered with her love before they retired back to the bedroom and dozed off into a deep slumber.

***

Dinero bobbed his head to Drake's "Mob Ties" as he watched a slim chick dance in an attempt to get his attention. He was posted at the bar with Kiyan, Keece, and Big, enjoying a night out with his brothers. He checked the time on his phone and noticed that it was a little after ten o'clock.

Dinero turned to Kiyan. "Aye, don't call me no more this week to come out with you."

Kiyan scowled. "Man, fuck you. I don't need you to come out with me."

"Yes, the fuck you do," Dinero argued. "Nigga be damn near beggin' me and shit. I actually like my wife unlike your fat lip ass, so I'm chillin' at the crib for the rest of the week."

Keece laughed. “Cam gon’ leave his ass if he keeps on with the bullshit.”

“Right,” Big chimed in, “his ass be kickin’ it like he don't have a family at home and shit.”

Kiyan flipped them off. “Fuck all three of y’all, and Cam ain't leaving me.”

“Shit, that’s what you think. She’s looking for a place right now,” Dinero announced.

Kiyan quickly spun his neck in his direction. “Who told you that?”

Dinero burst out laughing, “I'm bullshittin’ with your scary ass. You keep fuckin’ up, and she will be looking for her own shit. Sorry-ass nigga.”

Dinero returned his sight on the dancing girl and sighed. She was shaking so hard but not shaking anything at the same time.

“What the fuck you lookin’ at?” Dinero barked.

The girl smiled and sauntered closer to him. “Were you talking to me?” she flirted.

“Yeah, I'm talking to you. Why yo’ stiff, ironing board built ass keep looking at me?”

Keece and Kiyan cackled as the girl tried to keep a smile on her face. Dinero could tell she was embarrassed as she looked around.

“Well, maybe I thought you were cute,” she replied.

"Well don't," Dinero retorted. "I got a wife, and she knows how to fight."

She scoffed. "That ain't stopping shit, and I'm sure I look better than her ass."

"Yo' ugly ass will never look better than my girl. Now get your Skeletor lookin' ass on somewhere."

The woman stepped closer to Dinero. "Let me see a picture of your wife."

"Damn, girl, why?" Kiyan asked annoyed.

"Because I wanna see if she looks better than me."

Dinero peered at her mischievously. "What's your name?"

"Naomi."

Dinero took his phone out his pocket and tapped on his photo gallery. He scrolled to a picture of Asia and showed it to Naomi.

"Oh my God," she gushed. "I follow her and her twin on Instagram. Which one are you married to? Asia or Aimee?"

"Don't worry about it. Now back your ass up," Dinero snapped.

Naomi stepped back. "Man, I love them. They're so down to earth and cool. Why you won't tell me which one you're married to?"

"'Cause you don't need to know all that. Now take your ass back over there."

She smacked her lips. "You're so damn mean but whatever. Tell them I said what's up."

"Like they know your ass," Big joked.

"You know what I mean." Naomi giggled, walking away.

"Man Asia and Aimee's IG stay poppin'. Y'all ever go through the comments?" Keece asked Dinero and Big.

Dinero shook his head. "Hell nah, 'cause I'll be ready to track all them thirsty niggas down and put a hot one in them."

"I don't even be on that shit like that," Big added.

When Dinero's phone buzzed, he looked down and noticed Asia had sent him a text.

Asia: Where are you?

Dinero: At Big's bar. Why?

Asia: My grandma just came in town and I want you to meet her.

Dinero sucked his teeth.

Dinero: I'll meet her ass later.

Asia: No, I want you to come now. Please and bring Big too.

Dinero had temporarily forgotten about Asia's grandmother moving in with them. He didn't like the idea of having another person in his home, but since Asia had damn near begged him, he reluctantly agreed.

"Aye, Big, the twins' grandma here, and they want us to meet her ass."

Big's forehead creased. "Right now?"

"Yeah," Dinero nodded. "Asia told me to bring you."

"She's living with you and Asia?" Keece asked Dinero.

"Nah, with Big and Aimee," Dinero snickered.

Big snorted. "Nah, nigga she gon' be over there with yo' ass. I already got a full house."

Dinero stood. "Man, ain't nobody tell you to keep getting Aimee pregnant. Now y'all got a fuckin' Tribe Called Quest in that bitch."

Kiyan chortled. "His ass had twins with a twin. I knew that shit was gon' happen."

"Fuck y'all," Big shot, standing from his seat. "Aye, y'all staying?" he asked Keece and Kiyan.

Keece nodded. "Yeah, we'll be here."

"A'ight, I'll be back."

Dinero followed Big outside where they hopped inside of his car since he had rode with Kiyan. The two made small talk as Big drove toward Dinero's home. After a twenty minute drive, they finally arrived. Dinero pulled out his keys and opened the door. He was greeted instantly by Mila running up to him.

"Look Daddy, it's mommy's grandma," Mila pointed.

Dinero looked up and noticed an elderly woman with sand-colored skin and long black hair. She was very short and if he had to guess, she was maybe four-foot-ten.

"Damn, where y'all dig her ass up from?" Dinero questioned, picking up Mila.

Big cackled loudly. "Bro, you gotta chill."

"What?" Dinero quipped. "I thought her ass was a fossil."

"Dinero," Asia scolded. "Don't be an ass."

He smirked. “I'm just playing.”

“You see, Lola, Asia married the one who requires medication,” Aimee jested, emerging from the living room.

“Shut up, Ming Lee,” Dinero retorted.

An older gentleman came from the living room and stood next to Aimee. He was Filipino with short spiky hair and tanned skin.

“Oh this is our, Uncle Angelo. He brought grandma here for us. Uncle, say hi to our husbands,” Aimee introduced.

Angelo smiled. “Nice to meet you,” he greeted with an accent.

Dinero offered a nod while Big said, “What's up?”

Asia grabbed the older woman’s arm and stepped over to Dinero and Big.

“Lola this is my husband, Dinero, and that’s Aimee’s husband, Dakaden. Say hi.”

She waved and smiled warmly. “Kamusta.”

“Aw shit, Asia,” Dinero griped. “Her ass don't speak English?”

“Only a little,” Asia responded with a wince. “But she understands some English.”

Dinero waved his hand. “A little my ass. You think I wanna hear this guala guala shit every day.”

Asia grabbed Mila from his arms and placed her on her feet. “Boo, go upstairs and watch TV in my room, okay.”

Mila nodded and ran up the staircase. Big hung his head down and chuckled under his breath. Dinero looked over at him, not happy that he thought this situation was humorous.

"Fuck you laughing for, Big? You know this shit was a set up."

"It wasn't a set up," Asia denied.

"Yes, the hell it was," Dinero countered. "You ain't say shit about her not speaking English."

"Dinero, she speaks a little but not much. Why do you care? You act like you're going to be dealing with her one-on-one?" Aimee quipped.

"She's about to be living here. What the fuck you mean why I care?" Dinero snapped.

"Hey, young man," Angelo stepped up. "Is there a problem with my mother being here because we can make other arrangements?"

"Ah shit," Big snickered, walking over to the kitchen island to take a seat.

Dinero eyes glowered at Angelo, who was standing with his hands in his pockets. Dinero swiftly invaded his personal space, wearing a mean scowl and furrowed brows.

"Who the fuck you calling young man? You in my fuckin' house nigga, so you better watch what the fuck you say to me."

Dinero stared down at Angelo, waiting for him to say the wrong thing. Asia wedged herself in between the stare down and planted her hand on Dinero's chest.

"Babe, he didn't mean anything by that. He's older, so if he sees someone younger he always says young man or young woman."

"I don't give a fuck what he always say," Dinero seethed. "He better not try to son me again."

Angelo inhaled a deep breath as Dinero walked over to the stool and took a seat. He didn't like the vibe he got from Angelo, and he wanted him out of his house immediately.

"It's time for him to go, Asia," Dinero announced, pointing at Angelo.

Angelo tipped his head. "Yeah, I'm going to start driving back tonight. I will talk to you ladies once I get home."

Angelo gave Aimee and Asia a hug and then kissed his mother goodbye before walking out the house. As soon as the door shut, Asia turned to Dinero with a frown on her mug.

"You told me you were gonna be nice, Dinero," she fussed, walking toward him.

Dinero smirked. "I ain't never tell you that. Shit, you know I'm not nice."

"He ain't lying about that," Aimee chimed in. "Asia, is grandma gonna be safe with Rude Boy?"

"What you think I'ma do to her old ass?" Dinero shot.

Asia smacked his arm. "Stop being disrespectful."

Their grandma ambled over to Dinero and held her arms out. Dinero gave Asia a puzzled look.

"She wants a hug," Asia informed him.

He wrapped one of his arms around her shoulder and gave her a soft hug. When he pulled back, she offered him a gummy smile.

"Damn, Asia, I think grandma want me. Look at how she's smiling at me," Dinero laughed.

Asia chortled. "Don't nobody want you but me."

"Okay!" Aimee agreed.

"Come on, Lola. Let me show you your new room," Asia said, grabbing her hand and walking her down the hallway.

Big stood, wrapping his arm around Aimee's shoulder. "We 'bout to go. Have fun with your new grandma fam."

"Yeah don't be mistreating my Lola or else I will be over here to tase your ass and then Asia gon' lay hands on you."

"I'll beat both of y'all ass, then pop ya man if he feeling some type of way," Dinero laughed.

Big snorted. "Picture that shit."

Dinero watched as the two walked out of the house and closed the door. Just as he was about to go upstairs, Asia stopped him.

"Dinero, I need you to promise to be nice to my Lola. Don't make her feel uncomfortable. She's is now a part of this family so don't be an ass."

"Man, I'm not gon' do shit to her. Now go put Mila to sleep so I can put you to sleep."

Asia grinned. "I'll think about it."

FOUR

Camara wiped her wet face with a towel and then studied her reflection through the mirror. Her round eyes held grocery-sized bags underneath. Her pixie cut was in desperate need of a trim and despite just washing her face; her wheat-colored skin lacked the natural glow it used to possess.

Camara was exhausted.

Not only was she tired physically, but she was drained emotionally. Her joyless marriage was weighing her down, and Kiyan seemed to be oblivious to the state of their union. Her love for him was vanishing by the day. She no longer got the jittery feeling in the pit of her stomach when he laid eyes on her. Her heart didn't palpitate when he touched her in her most sensitive spots. Nothing about Kiyan satisfied Camara, and she often wondered why she was still holding on to her marriage.

Snapping out of her somber thoughts, Camara went to the laundry room to wash some clothes. While separating the whites from the colored clothing, the door crept open slowly. Kiyan stood dressed in a grey Nike jogger's suit and a pair of Air Max. His 'fro was covered by a black snapback that sat backwards on his head.

Camara glanced at him but she didn't say anything. These days, she really didn't have much to say to him. She bent over and continued separating the clothes.

"What's up?" he asked.

"Hey," she responded dryly.

"How was your day?"

"Busy."

"You wanna watch a movie or some shit?" he offered.

"I don't want to do shit with your ass."

Suddenly his lips smacked. "Fuck you then. Don't complain when I just tried to spend some time with your unpleasant ass."

She snorted. "I'm done complaining when it comes to you. You can do whatever you want, and I promise you won't hear a peep from me."

Camara meant every word she'd spoken. She was no longer going to consume her energy with the behavior of Kiyan. It was a waste, and she was tired of constantly fighting.

He shook his head. "How the fuck you wake up with an attitude and go to sleep with one? You so damn miserable Cam."

She stood up straight, her face neutral as she bore into him with intense eyes. "Have you ever questioned why I'm so miserable?"

"Hell no," he scoffed. "That shit ain't my problem why you're bitter."

"Hmmph," she chuckled. "You don't have a fucking clue."

"Nah, you don't," Kiyan countered. "You just love being mad all the fuckin' time, and you wonder why I don't be home like that."

"You wanna know something Kiyan, I'm unhappy with you."

Camara had had enough of Kiyan's shit. It was time to tell him what was truly on her heart instead of bottling up her feelings just to spare his.

She stepped into his personal space. "You make me miserable, Kiyan. You leave me out to rot all the fucking time. I feel like a single parent because you don't participate in helping me raise our kids. I have to call other family members to help me with shit you should be helping with. You're never home because you don't want to be, so don't blame your fucked-up behavior on me. My attitude is a reflection of you and your lack of support. You don't take me anywhere. You don't support my business. You just ain't shit and quite frankly, I'm starting not to give a fuck about you!"

Camara's chest was rising and falling at a rapid rate. Tears burned the brim of her eyes because she'd been longing to say that to Kiyan for months. She felt relieved but at the same time it pained her that she had to tell him what was wrong instead of him figuring it out on his own.

Kiyan stared at her for a moment before smirking. "It ain't my job to make you happy."

Camara jerked her head back, appalled by his statement. "It's not your job? Really? Well, whose job is it?"

"Shit, it's yours," he responded casually. "You ain't never satisfied anyway so I wouldn't even waste my time."

She peered at him with a disgusted countenance. Her stomach had suddenly turned sour as she looked at the man she called her husband.

"You're a fucking waste. Get out of my face, Kiyan."

"If I'm such a waste, then why are you still here? I'm not holding you hostage, Cam."

"You're right; you're not holding me so maybe I'll look into moving out and allowing you to be the bachelor you really want to be."

"Shut the fuck up," he hissed. "You ain't going nowhere. Ain't no nigga gon' take care of you like me. You get to buy whatever the fuck you want. You ain't gotta worry about a fuckin' thing so stop talking that dumb shit 'cause we both know you ain't gon' go anywhere."

The fact that he didn't believe she would leave angered Camara. Kiyan had gotten so comfortable with his treatment against her that he thought she would stay and endure his bullshit forever.

"Bye, Kiyan. I don't want to be bothered with you."

"Bitter ass," he mumbled as he turned and exited the laundry room.

When he closed the door, Camara dropped the clothes and covered her eyes with her hands. She didn't want to cry; Lord knows she was tired of the liquid pain running from her eyes. But she didn't know why Kiyan didn't see how much he was hurting her. Why had their marriage been reduced to a loveless bond?

Why did their only communication consist of bickering and malicious words against each other?

Camara was no longer present in her marriage. She didn't care about anything regarding Kiyan; so again, she questioned why she was still there?

***

Paris pulled a T-shirt over Deuce's head and helped him pull his arms through. She smiled at her baby boy who looked exactly like Keece. They possessed the same golden-wheat skin, round eyes, and low curly cut.

"Guess who you look like?" Paris said.

Deuce grinned widely. "My daddy."

"No, you look like me," she teased.

He shook his head. "Unt uh, I look like daddy."

"No boo, you look like me. I'm the one that carried you and pushed you out so you came out looking like your mommy."

Deuce giggled. "No, Mommy. Parker looks like you, not me."

Paris kissed his cheek just as Parker entered the room. "Mommy, where are we going today?"

"Do you guys wanna go see grandma today?"

The kids jumped up and down with glee, making Paris smirk.

"Ooh yeah, can Kya come too Mommy?" Parker asked.

Whenever Kya went away with Riley, Parker and Deuce always missed her.

"Yes, she's going to come. Her mom is going to drop her off soon."

Paris helped Deuce put his shoes on and then she went back to her room so she could finish getting dressed. Keece was out running the streets and since it was a nice day outside, she wanted to go take the kids out. Their first stop was going to be her mother's house, and then she figured they could go to Monkey Joes.

Just as Paris dropped her robe, the doorbell rang. She put it back on and made her way downstairs. When she opened the front door, Kya stood with Riley next to her.

"Hey boo," Paris sang as she leaned down to hug Kya.

"Hey, Mama," Kya responded with a huge grin.

"Did you have fun with your mom?"

Kya nodded. "Yes, we went to Discovery World."

"You did?" Paris stood. "That's great."

"Yeah, I took her since one of my cousin's daughters was having a party there," Riley explained.

"Oh, well, that's nice."

Kya ran into the house and up the stairs. Riley stood with an expression that displayed she wanted to say something. In the past, Paris and Riley didn't get along and even had a fist fight. For months, they went without speaking until Paris decided to call a truce for the sake of Kya. Riley agreed and they had been cordial ever since.

"Is Keece here?" Riley questioned.

"No, he's gone."

"Good," Riley breathed a sigh of relief. "Can I talk to you?"

Paris nodded, stepping to the side to allow her access in the home. She led Riley toward the dining room where they took a seat at the table.

"What's going on?" Paris asked.

Riley licked her lips. "I'm thinking about moving to Atlanta to expand my hair business. I was wondering if you thought Keece would allow Kya to come down there for half the year."

Immediately, a queasy sensation seized Paris' stomach. The thought of Kya being gone for six months had her feeling uneasy.

"Half the year?" Paris questioned with a chuckle. "Are you serious?"

Riley nodded. "I am. I feel like it's a better opportunity down there than here in Milwaukee. I don't want to move and not see my baby at all so I thought that maybe you could talk Keece into allowing me to have her for six months."

"Riley," Paris pinched the bridge of her nose. "Keece has full custody."

"I know, and I was thinking maybe we can have joint custody and come to some type of an agreement."

Paris looked at Riley as if she'd sprouted two heads. She didn't take great care of Kya with the days she was offered. She either didn't show up or would come days later and keep her for a maximum of two days.

"I'm going to be honest with you, Riley; I know Keece is not going to agree to that. He would never be able to handle Kya being away from him for months at a time. Honestly, I wouldn't be either."

Riley sat back in her chair and released a deep sigh. "Paris, what am I supposed to do then?"

"Stay."

Her face scowled instantly. "Stay here for what. I want my business to grow, and Atlanta is the perfect place. I would be able to get more clientele and even book some celebrity clients."

"Well, what's going to happen when you get a celebrity client that requires you to travel? What would you do with Kya then?"

Riley shrugged. "I would have to work something out. I haven't thought this all the way through, Paris."

"Well, I think you should, especially if you want Keece to agree to it. Did you ask Kya about moving to Atlanta?"

"Not yet. I wanted to discuss it with you and Keece first… if he doesn't agree to this; I'm going to go anyway. I would just have to see Kya on the holidays and summer break."

It pained Paris that Riley could be so selfish. She was so inconsistent with Kya, and she seemed as if she didn't care how badly it affected her daughter.

"That would break Kya's heart Riley," Paris said with disdain in her tone.

"I know, but I need to focus on my career so me and Kya can be straight in the long run."

Bitch please.

Paris had had enough of this conversation, so she stood. "I'll let Keece know and then we'll go from there. I will say not to get your hopes up too high."

"Trust me, I never do when it comes to Keece." Riley stood, grabbing her purse.

Paris walked her to the door and watched her get in the car. She had been in a great mood before her conversation with Riley, but now she was bothered. Kya was just as much her daughter as she was Riley. Paris had been there for her ever since she was two years old. She couldn't fathom the thought of Kya living miles away for six months just because Riley was trying to chase after her career.

Paris planned to bring up the discussion to Keece when he got home. She knew he would probably be ready to go and curse Riley's ass out and a part of her couldn't say she didn't blame him.

***

"Dada…Dada."

Big slowly opened his lids and found Devyn and Dylan standing next to his bed. They were wearing matching onesies with pull ups. Their wild tresses were scattered all over their heads as they smiled at him.

Big rubbed their cheeks before reaching for his phone and checking the time. It was a little after eight o'clock in the morning.

He had forgotten Aimee had a doctor's appointment, leaving him to watch the twins until she got back.

He slowly lifted his upper body and rubbed his eyes. "Y'all hungry?"

The girls nodded eagerly, prompting him to smile. Before he took care of them, he went to relieve his bladder and handle his morning hygiene. Once he was finished, he grabbed his phone, picked the girls up, and went downstairs to the kitchen. The house was very quiet since Zaria and DJ were at school. Big placed them in their high chairs and decided to fix them some eggs.

Just as he was getting the carton of eggs out the fridge, his phone rang. He glanced at the screen and noticed Zaria's mother, Tara, calling.

"Fuck she want?" he mumbled, pressing the end button.

Big and Tara had a volatile relationship that resulted in him taking her to court for visitation with Zaria. There were many instances when Tara would withhold Zaria from him because she was mad about the ending of their relationship. Tara had also disrespected Aimee on several different occasions. It had gotten so bad that Big hated Tara. They barely communicated, and when they did, it was mainly through text messaging.

"Dada, food," Dylan reminded him.

He chuckled. "A'ight. Daddy got you."

Big quickly cracked the eggs open and whisked them up. Before he could grab a skillet, his phone rang again. He huffed when he saw that it was Tara calling for a second time.

He snatched the phone and answered with a, "Yeah."

"I need to talk to you," Tara requested.

"About what?" Big asked with irritation in his tone.

"My car is broken down, and I need you to help me get it fixed."

Big took the phone away from his ear to check and see if he was actually on the phone with Aimee or Elle. Those were the only two women he was willing to do anything for.

"You must got the wrong number."

"No, I have the right number Big" she sassed.

"Nah, you don't when you calling me asking me to do shit for you like I'm your man."

"You're my child's father, and if you want Zaria to get to school, then you'll help me with my car."

"Listen, Zaria can stay here for the week, and she'll get to school just fine. I'm not helping you with shit, Tara. You know that."

"Y'all are not keeping my child for the whole week," she scoffed.

"Well, what the fuck you think you gon' do with her? Keep her out of school?"

"If I have to, I will."

Big shook his head, not understanding why Tara was being so damn silly. She had always made immature decisions when he didn't do what she wanted.

"I ain't giving you shit," he spat with finality.

"Well, let me use one of your cars then," she commanded.

"You must be crazy," he snorted. "I wouldn't let you use a skateboard if I had that shit."

"You know what? You ain't shit. I need my fucking car fixed and you got all that fucking money and won't throw me a couple hundred to get my car right. What kind of man are you?"

"Bit–," he chuckled in an attempted to stop himself from cursing her out. "So, you must've forgot how hard you made it for me to be an active father in Zaria's life. I had to take your bitter ass to court just to see my fuckin' daughter. If you would've been a pleasant baby mama, I would've had no problem helping you out, but because you've been hard to deal with, I'm not helping you with shit. Call your fuckin' man for your personal needs because I'm not the one."

"I don't have a man. We broke up so you need to step up and help me out."

"I'm broke, baby. I ain't got no money." He laughed.

"Fuck you!" she hollered.

Big ended the call and immediately placed her on the block list. He decided he was going to keep Zaria with him for the entire week, since he didn't want to risk Tara keeping her out of school. Big pushed thoughts of Tara out of his mind and proceeded to fix the twins eggs. Once he served them, he sat at the table and checked his text messages.

After the twins ate, Big cleaned them up, and they went to the living room to watch TV. He watched them jump around and play with their toys until Aimee came through the door.

Big instantly devoured her with his eyes as she entered the room. She was still the most beautiful woman in the world to him. Her hair was slicked back in a sleek ponytail. Her golden caramel skin was free of any blemishes. Big loved her angular, small eyes that held long beautiful lashes. Aimee's juicy lips were his favorite feature on her face. After birthing three of his children, her body had become much thicker to the point where he couldn't keep his hands off her.

"Hi, babies," Aimee greeted the twins with kisses. "Did you have a fun morning with your daddy?"

"Why you go to the doctor?" Big asked.

"It wasn't for me. I had to take grandma so she could establish care with a primary doctor."

"Oh word? The girls ended up waking me up," Big chuckled.

Aimee rolled her eyes. "I woke you up before I left. You must've fallen asleep again. Let something would've happened to my babies. I would've been at your head."

He smacked his lips. "You wasn't gon' do shit. Aye, guess who called me beggin'?"

Her forehead creased instantly. "Who?"

“Tara’s ass.”

“What the hell she beggin’ for?”

“She asked me to help her get her car fixed. She tried to use that she needed to take Zaria to school.”

“Um, Zaria can stay here, and I’ll take her to school,” Aimee quipped.

“That’s what I told her. But then she tried to say if I didn’t get her car fixed, she would keep Zaria out of school all week. So now I'm making sure Zaria stays here with us. I don't want Tara’s dumb ass to take her out of school.”

Aimee snorted. “She is so damn ignorant. I can’t believe she had the audacity to even call and ask you to help her with her car. She better use that damn child support.”

“She probably spent it going on her many trips. I swear she be out of town every month, partying like she ain't got no responsibility.”

“Well, that’s on her. She better not call and ask you for nothing else. You ain't her damn man.”

Big smirked at the scowl on her face. “Come over here.”

Aimee simpered and sat next to him. He pulled her face toward his and kissed her lips. “When do the kids take their morning nap?”

She burst into laughter. “Why Big?”

“Because, my mans need you,” he said, referring to his dick.

She playfully rolled her eyes. “Not for another hour.”

"Speed that shit up, so I can give you this morning dick."

She tittered. "I'll handle it."

FIVE

Dinero looked in the mirror, inspecting his fresh lining. He handed the hand-held mirror back to his barber, Vee, and nodded.

"You better have my shit crispy, or I was gon' knock you on your ass," Dinero joked.

Vee laughed. "Man don't come at me like that. You know I'm official."

"Shiiit," Dinero stood. "Nigga when you high you be having mothafuckas linings behind their ears and shit."

Vee cackled loudly. "Fuck you, bruh."

Dinero reached into his pocket and pulled out a knot of money. He peeled off a fifty dollar bill and passed it to Vee.

"Good looking, fam," Vee said.

Dinero nodded and gave him a hand shake. He made his way to the front door and spotted Case walking in.

"Man, where your ugly ass been?" Dinero questioned, giving him a brotherly hug.

Case chuckled. "I had to go to this tattoo convention out of town. Why? You missed me gay-ass nigga."

"I'll beat yo' ass." Dinero laughed. "You think you the shit because you got some clout now. You still ain't finished my fuckin' tattoo on my back and I'm damn near about to go on IG to expose you."

Case chortled. "You would hate on your own brother like that?"

"Hell yeah. Nigga, you ain't exempt from shit," Dinero ranted.

"You ain't shit. Come to the shop later on, and I'll finish that weak-ass tattoo."

"Good looking. Aye, I saw Miss Daisy driving the other day. Nigga, she made a left turn so wide, I thought her ass was gon' end up on the sidewalk."

Case and Dinero doubled over in laughter. Diar wasn't a very good driver and Dinero often made fun of her for that.

"Man, get off my girl. She got a lil' better," Case defended.

"Yeah right. I bet y'all insurance premium high as fuck because of her ass."

Case swayed his head back and forth. "Man, I don't even wanna talk about it."

"I know you don't, but I'll get up with you later on."

"A'ight."

The two brothers shook hands, and Dinero exited the barbershop. He pulled out his phone on the way to the car and dialed Asia's number.

"Hey baby," she answered sweetly.

"Aye, I was in the neighborhood and wanted to know if you needed some dick dropped off?"

Suddenly, a loud cackle sounded through the phone causing Dinero to smile.

"Why are you so damn ignorant?" she questioned still laughing.

"What?" he feigned innocence. "I thought you might need some."

"Yeah, I bet you did. Come through."

"A'ight, I'm on my way."

Dinero ended the call and hopped in his matte black Audi. He was only five minutes away from Asia's photography studio so he arrived fairly fast. He'd purchased the space for her on their second anniversary. Asia thought he had bought the studio to be supportive but Dinero did it for an entirely different reason. She was starting to gain some notoriety since she had been rapper, Fabian's, photographer. Dinero was selfish when it came to Asia, and he wanted her home with him instead of traveling to photograph other people. So he purchased her a studio, hoping this gesture would suffice to keep her home, and it did.

He got out the car and walked inside. Summer Walker's "I'm There" serenaded through the space as Dinero ambled over to where Asia was standing. He snuck up behind her and wrapped his arms around her waist. Her body jumped but relaxed when he kissed her ear.

"Boy, you scared me," she hissed, turning to face him.

He gently pecked her lips and cuffed her ass that was sitting up nicely in some leggings. "Let's go to your office. Anybody else here?"

"Yeah, Cam and her staff are in their area. It ain't like you care."

"You know I don't. I was just asking. Come on."

Dinero led Asia up to her office and closed the door. Her office was huge with an adjoining bathroom and wet bar. The color of the walls was teal with gold pictures adorning the room.

"My dick been getting hard all morning since you ain't give me my morning fix."

"First off, I had to go pick up some equipment, so calm down. Plus, you sleep until noon, and ain't nobody got time to be waiting for you to get up."

"Yeah whatever."

Dinero stepped over to the sofa, threw the pillows on the floor and pulled out the let out bed. He looked back at Asia who was smiling widely.

"You want me to get naked, naked?" she flirted.

"What the fuck you think? And lock that door because I don't want nobody walking in while I'm dicking you down."

Asia locked the door and removed all of her clothing. Dinero licked his lips at her body as she sauntered toward the bed. His appetite for Asia was endless. He loved every part of her being from her thick tresses down to the stretch marks on her ass. Dinero pulled off his hoodie, unbuckled his jeans and stepped out of them. He crawled between Asia's legs, wearing only his boxers.

"You so damn sexy, baby. I can't imagine not being the one to fuck you every day."

Asia smiled, biting her bottom lip. "Me either."

He kissed her before trailing his lips down to her breasts. He cupped them softly before sucking on her hardened nipples.

Asia rubbed her fingers through his dreads as faint moans escaped her lips. He went down further pecking her stomach before being greeted by her honey pot that was glistening with her juices. His mouth watered as he stared at his favorite part on Asia's body.

In one swift motion, Dinero flicked his mouth against her clitoris, causing her to buck in pleasure.

"Baby," she whimpered.

He locked her legs with his forearms and hands while feasting on the best pussy he'd ever tasted. Before Asia, Dinero wasn't one to perform oral sex on a woman. But with her, he couldn't halt himself from savoring her sweet nectar.

Dinero dipped his tongue in her opening before hovering his mouth over her clit. He glanced up at Asia, who had her eyes closed while sucking on her bottom lip.

"You like my tongue baby?"

Asia slowly nodded.

"Tell me that shit. Don't nod," he ordered as he slid two fingers into her pussy.

"I love your tongue, baby."

"You ready to cum?"

"Yes," she said breathlessly.

Dinero kissed her clitoris before sucking it. His fingers worked her middle as he slurped relentlessly on her bud.

"Oh…shit," Asia groaned.

He knew she was near her peak so he sped up the pace of his fingers. After seconds of attacking her pussy, Asia released her essence all over his fingers. Dinero lapped up most of her juices and then brought his fingers to her lips. Asia sensually licked the remnants of her center, causing his already stiffened dick to become harder.

Dinero sat up on his knees and pulled down the waist band to his boxers. His manhood stood at attention as he leaned over Asia. Within seconds, he was invading Asia's wet pussy, provoking a moan to sound from her lips.

"How this dick feel?" he kissed her chin.

"So good, baby," Asia whimpered.

Dinero fell into a familiar trance as he thrust deeper into her walls. The wetness that was encompassing his dick was causing him to become feeble. He pinned her wrists above her head as he picked up his pace. Asia's fuck faces were so sexy that he was on the verge of nuttin' prematurely.

"Tell me something baby," he requested, pounding into her center.

"You got the best dick in the world," she professed breathlessly.

Dinero placed her legs over his shoulders. "And what else?"

"I love you so much," she moaned.

He kissed her hungrily, her tongue invaded his mouth while he pounded into her slit.

Don't nut…don't nut.

Dinero was trying to coach himself into not reaching his peak, but Asia's wetness was pulling him deeper into a spell. When Asia's legs vibrated against his shoulders, he knew she was about to cum again.

"Ooooh," she grumbled, sinking her nails into his skin.

Dinero looked down and noticed her cream coating his dick. After appreciating that beautiful sight, he could no longer contain himself.

"Shit," he grunted, releasing all his fruits inside her.

Once he came down from his sexually-induced high, Dinero pulled out and kissed her lips.

"I'm ready to go take a nap now," he chuckled.

Asia laughed as he helped her out of the bed. "I wore you out babe?"

He wiped the sweat from his forehead with the back of his hand. "That pussy always wears me out."

She tittered. "Let's go clean up."

The couple walked into the bathroom and showered together. Once they were cleansed, they got dressed.

"Where Mila at?" Dinero asked, pulling his dreads in a ponytail.

"Where do you think she's at? School."

"I'm about to go pick her up early so we can go out to eat."

Asia smacked her lips. "You can wait until school is out."

"Nah, I feel like spending time with her now."

"You need to stop getting her from school early just so y'all can kick it. You get on my nerves with that."

Dinero shrugged, not caring what Asia thought. He often picked Mila up from school early so they could go have fun together.

Dinero and Asia walked out of the office where they ran into Camara in the hallway.

"What's up, Killa Cam?" Dinero greeted. "Aye, where my damn earrings at?"

"What earrings?" Camara questioned.

"I ordered some earrings for Mila yesterday, and I want my shit."

Camara chuckled. "Did you really order?"

"Yeah, I wouldn't jack to you." he smirked.

"Did you not read that there was a five day processing time?" Camara questioned.

"Nah, I ain't got time for that. I want my earrings, or I'm going to go on your site and leave a bad review."

Asia smacked his arm. "Why are you always threatening somebody? She gets so many orders a day that she needs time to process your order."

Ignoring Asia, Dinero said, "Cam, have my shit today."

"Boy, fuck you." Camara laughed, walking back to her packing room.

Dinero chortled. "Man, she ain't shit."

"You're horrible, babe. You're always trying to strong-arm somebody into what you want. You're a bully."

"You don't say nothing when I'm bullying that pussy."

Asia smirked at him and walked off.

Dinero snorted. "That's what I thought."

When they got to the photography area, they noticed a man walking inside. He was average height with a medium build and low fade.

"Can I help you?" Asia asked.

"Uh, yeah, I'm looking for the photographer of this studio."

Dinero eyed him suspiciously as he made his way toward Asia.

"I'm she. What can I do for you?"

The guy held his hand out for a shake but Dinero intercepted and slapped his hand away.

"She don't shake hands," Dinero said coolly.

The man chuckled and scratched the back of his neck. "I understand. I was looking to hire a photographer to take pictures in my club."

"I'm sorry, but I don't do club pictures," Asia informed him nicely.

"Not even for the right price?" he questioned.

"Nigga, she ain't pressed for money, and she ain't about to be in your weak-ass club taking pictures," Dinero snapped.

Asia rubbed Dinero's arm in an attempt to keep him cool.

The guy nodded. “A’ight, I guess your man has spoken. If you change your mind–”

“She won't, now get the fuck on,” Dinero cut him off and shot him a death stare

The man quickly bowed his head and turned to leave. Dinero’s jaw was clenched as he watched him exit the building.

“Babe, why do you have to be so mean?” Asia fussed.

“’Cause, he wasn’t looking for no pictures. That nigga wanted you to get to his club so he can try and fuck you.”

“Oh, so you figured all that out within five minutes, huh?”

“I'm a man, Asia. I know what niggas be on. Now drop the damn subject, and give me a kiss before I don't want it no more.”

Asia giggled and puckered her lips. They kissed intensely for a while before he pulled back.

“I’ll see you later.”

“Bye, baby.”

Dinero walked out the studio and hopped inside his car. He cranked the engine and headed toward Mila’s school so he could spend some time with his baby.

***

Diar stuck the key into the door and twisted the lock. She opened the door and sat her keys and purse on the foyer table. She shut the door with her foot and voyaged to the kitchen. Diar stopped in her tracks when she spotted Case’s mother, Celine, preparing a meal on the island.

What is this bitch doing here?

Diar couldn't stand Celine and Celine seemed to possess the mutual feeling. Diar found her to be quite snobbish and bourgeois. There had been times when Diar wanted to curse Celine out, but she never wanted to disrespect Case. She hated that Celine never treated her with respect; she mostly tolerated Diar.

Celine looked up with a fake smile plastered on her face. "Oh, hey. I see you made it to my *son's* house?"

An instant attitude surfaced, prompting Diar's lips to press together. "No, it's *our* house."

"Well, my son did pay for the property."

"I don't care what he paid for. If Case says it's our house, then that's what it is," Diar countered.

Celine smirked. "I guess you put me in my place."

"Why are you here?"

"Well, my son is getting married, and I want to help in any way that I can."

Diar opened the fridge to retrieve a bottle of water. "I don't need your help with *my* wedding. Me and my mama got it."

"Diar, I would like to have some input," Celine explained. "Case is my only child, and it would kill me if I didn't have a say so in the wedding."

"This isn't your wedding, so your input doesn't matter," Diar hissed with wrinkled brows. "And I don't care about Case being your only child. Like I said before, this is my wedding."

Celine scoffed. "Whatever you say, dear."

Diar turned to leave but Celine stopped her. She slowly turned around and glared at the woman who was set to be her mother-in-law in just a few months.

"I know you think I don't like you, but that's not the case."

Diar shrugged. "I actually didn't care if you didn't like me."

"Now, granted, I wouldn't have chosen you for my son, but he seems to be in love with you so I guess I have to adapt to that."

Diar simpered. "Yeah, he's very much in love, so much so that he asked me to be his wife," she gloated, flashing her six carat, diamond ring.

Celine offered her a tight-lipped smile. "That's cute, but I want you to know that whatever you come into this marriage with, you're going to leave with the same thing. You won't be taking my son's money."

Diar stepped closer to the island so she could look Celine in her face. "For your information, I don't want Case's money. I'm marrying him because I'm deeply in love with him, so you need to fall back and mind your business."

"Great, then you won't have a problem signing a prenuptial agreement."

Diar jerked her head back, confusion written all over her visage. "A prenuptial agreement? Me and Case never discussed that."

"Well, you should because he's gonna have you sign one."

Diar swiftly turned around and stomped out of the kitchen. She hiked the stairs two at a time until she reached her bedroom.

Case sat on the chaise going through his phone. When he glanced up, he smiled.

"You ready to go to lunch?" he asked, his eyes glued back to his phone screen.

"So you want a prenup?" she quipped, getting straight to the point.

His brows furrowed immediately. "Who told you that?"

"Your mother told me." Diar folded her arms over her breasts. "Is that what you want, Case?"

Case sat back and sighed deeply. She knew by the stillness in the room that Celine was telling the truth.

"I actually wanted to talk to you about it first before my mama ran her damn mouth."

"Why do you want one? I mean I would never try to take your money if that's what you're thinking."

"Diar, that's what all women say until mad day comes. Then they'll be ready to take you for everything you have and shit."

Her mouth gaped open with astounded eyes. "Are you serious, Case? So now you don't trust me?"

"I didn't say all that."

"So, why the hell do we need a prenuptial agreement? That shit is a fuckin' curse on our marriage."

He chuckled. "No, it's not."

"Yes, it is. I'm not getting married just to get divorced Case. I wanna be married for a lifetime, but I can see that you're not on the same page."

Case stood, ambled to where Diar was standing and grabbed her hands. "I wanna be married for a lifetime too, so don't ever question that again. I just want our assets to be protected."

She snatched her hands out of his grip. "Our assets? No, you're just thinking about yourself so don't try to put me in it. I can't believe you really want a prenup."

"Diar, you're making this shit more complicated than it needs to be. Why are you looking at it so negatively? It ain't shit but an agreement that's making sure we're both protected financially."

"Because I feel like you're already preparing for a divorce when we should be preparing to be married. Aren't you the one always preaching what's yours is mine and vice versa? So now, why you all of a sudden trying to protect your shit?"

"Because I think it's necessary for both of us. Besides, I don't want to be on the losing end if we were to ever get divorced."

Diar peered at him, not believing that he was actually thinking about them possibly divorcing. Her views on a prenuptial agreement had always been negative. She always thought that it was some kind of jinx that would prohibit a marriage from lasting forever. Hearing that Case wanted a prenup left a sour taste in her mouth.

She exhaled deeply. "I'll be back later," she muttered.

Case quickly grabbed her. "Where you going? I thought we were going to lunch."

"I'm not hungry anymore. I'll see you later, though."

Case smacked his lips and reluctantly let her go. Diar wasn't in the mood to be in his presence anymore. She needed to be alone, so she could digest her fiancé wanting to protect himself if they were to ever divorce.

***

"Fuck," Case mumbled as he watched Diar walk out of the room.

He was aware that she wouldn't like the idea of getting a prenuptial agreement and that was one of the reasons he wanted to talk to her privately about it. But now that Celine had spilled the beans, Case was ready to take his anger out on his mother. He exited the room and descended the steps.

He knew Celine was in the kitchen because of the soft jazz music playing. When he entered, Case glowered at her like she was crazy.

"Why would you do that?" he seethed.

"Do what?" she asked oblivious to his scowl.

"Why would you tell Diar about the prenup? I didn't get a chance to talk to her yet, and that shit looked bad coming from you."

"Well, how was I supposed to know you didn't tell her? Shit, she needed to know anyway."

"You should've minded your damn business instead of getting involved in my shit with Diar. I don't know why you thought it was cool to even bring that up to her."

Celine cocked her head. "Case Anthony DeMao, you will not talk to me like that! I am your mother!"

Case shook his head, not willing to go back and forth with Celine.

"Ma, you gotta go. You can't stay here with me and Diar. Go to your own crib."

Celine's mouth dropped. "Case, I always stay here when I come to town."

"Well, you're disrupting my household so you gotta go. You have your own house so you'll be a'ight."

Case walked out of the kitchen and went back to his bedroom. His mood was shitty now that Celine had interfered in his relationship with Diar. If he'd known Celine would run her mouth, he would've never talk to her about the topic. Case fell back on the bed, wondering how he was going to get back in Diar's good graces, while hoping she did actually sign the prenup.

SIX

Kiyan rang the doorbell and stuck his hands in his pockets. He looked back at his car and then returned his sight on the door. Seconds later, his mother Rochelle opened the door with a pleasant smile on her face.

"Well, hello my man child," she greeted.

Rochelle opened her arms for a hug, and Kiyan happily stepped into her embrace. He pulled back admiring the youthful look his mother possessed. Rochelle's skin was the shade of toffee with brown eyes and full lips. Her jet black hair was styled in a wrap that sat on her shoulders.

"Come in," she requested.

Kiyan stepped inside and watched her close the door. Rochelle then led him to the living room, and the two sat on the couch.

"What's up, son? You just stopping by because you missed your mama or you need something?"

Kiyan smirked. "It's both."

She playfully rolled her eyes. "I bet it is. So what's up? How's my grandbabies and Cam doing?"

He sighed and rubbed his hands down his face. "That's what I came to talk to you about. Cam is getting on my nerves, and I don't know what to do."

She chuckled, grabbing her coffee mug and taking a sip. "How is she getting on your nerves?"

"She's a fuckin' nag, and she's always angry. Every time I look up, she's got an attitude about some shit. She gets mad when I'm not home, but I don't want to be around her angry ass. She be fuckin' up my mood with her bullshit."

"Kiyan, have you tried to talk to her about why she's always mad?"

He waved his hand dismissively. "I don't want to talk to her annoying ass no more."

"Kiyan," Rochelle said with disdain. "It's your job as Cam's husband to figure out why she's not happy, and from what I hear; you're the main source to her misery."

He quickly cut his eyes at her. "She talked to you?"

"Yes, and you aren't handling your business as a husband and a father. She feels like she's in this marriage by herself, and you don't seem to understand that."

Kiyan snorted. "I don't see how she feels that way. I make sure all the bills are paid and make sure she don't have to worry about spending money. She don't be complaining when she's doing all that fucking shopping and shit. And I fronted her the money to help her start that damn business of hers. She can gone somewhere acting like I don't do shit for her."

Kiyan always made sure Camara was straight financially, and when she approached him about starting her jewelry business, he spared no cost to make sure she had what she needed. He didn't appreciate how she was trying to paint him out to be this guy that did nothing for her.

"Kiyan, I don't think Cam cares about what you do for her financially. It seems like she just want your support and help when it comes to your family. Why didn't you go pick Milan up from school when she was sick?"

"Because I was busy. She wasn't doing shit so I don't see why she made a big deal about me not picking her up."

"Boy, she was working," Rochelle hissed.

Kiyan sucked his teeth. "She's got employees so they could've handled that shit. She didn't have that much shit to do."

Rochelle swayed her head back and forth with an expression of disappointment on her face.

"What mama?"

"Your ass better get a clue before you lose your family."

He snorted. "Cam ain't leaving me. Her ass is too comfortable."

"You keep thinking that, and when you look up one day and all her shit is gone, don't come crying to me."

"I won't because it ain't gon' happen."

Rochelle nodded. "Okay. When's the last time you've spent time with Milan and Kamryn?"

He shrugged. "They like being under Cam all day so I really don't try to do anything with them."

"Kiyan, you gotta do better. This shit you telling me is not sitting well with me. If crazy-ass Dinero can spend time with Mila, then your ass can spend time with your daughters. I don't care who they like to be under. They need time with their dad, so don't come to me with that lame-ass excuse about why you don't spend time with them."

Kiyan allowed Rochelle's rant to marinate in his mind. He often used the excuse that his daughters were mama's girls so he didn't attempt to spend much time with them. He figured that providing them with an exquisite lifestyle would make up for his lack of presence in their life.

"You right mama; I gotta do better when it comes to them."

"And you have to do better with your wife. I've seen Cam be a good woman to you so if she's been angry with you that tells me you're not doing your job as her husband."

He sighed deeply. "I hear you, Mama."

"Now when's the last time you two went out on a date?"

The room became silent as Kiyan pondered when he and Camara had actually had some one-on-one time.

"If you gotta think that hard, that means it's been long overdue," Rochelle clipped. "Take her out, and say sorry for being an ass."

Kiyan grinned. "A'ight, I'll admit I ain't been on my shit, but that don't mean Cam ain't been getting on my nerves."

"Well, I'm sure the feeling is mutual. If you need a babysitter, you know you can bring the girls by."

He nodded. "Thanks. Where is Carlos?" he asked, referring to her husband.

"He went out for a while. He'll be back later on."

"Have you seen Keece and Dinero lately?"

"Not since I got back in town, but I'm sure they'll stop by this week."

"Can you cook this weekend?" he begged.

Rochelle chuckled. "What your beggin' ass want, Kiyan?"

"I got a taste for some fish and spaghetti."

She rolled her eyes. "I'll see what I can do, boy."

"Good looking out." he stood. "I'll call you later. I'm about to go to the crib for a lil' while."

"Okay, and remember what I said. Go take care of your family, alright?"

Kiyan nodded and headed to the front door. When he walked outside, his phone rang. He looked at the screen and noticed Fabian calling.

"What does your extra busy ass want?" Kiyan answered.

Fabian laughed. "Shit, I've been busier than a mothafucka. What you been on?"

"Shit, getting money. Where you at?"

"That's why I was calling. I got a show in Houston tonight and was calling to see if you wanted to come down. You know it's always a movie when we hit H-Town."

Kiyan grinned because they always had fun whenever they would visit Houston. Instantly, his plan to take Camara out on a date surfaced. He wanted to try and rectify their marital issues, but partying with Fabian seemed to be more enticing than being with Camara and her attitude.

"Shit, I'm down. I'm about to catch a flight down there."

"That's what's up. Aye, I know it's short notice, but ask the bros to come down too."

"A'ight, I got you. I'll hit you up when I touch down."

"A'ight fam."

Kiyan quickly jumped in his car and made his way home to pack. He figured he would take Camara on a date when he got back in town, so they could figure out how to get their marriage back on track.

***

Diar took a huge gulp of wine and sat the glass on the coffee table. She stared at her best friend, Kayla, anxiously awaiting her reply. Diar had fled to her house so she could vent about the prenuptial dilemma and she needed her advice.

"Well," Diar urged.

"Well," Kayla began, "I can see why you're bothered, but don't you think it's smart on both of your parts to get protection?"

A grimace appeared on Diar's face. "No, it's not. We don't need protection from each other when we're planning on being married forever."

Kayla flicked her long weave. "Let's be realistic, marriages don't last these days."

"Well, mine will. I'll never want to be with anyone else except Case."

"That's sweet, but what if he cheats on you?" Kayla challenged.

"I don't think it would happen but if it did, I'll forgive him after he receives my wrath."

Kayla chortled. "Okay, what if he has a baby on you?"

"That won't happen. Case ain't that reckless."

"I guess so…but Diar, don't give him such a hard time about this prenup shit. It's not that big of a deal."

Diar pouted while folding her arms across her chest. "It's a big deal to me. That shit is a curse. Couples who get that prenup shit always get divorced."

"Not always."

"Yes, they do, and I'm not willing to put my marriage in jeopardy like that."

"So, what if you don't sign and Case calls off the wedding?"

That thought hadn't crossed Diar's mind. She was hoping he didn't turn this into an ultimatum because she was prepared to stand her ground.

"If he does, then I'll be fine with that," she lied.

Kayla twisted her lips. "Bitch, I know you, and you will not be fine with him pulling out of the wedding."

Diar shrugged, opting not to respond verbally.

"Oh and Case needs to check his damn mama. Her uppity ass is always trying to throw shade at somebody. She's just mad his daddy left her ass."

Diar tittered. "She's so miserable. I hate when her ass comes to visit because she's always trying to ruin shit. When I get back home, I'm going to tell her ass to leave. I don't want to deal with that bitch."

"I know that's right," Kayla agreed. "She don't need to be interfering in your relationship. Kick that hoe to the door."

Diar laughed, appreciating Kayla's candid hilarity. "So you think I'm trippin' on Case?"

"I wouldn't say trippin', but don't take it so personal. He has businesses as well as you. Would you want him to take the stores you share with Stefani?"

Diar and her sister, Stefani, owned two boutiques together. Stefani had extended the offer for Diar to be a co-owner, and she happily obliged.

"Case wouldn't do that, and I wouldn't want to take his tattoo shops."

"Well if you know that, then signing the agreement shouldn't be that difficult," Kayla noted.

Diar understood what Kayla was saying but it still didn't sit well with her.

"Maybe I should go talk to his brothers' wives to see if they signed one. I know Case's family is wealthy, and maybe they all just want to protect their money, so if the other women signed, maybe I wouldn't be opposed to signing either."

"That's a good idea. They can maybe get you to see that it's not that big of a deal since they've possibly gone through it."

Diar nodded. Maybe speaking to one of Case's sister-in-laws would help her see that a prenuptial agreement wasn't all that bad.

***

Camara bore into the pool in her backyard while becoming lost in her thoughts. She had just put the girls to bed and was enjoying a much-needed night cap. She gazed up at the night-time sky, admiring the shimmering stars that shined on the horizon. Camara often retreated to the backyard and contemplated the trials in her life. This was her only escape from her hectic life. She picked up her glass and swallowed a gulp of red wine. She closed her eyes as the smooth liquid flowed down her throat. Just as she was about to take another sip, her phone rang.

Camara smiled when she noticed her best friend, Paris, calling. They hadn't spoken all day which was unusual for them because they always communicated throughout the day. She quickly grabbed her phone and answered.

"Oh, so you're just now calling me? I haven't heard from you all day," Camara playfully sassed.

"Girl," Paris began, "my day was so damn busy. I didn't even have time to eat lunch. I had court and a bunch of meetings with clients today. I am beat."

Camara smirked. "The life of a lawyer never ends."

"Tell me about it. What are you doing?"

"I'm sitting in my backyard, having a glass of wine. I just put my rug rats to bed so I decided to unwind."

"Shit, my kids are still up worrying me," Paris ranted. "I told them to give me five minutes to get my mind right."

"You're terrible," Camara laughed. "Where's daddy Keece?"

"He's in his man cave watching the game. Where is your man?"

Camara shrugged as if Paris could see her. "Your guess is as good as mine."

"You don't be asking Kiyan about his whereabouts?"

"Girl, fuck that nigga."

Paris cackled. "Damn, Cam, why so much hostility in your tone?"

"Because I'm tired of him and his bullshit."

"It's not getting any better, huh?"

Camara had confided in Paris about her failing marriage. Other than her mother, Camara trusted Paris with her marital woes.

"It's actually gotten worse. He doesn't respect me or seem to care about me. I'm tired of talking to him and telling him what I need only for him to keep doing what he wants to do. He thinks because he has money that I won't leave his ass, but he just doesn't know, I have one foot out the damn door.

"I never thought Kiyan would revert back to his old antics. As much as I want you guys to make it, I don't want you to sacrifice your happiness either."

"Yeah and truthfully… I'm not even in love with Kiyan anymore."

Camara had never uttered those words and a part of her was relieved now that she had admitted it. Her love for Kiyan had faded months ago. She loved him because he had helped her create two beautiful little girls, but he no longer held her heart.

Paris gasped. "Really, Cam? It's that bad."

"Yeah, Paris. There's no need for me to keep up this front. I'm not in love with my husband anymore."

There was dead silence on Paris' end. Camara figured she may have been shocked by her revelation.

"Wow, I'm stunned. So what are you going to do? You can't stay in a marriage when you're not in love."

Camara sighed heavily. "I haven't decided yet. I never wanted my kids to grow up without being in a two-parent home. Somehow, I'm trying to stick it out for them, but this shit is becoming more difficult by the day."

"Cam, I understand that you want your kids to grow up in the same household with their mother and father, but what about you? Are you willing to be unhappy for the sake of them? They don't need to see their mother upset and stressed out because you're trying to keep your failing marriage together, especially if Kiyan isn't trying to help you keep it together. In this situation, I recommend that you be selfish just this one time so that you can be one hundred percent happy for the girls."

Camara carefully considered Paris' advice. She had been willing to bite the bullet for her daughters, but she didn't know how much she was willing to endure from Kiyan.

"I know, Paris…I know."

"Plus, I need my crazy friend back. You've been down, and I can tell it's because of Kiyan. Don't let him steal all your joy. Hey, maybe you guys should try counseling."

"I suggested it a while back, but he won't do it."

"Why not?"

Camara snorted. "Because he's a fucking asshole. He came up with some bullshit excuse, so I never suggested it again."

"Well, what about separating for a while."

"Paris, if I leave, I'm never coming back to him," Camara declared.

"I understand. Well, whatever decision you make, you know I'm here for you."

"I know, and I appreciate you."

"Of course. Well, let me get these kids together. I'll talk to you tomorrow."

"Okay, bye."

Camara ended the call and quickly quaffed down the rest of her wine. She stood, grabbed her glass and entered the house. After locking the doors and washing the few dishes in the sink, Camara traveled upstairs to her bedroom. She hadn't seen nor spoken to Kiyan since this morning. That was the norm for the couple unless there was something Camara really needed. Rarely did they communicate throughout the day. Camara found that reality to be sad because at one point in time, Kiyan was her best friend.

She pulled back the comforter and settled into bed. She was beyond exhausted, and as soon as her head hit the pillow, she was out like a light.

***

Hours later…

Camara opened her eyes and slowly rolled over. She ran her hands down the other side of the bed and noticed that it was empty. She quickly sat up and looked at the time on her phone. When she realized it was almost five o'clock in the morning, she got out of bed in search for Kiyan. Sometimes, he fell asleep in the living room, so she voyaged there. When she didn't see him, Camara went back up the stairs and checked the girls' room.

"Where the hell is he?" she mumbled when she saw that he wasn't there.

Camara went back into their bedroom and checked the bathroom. When it was determined that Kiyan wasn't in the home, she grabbed the phone and quickly dialed his number. Her heart was thumping erratically at the thought of something being wrong with him. Kiyan usually came home and never did he come home this late.

Please God let him be okay.

"Hello?" Kiyan answered in a groggy tone.

The anxious expression Camara had worn for the last five minutes had quickly vanished. Kiyan didn't seem to be in distress and that instantly angered Camara.

"Where are you?"

"I'm in Houston," he told her as if he'd informed her before.

"In Houston?" she questioned incredulously. "Why are you in Houston, Kiyan?"

"Fabian invited me down since he had a show. I meant to call you earlier, but I had forgot and shit."

This mothafucka.

At this point, Camara was suffused with rage. She couldn't understand how he could be so inconsiderate and not inform her that he was going out of town for the night. Kiyan often moved around as if he was a bachelor with no wife and kids, and Camara was officially done with his bullshit. She had already been fed up with his behavior, but this stunt he'd pulled had her beyond furious. Instead of cursing him out like she normally would, she decided to try a different approach.

"Well, I just wanted to make sure you were okay. Enjoy your time down there," she said with a softer tone.

"I'll be back in the afternoon. Maybe we can go somewhere to eat," he suggested.

She chuckled, but she was far from amused. "We'll talk about it once you get home. Like I said, enjoy your time."

"A'ight, aye—"

Camara swiftly hung up and placed his number on the block list. Her patience for Kiyan's flippant decorum had run its course. She was no longer going to tolerate his blatant disregard for her or their children. Camara had to go just to keep what sanity she had left.

She hopped up and entered her walk-in closet. Camara pulled out her suitcase and began to throw all of her belongings inside. Kiyan had disrespected her for the last time. Camara knew there was possibly no way he would come back from this, so she made sure to take everything she owned before going to her girls room and packing their things as well.

***

Paris cleaned off the center island from the mess the kids had made from breakfast. She'd just saw them off to school and was straightening the kitchen before she headed to work. She wiped down the marble top with a dish rag before tossing it in the sink. The sound of Keece's voice turned her head as she noticed him entering the kitchen on the phone. He walked up to her and kissed her cheek before continuing his conversation.

Paris turned on the Keurig coffee maker and decided to fix her some coffee. After a couple minutes, Keece ended the call.

"What time you gotta be at the office?" he queried.

Paris glanced at her Cartier watch. "In like thirty minutes. I have a meeting with a client. What are your plans for today?"

"Work," he smirked.

"What kind of work?" she quipped playfully.

"The usual."

She twisted her juicy lips. "Yeah, okay. I want to talk to you about something."

Keece took a seat at the island. "What is it?"

"Well, when Riley dropped Kya off the other day, she asked to talk to me. I agreed and she proceeded to tell me that she was moving to Atlanta, and she wants you to give Kya up for six months so she could spend half the year with her."

A grimace immediately surfaced on Keece's handsome face. Paris knew by the bulging vein in his neck that he was vexed.

"She got me fucked up if she thinks that's about to happen. Kya ain't going nowhere with her trifling ass"

"I told her not to get her hopes up."

"You should've told that bitch that it's not happening," he clipped. "She don't even take good care of Kya now, so why would I be dumb enough to send her to another state with Riley's inconsistent ass?"

"I know, babe, and I brought that to her attention. She made it seem like she had it all figured out, so I don't know."

Keece abruptly stood and began to pace. "Why the fuck she just won't stay here? I mean this is where her daughter is. Riley knows I'm not sending Kya with her so I don't know why she fuckin' trying me," he griped.

Paris stepped over to where he was pacing. Keece was clearly agitated so she grabbed his hands in an attempt to calm him down.

"I was thinking, maybe you should ask Kya what she wants to do," she suggested.

He cut his eyes at her. "I ain't asking Kya shit. I'm not about to let a seven-year-old tell me what she wants to do."

Paris quickly released his hands from her hold. If there was one thing she could change about Keece, it would be his controlling nature. He always wanted things to go his way and if you went against him, he would make situations more difficult.

"At least you could see how Kya would feel being without her mother. I figured either way, she'll be lacking if she was to go with Riley or stay with us."

He scoffed and then waved his hands dismissively. "I ain't trying to hear that shit you talking. Kya don't need to be away from me. I'm the one that takes care of her."

"Oh, it's just you?" she quipped.

Keece gave her a knowing look. "You know what I mean."

"Oh, okay," she replied unconvincingly.

"You know what I don't understand? Paris, why would you ask me to ask Kya how she feels about going with her mama? Why the fuck it seems like you on Riley's side all of a sudden?" he hissed.

Paris held her hands out in confusion. “I'm not on her side, Keece. I just thought it would be a good idea to ask Kya what she wants to do.”

“Nah, you be letting Riley punk you. That’s why she talked to you about it before she told me. She knows what the fuck she be doing and you be falling for the shit”

“I am not letting her punk me. I'm only trying to be neutral and keep the peace for your information.”

“You don't need to be neutral. You're my wife, and you don't owe that bitch shit. You should always be on my side.”

Paris shook her head before pinching the bridge of her nose. She refused to go into work with an attitude because of Keece.

“You know what? I’ll see you later.”

“Why you running?” he taunted her. “You know I be spittin’ the truth.”

“Actually, you be spittin’ bullshit with your mean and controlling ass. Have a good day.”

Paris’ heels clicked loudly against the marble floor as she grabbed her purse and exited the house. Every time she tried to be the peacemaker between Riley and Keece, it always backfired on her. A part of her wanted to stop all communication with Riley just so Keece could see how much help she was when it came to dealing with her. Paris made a pact with herself that she would force Keece to communicate with Riley since he didn’t appreciate her efforts.

SEVEN

Diar entered the studio in search of Asia. She wanted to discuss this prenuptial business, and since she and Asia had established a relationship, Diar figured she would be the first stop. She spotted Asia taking pictures of a woman who was styled in a beautiful white gown. When Diar spotted her baby bump, she figured they were shooting maternity pictures.

Asia looked up and smiled. “Hey, Diar. What brings you by?”

“I was just…I was hoping to talk to you, but if you're busy, I can come back another time.”

“No, I have time for you. I'm almost done with this shoot. You can go sit in my office if you like.”

Diar nodded. “Okay.”

She traveled upstairs to Asia’s office and took a seat. Diar was familiar with the studio since she had hired Asia to take pictures for their new inventory for the boutique. After twenty minutes, Asia came into the room.

“Okay, girl, I'm ready. I've been booked all morning so you came at the perfect time. What's going on?” she asked, taking a seat behind her desk.

Diar smiled at Asia as she soaked up her beauty. “You look pretty today.”

Asia beamed. “Aw, thank you. You look fly as hell like always. No wonder Case put a ring on your ass.”

"Well, that's what I came to talk to you about."

Asia's eyebrows furrowed. "Don't tell me you're getting cold feet?"

Diar tittered. "No, nothing like that, but Case's mother told me that he wants me to sign a prenuptial agreement. I thought her evil-ass was lying so I went to confront him about it, but he actually wants me to sign one, and I don't know how to feel about that."

"Celine is so damn messy," Asia complained. "Why would she run her mouth like that?"

"Because she's a bitch. She doesn't like me, and I damn sure don't like her ass."

"Don't nobody like her miserable ass."

"I'm sure, but I don't mean to get in your business or anything like that, but I was wondering if Dinero made you sign a prenup."

"Girl," Asia began, "he didn't. Actually both times we got married he didn't say shit about a prenup."

"Wait a minute; you guys were married twice?" Diar asked in disbelief.

Asia smirked. "Yes, my dumb ass married the same guy twice."

"What happened the first time y'all were married?"

"Girl, Dinero showed his entire ass. He cheated, and then he wasn't there for me when I had a miscarriage so I divorced his ass. We got back together after I had Mila though."

"Wow, that's crazy. I never knew y'all went through all that."

"Yeah, it was a journey, but we're good now. So, Case must've rubbed you the wrong way when he asked for you to sign the prenup, huh?"

"Yes," Diar sighed. "I know I can be dramatic, overly emotional, and sensitive sometimes, but I always felt like a prenuptial agreement was a curse, and I don't want that shit over our marriage."

Asia chuckled. "I understand, but you two are very successful, and y'all have businesses that y'all share with your siblings. In a way, the prenuptial agreement will be protecting Stefani as well as Keece."

Diar considered her statement because she hadn't really seen it as a way to protect their siblings, who were also their business partners.

"I guess I really didn't look at it that way."

"Yeah, and it's not such a bad idea, because it would be unfair for Stefani and Keece to be in the middle of something that really has nothing to do with them."

"But I don't plan on getting divorced," Diar professed sadly.

"Listen, we all plan to stay married forever, but shit, sometimes things happen. But I don't want to excuse your feelings because prenuptial agreements can be tricky. If you know Case is the one and you and him both plan to be married for the rest of your lives, then signing the agreement shouldn't be a big deal."

Diar nodded, feeling a little better since Asia was making her see things in a much clearer way.

"Okay, I understand. Thanks for making me feel better about the situation because my extra ass had overdone it. I stormed out the house all dramatic and shit. I swear I don't know how Case loves me," Diar kidded.

Asia chortled. "I'm sure he knows what he's dealing with so your episode wasn't all that surprising."

"Yeah, I guess I should talk to him now that I've calmed down."

"Good and Diar, you got the best brother out of the DeMao bunch, so I don't think you have anything to worry about with Case. We got the difficult-ass niggas so you're lucky," Asia jested.

Diar giggled. "I guess you're right because I don't know how you deal with Dinero."

"Chile, me either. With prayer and fasting you can achieve anything."

The girls cackled loudly while talking for another twenty minutes. Diar stood and smooth down her midi dress.

"Thank you and I'm going to email you later because we're doing our summer campaign, and we'll need you to shoot it."

"I got you," Asia assured.

The two women hugged before Diar left and made her way to make things right between her and Case.

***

Kiyan opened the door to his home and dropped his bag on the floor. He threw his keys on the foyer table and walked to the kitchen. He noticed that the house was quiet, so he figured Camara and the girls were gone enjoying the beautiful weather. He grabbed a bottle of water out of the fridge, traveled upstairs, and entered his bedroom.

"Shit, I'm tired," he muttered, taking off his hoodie.

Kiyan stepped into the closet and abruptly stopped in his tracks. His heart pounded profusely against his chest as his almond-shaped orbs roved over the emptiness of the closet.

"What the fuck?" he whispered, ambling toward the bare racks on Camara's side of the closet.

Kiyan quickly left out the space and traveled to Milan and Kamryn's room. When he noticed that all of their belongings were gone, he ran back to his bedroom to grab his phone. By this time, sweat beads had surfaced on his skin while his chest began to tighten. The sour sensation settling in the pit of his stomach caused him to feel nauseous. Kiyan dialed Camara's number while holding his breath.

"The number you've dialed…"

"Shit," he grumbled before ending the call.

Camara had blocked him, so he pulled out his second phone and dialed her again. When he realized that she had blocked that number, Kiyan threw his phone against the wall.

"Fuck!" he yelled, feeling like he was about to have a panic attack.

This was a reality that Kiyan hadn't prepared for. Despite his inconsiderate conduct, he never thought he would return home to find not only all of his wife's belongings missing but his daughters too. Camara had made several threats to leave him over the past months, but Kiyan knew she was just bluffing. He always thought Camara would adapt to him wanting to do what he wanted even though they were married. Being a family man was great at times, but Kiyan loved to party. He liked going to clubs or booking a flight just to attend a party. He knew Camara had been fed up with his antics, but he didn't see this coming at all.

Kiyan quickly snatched up his hoodie and threw it back on. He ran down the stairs, grabbed his keys and left out the house. He needed to talk to someone before his thoughts ran him rampant, so he dialed Dom's number. Just as Kiyan got into his car, he answered.

"What's up, Kiyan?"

He sighed. "I just came home and all of Cam's shit is gone, including the girls."

Dom chuckled. "What the fuck you want me to do?"

"I don't know," Kiyan snorted. "I just…I don't know."

"Well, what happened that made her leave?"

Kiyan shrugged like a kid who hadn't received a snack. "I don't know."

"So you're just oblivious to what goes on in your house? Or you're not man enough to admit that you fucked up."

"Nah, it's not that. Pops, Cam just ain't never satisfied. She's always naggin' me and shit, especially when I don't do what she wants me to do."

"Tell me this, have you been handling your responsibility as a husband and a father well?"

Kiyan grew quiet because he didn't want to admit that he was failing in both areas.

"I'll take your silence as a no. How come Camara had to call me the other day and ask if I could pick the girls up from school? Why couldn't you do it?"

"Because I was busy," Kiyan huffed.

"Too busy to pick your daughters up from school? I don't know about you, Kiyan. I think you got life fucked up."

"How?"

"Because you don't see the shit you're doing to Cam and now you're surprised when you come home and find your family gone. You don't handle your shit when it comes to them and you know it. Cam shouldn't have had to call me to get the girls when she has a fuckin' husband. What the fuck is wrong with you?"

Kiyan was aware that Dom was speaking the truth but the stubborn side of him wouldn't accept it.

"So now I gotta stop what I'm doing whenever Cam calls me? I'm not her bitch."

Dom snorted. "You've got a lot of growing up to do, son. I would never want someone else to come to the rescue of my wife when I'm capable of meeting her needs. But hey, that's me."

"Man, I didn't call you for a lecture, pops. I wanna know how to get my wife back home."

"Lil' nigga, I don't know the answers to your problems. Now get off my line since you don't wanna hear the truth."

When Dom hung up, Kiyan threw his phone in the passenger seat. He was frustrated and hearing how he had caused all the turmoil in his marriage wasn't something he wanted to digest at the moment. Kiyan started the car and headed to Camara's mother, Celeste, house. When he arrived, he spotted her outside, pulling weeds from her garden. He got out and tucked his hands in his pockets.

"Hey, Ms. Celeste."

The older woman looked up while holding her hand above her eyes to shield the bright sun.

"Oh, hello, Kiyan. What brings you by?" Celeste asked, standing to her feet.

Kiyan looked through the windows of the house to see if he spotted Camara. "I um…I was wondering if Cam and the girls were here."

"I'm afraid not. What's going on?"

I know you fucking know already.

"Nothing," he lied. "I just wanted to take them out, but they weren't home and Cam's not answering her phone."

"Hmmph," Celeste grunted with a smirk. "Well, she's not here."

"A'ight thanks."

Kiyan trudged back to the car feeling defeated. Deep down, he felt like this was the beginning of the end for his marriage. Camara had never pulled a stunt of this magnitude and a part of him was fearful that she was officially done with him. Kiyan's pride wouldn't allow her to walk away. He knew he hadn't been a great companion to her, and for that, he was willing to fight to bring his family back home. He pulled out his phone and dialed her number, but he'd forgotten she had blocked him.

Fuck!

***

Camara grinned as the girls raced down the hallway of the hotel. They had just come back from the indoor water park after having some much-needed fun. They were now headed back to their suite so they could eat and unwind from their amusing day.

Camara approached the door and slid her key card inside. The three of them walked in, and before the girls went to take a shower, Camara stopped them.

"Hey, I want to talk to you guys for a minute."

Milan and Kamryn came to sit down on the sofa as Camara took a seat across from them. She had dreaded this part of her transition ever since she decided to flee her home. She didn't know how the girls would take her breaking up with Kiyan. Camara never wanted to disrupt their lives like this, but she couldn't take any more of his bullshit just for the sake of keeping their family together.

"So, I wanted to ask you guys something and I want you to tell me how you feel, okay?"

The girls nodded.

"Okay...how would you feel if the three of us got our own house?"

"Only us three?" Milan questioned, curiosity written on her beautiful face that resembled a perfect blend of Camara and Kiyan.

Camara quickly placed an inviting smile on her face just so they wouldn't be alarmed. "Yes, just us three, sweetie."

"What about daddy?" Kamryn asked.

Camara hesitated and carefully chose her words before responding. "Daddy will stay at the house we were in last night, and we'll get our own place."

"Are you guys getting a divorce?" Milan asked.

Milan was six years old but she was wise beyond her little years. She wasn't a kid you could tell anything to because she would always figure out the truth.

With much reluctance, Camara nodded while cringing on the inside because she didn't know how they would react.

"Is it because he makes you sad?" Kamryn questioned innocently.

Camara attempted to keep her eyes from tearing up, but it was almost impossible. She hated that her daughters were aware of how badly Kiyan treated her.

"Yes, it's because he makes me sad, and mommy wants to be happy for you guys. That's why I want to get our own house so we can start over with just us three."

"Can we get a house with a pool?" Kamryn asked excitedly.

Camara chuckled. "Sure, if I can find one at a decent price."

"And can I paint my room aqua green?" Milan asked.

"Sure you can. You guys can do whatever you like to your new room."

Kamryn shimmied her shoulders. "Can we stay at the hotel a little longer Mommy? Please."

"Of course. So how do you guys feel about what I just told you? Do you have any questions for me? Are you guys gonna be okay with us living in one house and daddy living in another?"

Kamryn nodded eagerly.

"Well, we didn't see daddy a lot so I'm not sad," Milan noted.

"Yeah, daddy never comes home," Kamryn agreed.

It broke Camara's heart to hear how content the girls were with not seeing Kiyan. She wished he would realize how much his presence was needed in their daughters' lives.

"Well, hopefully that'll change," Camara said with not much confidence. "Now give me a hug so you guys can go shower."

The two girls hugged Camara before they ran off toward the bathroom. Once they were out of her sight, Camara breathed a sigh of relief. She thought that the girls would be bothered that they were moving out of their house, but they'd surprised her with their support. Camara stood and headed to the bedroom. She left her phone in the suite while they went to the water park and she wanted to check her messages.

When Camara saw that Rochelle had sent her a text, requesting that she call her, she immediately dialed Rochelle's number.

"Hello?"

"Hey, Rochelle, it's me, Cam."

"Hey sweetie. Kiyan just called me asking where you were, and I wanted to make sure you and the girls are good."

"Yeah, we're currently at the hotel right now. Please don't tell Kiyan because I'm leaving him."

"Really? You've had enough, huh?"

Camara nodded. "I have Rochelle. You know all about what I've been going through with your son. He just doesn't care and the last straw was him going to Houston without telling me. That kind of inconsiderate shit pisses me off, but when I realized he saw no wrong in what he'd done, I knew it was time for me to go."

"Listen, you don't have to explain anything to me. I'm a woman so I can understand when you're officially fed up. So you have my support. Now where are you going to stay while in this transition?"

"I'll probably stay here."

"Cam, no, you guys can come to my house. I promise to keep Kiyan away."

Camara smiled. "I appreciate that Rochelle, but I think I'll just stay here. I'm sure it won't take me long to find a place."

"Are you sure?"

"I'm positive, but thanks for the offer."

"Okay, well, keep me in the loop, and I promise not to tell Kiyan anything."

"I will, Rochelle. Thank you."

"Bye, sweetie."

Camara hung up and placed the phone on the nightstand. She was relieved that Rochelle was a woman who was unbiased. She never sided with her sons just because she was the one that birthed them. She always held them responsible for their actions, and Camara appreciated that. Distancing herself from Kiyan was necessary, and she knew in his mind, he would make it like she was the bad guy. For once, Camara was putting herself first and it felt great.

***

Aimee posted a promo video to her Instagram account that she shared with Asia before sitting her phone down on the counter. She prepared herself to make some lunch before she was interrupted by the doorbell. Aimee headed toward the door as she glanced over at the twins playing with her grandma who was visiting for the day.

“Don't be so rough with Lola, girls,” she called out before opening the front door.

Aimee’s pleasant face contorted into a grimace as she peered at, Tara, who had her hands propped up on her hips. Aimee sighed deeply, hoping this unannounced visit wouldn’t be consumed with them fighting.

“Can I help you?” Aimee asked in a flat tone.

“I'm here to get my baby since y’all had her all damn week,” Tara shot nastily.

“I’m sorry, but she's not here.”

Tara snaked her neck. “Well, where is she?”

“Big took her out for daddy and daughter time. They’ll be back later on.”

Tara became quiet for a moment as she folded her arms over her chest. “Y’all need to return my damn daughter asap. Y’all done had her all week acting like y’all the damn Brady Bunch family.”

Aimee pursed her lips. “Is your car fixed?”

Tara smacked her teeth before looking off into the immaculate lawn. After a moment, she then returned her sight on Aimee. “Why do you care?”

“Because if it’s not, Big is not going to send Zaria home to you. You're not about to keep her out of school because you're trying to spite Big because he wouldn’t get your car fixed.”

“Well he should have. I'm his daughter’s mother, and he should be available when I need help.”

"That's not his place, Tara. Big is married, and he is not about to come to the rescue of you. Besides, he pays child support, so you should be good with that."

"I use that for my bills and for Zaria."

Aimee rolled her eyes, growing tired of the conversation. "Like I mentioned before, Zaria will remain here until your car is fixed."

"You ain't her damn mama. I am," Tara griped defiantly.

"Actually, I'm her step-mother, and I help take great care of Zaria, so save your fucking breath."

"I don't care what you are. You ain't give birth to her so you ain't her mother. Now when can I come back to get my baby?"

Aimee smirked. "Big will drop her off tomorrow. We have some family time planned tonight."

"Aimee, stop trying to include my baby in your little family. She is not yours. I am her mother, and I don't need you trying to take my spot."

Aimee was baffled that Tara didn't want her to include Zaria even though she was a big part of their family.

"Tara, get off my doorstep before you get your ass whooped again."

"That shit doesn't count. You and your twin jumped me."

Aimee snickered. "Trust me. If I was to fight you by myself, the results will still be the same. If you need me to show you again, you know it can be arranged."

Tara backed up a bit before looking around. "Just have my child home tomorrow."

"No problem. Now you have a good day, and don't show up at my house again without calling."

Tara mumbled something under her breath just as Aimee shut the door. Tara was still the same ignorant woman she was when Aimee first met Big. Their journey had been tumultuous which included a fist fight. After that transpired, Aimee vowed to never deal with Tara, but since she had taken it upon herself to pop up, Aimee felt like she should lay down the law. Aimee entered the kitchen and sat at the table with Big, DJ, and Zaria.

"Who was that at the door?" he asked.

Aimee shrugged. "Jehovah's witnesses."

"Mama, what are Jehovah's witness?" DJ asked.

"They're people who come and take your kids away from you when they beg too much," Big joked.

Zaria laughed. "Daddy, that's not true."

Aimee shook her head. "Why are you always playing?"

Big chuckled. "I'm playing, DJ. They're people who try to teach you about the bible."

"Oh," DJ replied, nodding.

"Hey, did you guys figure out where we're going today?" Aimee questioned.

It was their day to spend as a family so they were trying to figure out what their activities would consist of.

"I want to go to the zoo," DJ requested.

"I wanna go to the water park," Zaria added.

"Okay, Big, which one are we going to do?" Aimee asked.

"Uh," he sat in thought. "I don't feel like that water park shit today. Let's hit up the zoo."

"Daddy, DJ chose last time," Zaria whined.

"No, you did," DJ countered.

"Yep, you sure did, Zaria. Remember when we went to the museum?" Aimee asked.

Zaria smirked as she rested her chin on her open palm.

"Don't be getting quiet now," Big teased. "Yo' little spoiled ass be forgetting that we do a lot of things you like."

Zaria playfully rolled her eyes. "Okay, Daddy."

Big's eyes landed on Aimee. "Aye, we gon' have to drive two cars since your grandma with us."

Aimee shook her head. "Big, I don't feel like driving. I drive all day, every day, and I need a break. We're just gonna have to pile up in the truck."

"Now you need a break," he snickered. "Ain't this what you wanted soccer mom?" Big joked.

Aimee enjoyed being a stay-at-home mom, but some days she needed a break, and this was one of those days.

Aimee tittered. "Yeah I did, but you need to chauffeur me around today."

"A'ight. I got you."

Aimee smiled, happy that she was getting her way. She loved spending time with her family. She wasn't going to allow Tara to ruin it by pissing her off and taking Zaria away from them.

Not today bitch…

EIGHT

Paris sat at her vanity applying her nightly face mask to her skin. Once it was applied, she pulled her hair into a ponytail and secured her robe tightly around her waist. Deuce ran into her closet and wrapped his arms around her neck.

"Goodnight, Mommy," he said sweetly.

"Goodnight, sweetie, and make sure you use the bathroom before you lay down."

He nodded. "Okay."

Deuce ran out the room, causing a simper to appear on her face. Seconds later, Keece entered the space with a slight frown on his face. Paris quickly turned back to her mirror because she hadn't been feeling him since their spat about Riley and Kya.

"Aye, why the fuck Riley keeps calling me? Have you talked to her?"

"Nope."

"Well, you need to. You know I don't like dealing with her ass."

"Actually, I'm not going to talk to her," she revealed with a smirk.

"Why?"

"Because I'm no longer going to be in the middle of you and Riley's shit. That's your daughter's mother, not mine so you deal with her from now on."

Keece stepped closer to where Paris was seated and towered over her. “Why you on that bullshit?”

“Because you don't appreciate my help when it comes to you and her. I try to keep the peace, but you would rather see all of us in chaos, so you deal with her because I'm done.”

He chuckled. “Is this some kind of way of trying to get me back for speaking the truth the other day?”

Paris stood, facing him. “No, it’s me dealing with my own problems instead of taking on you and Riley’s bullshit. Besides, I wouldn’t want her to punk me like you said.”

Paris attempted to walk around him, but Keece gently grabbed her arm.

“Listen, I do appreciate your help, but I don't like when you be trying to take her side.”

“I never take her side, I just try to get you to look at things from all sides, but you're incapable of doing that because you're so damn controlling.”

Keece snorted while letting Paris’ arm fall to her side.

“You know what? Keep your fucking attitude. You're a spoiled ass brat who throws tantrums when somebody tells your ass the truth.”

“And what's the truth, Keece?” Paris asked with a smirk. “For years, I've been the mediator between you and Riley. Even after this bitch came to my house and attacked me while I was pregnant, I still pushed that shit to the side for the sake of Kya. Riley calls me for everything because you refuse to deal with her.

So yeah, I'm tired of doing your damn work for you. You got that bitch pregnant, not me. So you deal with her from now on."

Paris had become tired of Keece acting as though it was her job to converse with Riley when it came to Kya. She needed him to realize that she didn't have to deal with his child's mother.

Keece bowed his head. "You on some bullshit, but okay. I'll deal with *my* child's mother."

Paris narrowed her eyes in his direction. "What the fuck is that supposed to mean?"

"What?"

"'*My* child's mother. Kya is mine too, so don't fucking play with me."

He shrugged before exiting the closet. Paris followed after him, not liking the silence he was giving her.

"Don't play with me, Keece. Kya came into my life the exact same time she entered yours so stop saying shit like that."

"Man, I ain't said shit," he laughed.

"Your ugly ass always fucking around," Paris accused.

Keece laid back on their king size mattress and propped his hands behind his head. "I'm just taking your advice, since I'm the one that got Riley pregnant. Just know that I'll never ask you to do anything else for me, okay?"

Paris closed her eyes and shook her head. Keece often tried to manipulate her and make her feel guilty for opting out of dealing with his situations. Sometimes, she felt unappreciated.

"You ain't threatening me by saying that. Shit, that's music to my ears."

There was silence for a moment before he said, "I was thinking maybe I should let Kya move with her mama since you think it's a good idea."

She cocked her head. "I never said it was a good idea Keece. I said maybe you should ask her how she feels about it."

He sat up, glaring at her. "Kya, come here!"

A minute later, Kya entered the bedroom wearing her pink, satin pajamas. "Yes, daddy."

Keece grabbed her hands. "Your mama is moving to Atlanta, and she wants you to move with her. You would be gone for six months, and then you would come back here with us and spend the rest of the six months at home. How would you like that?"

Kya stared at him for a moment before looking over at Paris.

"So you're not coming?" Kya asked.

"Nah, it would just be you and your mama," Keece replied.

Paris held her breath because she truly didn't want Kya to move with her mother. She only wanted Keece to ask Kya just to hear her thoughts about it.

"I don't know," Kya responded with uncertainty. "I don't want to leave now. Do I have to?"

"No, you don't have to. If you're not sure, you can think about it. You don't have to make a decision right now boo," Paris offered.

Kya nodded. "Okay, I'm going to think about it."

Keece pulled her in for hug. "You know daddy really don't want you to leave. I would cry if you left me," he said jokingly.

Kya pulled back, giggling. "Daddy, you don't cry. You're tough."

"Yeah, but I would be sad if you left me though. Just think about it, a'ight," he told her.

Kya nodded and ran out the room. Keece cut his eyes at Paris before standing up and walking out the room. Paris sighed and padded to the bathroom. She had no qualms about Keece having an attitude. She meant what she said when she declared that he deal with Riley instead of her.

***

Case entered his home after a long day of tattooing. He and Keece owned two tattoo shops in the heart of the city. In fact, Keece had been the person to introduce Case to the art. His career took off after tattooing Fabian and receiving a shout out on his Instagram. From that day forward, Case had been booked for events and different conventions. He'd appreciated the opportunities he received, but at times, he felt bad because he spent a lot of time away from Diar.

Ever since their debate regarding the prenuptial agreement, things had been tensed between the couple. Diar had been withdrawn and unusually quiet, and while Case decided to give her some space, he didn't like the tension between the two. When he stepped into the master suite, Case noticed that Diar was sitting in the bed with her MacBook on her lap. He took a brief second to marvel at her beauty. Diar had been the first plus-sized woman he'd ever been with, and now that he'd experienced her and all of her glory, he was no longer attracted to slim girls.

Diar's coils were piled into a ponytail on the top of her head. Her bare, gingerbread-toned skin glistened with moisturizer while her nipples poked through her thin T-shirt. She looked up at him with those doll-like eyes and offered a faint smile.

"Hey," she greeted him softly.

Case padded over to her side of the bed and sat near her legs. He gently moved the laptop from her lap and gazed at her.

"You still mad at me?" he asked.

Diar shook her head. "No, not anymore."

"You know I didn't mean to offend you, right?"

"I know," she sighed. "I just don't like the idea but after speaking to other married people, I kind of understand why you want it. I wouldn't want Stefani and Keece to suffer if we were to ever get a divorce because we're their business partners."

Case was relieved that she finally comprehended why he wanted a prenup. He had assets that he wanted to protect just in case they were to ever divorce. Not only did he own the tattoo shops with Keece, but he and all of his brother's own a construction company that was worth millions. After his parents divorced, Case watched his mother take a lot of money from his father since they didn't have a prenuptial agreement. Even though Dom wasn't hurting for any cash after the divorce, Case still didn't want to end up like his father.

"It's only in place for the businesses, right?" Diar questioned with doubt in her tone.

"Yeah, baby. It's only for our businesses. Nothing else."

Her mouth formed into a grin. "I still think it's a curse though."

He threw his head back, chuckling. "Stop being so superstitious, Diar. That shit ain't no curse because we gon' stay married forever."

"You promise?"

Case nodded and sealed his words with a kiss to her lips. "I promise. I don't want nobody but your dramatic ass."

Diar tittered. "I'm not that dramatic, Case."

He twisted his lips. "Yeah, right. You should've been an actress."

"Whatever…can I tell you something and you promise not to get mad?"

"Yeah."

"I don't like your mama."

Case chuckled because he was aware that Diar wasn't fond of Celine. Every time Celine came around, Diar copped an instant attitude and would make herself busy just to avoid conversing with her.

"I know that, babe. That's why I told her she can't stay at our house anymore. I don't want her causing drama in our household."

"Good, because I really hate when she's around. She always throws shade at me because I'm not the girl she would've chosen for you. And she was happy as hell to tell me that you wanted a prenup. I damn near don't want her at the wedding."

Case peered deeply into her orbs. "You want me to beat her ass?" he joked.

Diar cackled, holding her stomach. "Stop playing, Case."

"I'm for real," he grinned. "You know I'll fight anybody for you."

"Boy, not your damn mama though."

"I'm just sayin'. If you say the word, I'll tag her ass," he kidded.

She playfully rolled her eyes. "We both know you love Celine too much to lay a finger on her, so stop jackin'."

"Nah, but for real, I'll talk to her again just to get her to understand that you're not to be disrespected, a'ight."

Diar grinned. "Okay."

"Now come take care of me because you've been holding out for days."

***

It had been two grueling days since Kiyan had come home to find his family gone and things hadn't gotten better. Looking for Camara and his girls had become a task that seemed impossible.

She hadn't answered his phone calls, texts, or emails. So now, Kiyan was camped out in front of Asia's studio, preparing to go inside. He had only been there once before to drop something off to Camara, so he was hoping someone would direct him in the right direction to where she was.

Kiyan stepped out the car and strolled inside the studio. He spotted Asia right away, placing her purse over her shoulder and grabbing her keys.

"What's up, Asia?" he greeted.

She smiled warmly. "What's up, Kiyan? What are you doing here?"

"I'm looking for Cam. Is she in here?"

"No," she swayed her head back and forth. "She told her staff that she would be out of the office for the rest of the week."

Somehow, Kiyan didn't believe Asia. "Stop playing, Asia. Is she here or not?"

She smacked her lips. "I just told you she wasn't. If you don't believe me, then go look for your damn self."

Asia walked off without uttering another word and left the studio. Kiyan decided to take her advice so he wandered through the studio until he reached a room that looked like a mini warehouse. Boxes were everywhere and packing stations were set up in the room. Two girls looked at him curiously before one trudged over to him.

"Um… can we help you?"

"Where Cam at?" he asked rudely.

"She's not here and won't be here for the rest of the week. Do you need me to relay a message?"

"Yeah, tell her that her husband came by, and I'ma keep coming by until she brings her ass home."

The girl's eyes widened a bit before she responded, "Okay, I'll, uh, let her know."

Kiyan nodded and stomped out the room. Camara was playing games, and he wasn't here for it. He decided that he would come up to the studio every day if he had to for her to at least talk to him. Once he got outside, he noticed Rochelle calling so he answered.

"Yeah, Ma," he said, opening his car door.

"I just wanted you to know that I picked the girls up from school, and they're here if you want to see them. You have a couple hours before Cam come get them."

"Why you had to go pick them up? What was Cam doing?"

"She had some business to handle. Stop worrying about that, and come see your kids."

Kiyan sighed. "A'ight."

Since Kiyan did miss his kids, he started the engine and made his way to Rochelle's house. When he arrived, he got out the car and rang the doorbell. Seconds later, Rochelle appeared, wearing a cozy cardigan and slippers.

"Hey," she greeted.

"What's up?" he mumbled.

"Now listen, don't go in there interrogating them. Just spend some time with them," she advised.

He sucked his teeth. "Ma, I know what to do with my kids."

"Alright now. Don't be questioning them."

Kiyan ignored her and proceeded into the kitchen where the girls sat, eating a sandwich. When they looked up, they smiled at him and waved.

"Hey dad," the girls said in unison.

He smirked once he approached the table. "That's all daddy get is a 'hey dad'? What about a hug and a kiss?"

They got up from the seats and hugged his waist. Kiyan kissed their foreheads before they all took a seat.

"So what y'all been doing?" he asked.

"We went to the water park, daddy," Kamryn gloated.

"Oh yeah? Which one?" Kiyan quizzed, hoping to get some answers.

"We don't know the name. It's in a hotel," Milan replied.

"What hotel?"

"Kiyan," Rochelle scolded, who was standing near the fridge.

"What, Ma?" he groaned. "Let me talk to them."

Rochelle waved her hand. "You can talk to them but don't question them. Now stop playing with me."

Kiyan leaned back in his seat, releasing a hefty breath. "Y'all ready to come home?"

Milan shook her head. “Mama said we’re getting a new house, and you can’t move with us.”

“Y’all not moving nowhere. Y’all coming back home, including your mama,” Kiyan declared.

“But daddy I want my new room,” Kamryn complained.

“What's wrong with your room at home?” Kiyan asked.

“I just want a new room,” she pouted.

Kiyan shook his head, not believing that Camara was filling his girls’ heads up about them not coming home. There was no way he was going to allow Camara to move out and take his daughters with her.

Kiyan eyed Milan’s iPad on the table. Suddenly, an idea popped up in his head.

“Milan let me see your iPad.”

She quickly passed it to Kiyan and then continued to devour her sandwich. Kiyan stood, walked into the powder room and closed the door. He swiftly tapped on the FaceTime icon and pressed Camara’s name. His heart thundered inside his chest in anticipation of finally speaking to her after two days. After three rings, her face appeared on the screen.

“Why the fuck you playing games with me?” he gritted in a low tone.

Camara rolled her eyes and looked out what looked to be her car window. Her short cut was wrapped in a turban and her skin was clear of any makeup.

"Oh, you don't fuckin' hear me? You think this shit is cool to just move out without giving me any kind of warning."

"Are you fucking serious?" she asked incredulously. "Are you that removed from reality that you didn't see any signs of me being sick of your bullshit?"

"So you go straight to moving out? What kind of shit is that?"

Camara chuckled. "You a fucking joke, bruh. A real-life comedy."

"I'ma show you I ain't no fucking joke. Now when you bringing your ass home? You got my kids talking about getting a new house without me. Why are you trying to turn them against me, Cam?"

"Oh, so now I'm turning the girls against you? You wish that was the case. You're a piss poor father, Kiyan. I don't need to turn them against you because you've already done that yourself. Stop blaming people for everything and look in the got-damn mirror."

Kiyan swallowed hard at her words. He couldn't deny that her statement stung him because he never wanted to view himself as a bad father. Kiyan wasn't an average father, who took his girls to the nail salon to get pampered or sat with them and watched their favorite movies. He admitted that he wasn't hands on but he wouldn't accept being a bad father to Milan and Kamryn.

"You see how you disrespecting me as a father. I would never tell you that you're a bad mother."

"That's because I'm not, and you know it."

"Nah, all I know is I ain't a bad father. That shit wasn't cool Cam."

"And neither is your blatant disregard for my kids, but when they really stop fucking with you, I don't want you to blame nobody but yourself. Now stop trying to reach out to me because I don't want to talk to you. Just let me go so I can finally be happy without you."

The seriousness in Camara's tone caused a throbbing sensation to shoot through Kiyan's chest.

"So after all these years, that's it?" he asked, feeling his throat ache with each word he spat. "You just leave and not try to work on shit."

Camara peered deeply into the screen. "Kiyan, I'm not in love with you anymore. There's nothing else to work on."

Kiyan swore his heart temporarily went into cardiac arrest. The stone expression on Camara's face caused chill bumps to become visible on his skin. He'd known Camara for years, and he was aware of when she was being genuine. Kiyan just wished in this case that she was telling him a lie.

"Now you don't love me no more?" he quizzed.

"No, I'm not in love with you. Now stop calling me, and leave me alone. I'll reach out to you later this week so we can establish a schedule for the girls. I mean that is if you want to even spend time with them. Now, bye."

When Camara ended the FaceTime call, Kiyan sat the iPad on the floor and covered his face with his hands. Devastation coursed through his body like a deadly virus. Kiyan hadn't been completely oblivious to their marital woes but hearing Camara announce that she was no longer in love with him, knocked the wind out of his system.

Kiyan never wanted to confront his problems. He usually continued on with life without facing his reality, and now those actions had come back to bite him in the ass. Camara was his wife; the only girl he had been willing to marry, and now she didn't want him. She didn't want to continue being married and she didn't want to continuing living under the same roof as him.

"Damn," he murmured, feeling physically sick.

Kiyan's stomach rumbled with nausea as his body temperature spiked to a warmer level. He was officially love sick, and at that moment, he didn't know what his next move would be. He abruptly opened the door and headed for the front door. Kiyan left Rochelle's house without saying goodbye to his girls because he wouldn't be able to face them in this kind of state. He couldn't allow them to see that their mother had ripped his heart into shreds, even though it was him that had provoked Camara to do this.

***

Dinero walked into his home a little after eight o'clock at night. He was greeted with the aroma of something sweet, so he voyaged to the kitchen and spotted Asia and Mila cracking eggs in a mixing bowl.

"Look Daddy, me and mommy are making cakes," Mila announced excitedly.

"Oh word," he said, taking a seat at the island. "Y'all about to have all kinds of eggshells in that shit."

"Stop hating," Asia laughed. "We already have the chocolate cake in the oven and now we're making the one with sprinkles."

"Aye, where is Nero?" he asked, referring to their pit bull. "I ain't seen him since yo' grandma moved in."

"What's that supposed to mean, Dinero? He's around here somewhere." Asia shrugged.

"I just wanna make sure she ain't chop him up and throw his ass in a pot."

Asia gave him a knowing look. "You gon' stop trying to play my Lola."

"Man, you know how y'all Asians is. Y'all a fry a dog up in a minute and serve him on a plate with some shrimp fried rice," Dinero chortled.

Asia guffawed loudly. "I really can't stand you."

"Nero!" Dinero yelled.

Minutes later, the dog descended the steps and ran up to his leg. "What's up, fam? I had to make sure you were all in one piece."

Dinero played with Nero while Mila and Asia baked their cake. Once the last cake was in the oven, Mila went to watch TV as Asia sat next to him.

"Where is Grandma Fossil at anyway?" Dinero asked.

She smacked his arm. "Stop playing with me. Her name is Lola."

"Whatever."

"She's at Aimee and Big's for the night."

Dinero turned to face her. "Aye, I've been meaning to talk to you about something."

Asia placed her hand over her chest. "Oh my. What is it?"

Dinero chuckled. "Calm down. Why you geeked?"

"Because I always have to brace myself when you say that you need to talk to me."

"This ain't nothing bad so chill out."

"Okay, so what is it?"

"I want to give my car washes to Meesha and Terri."

Asia's face displayed that she was surprised as her mouth dropped open. Meesha and Terri had been two young girls that worked for him. They had done so well with his car washes that Dinero rarely had to show up.

"What made you come to this decision?"

He shrugged. "I'm ready to move on from my car washes and they basically run everything for me. I think they can handle it. What you think?"

Asia's mouth was still gaping open as she chuckled. "I mean, yeah they do run the car washes really well, but I always thought that those were your proudest accomplishments."

"It's not. You and Mila are."

"Dinero," she whined, kissing his cheek. "That was really sweet. How come you can't be like this all the time?"

"Because I ain't no soft ass nigga."

Asia rolled her eyes. "I see that moment didn't last long so let's move on. Now, what will you invest in when you give the car washes away?"

"So I've been doing some research, and I came to the conclusion that I'm gon' buy a couple of Starbucks and try to invest in a basketball team."

Asia's brows crinkled immediately. "I can understand the basketball team, but Dinero, you hate coffee," she pointed out.

"I know, but I went to sit at three different locations, and those mothafuckas was packed. I ain't know people drink coffee like that so, me and you about to buy some. I think it'll be a good investment. Plus that basketball team investment gon' make us richer than what we already are."

She smiled. "You're so damn random babe, but I'm down."

"I gotta go meet with my lawyer and shit tomorrow. You gon' come with me?"

"Of course," Asia assured. "I wanna be a part of this."

Dinero nodded, because he wanted him and Asia to own some businesses together so they could pass them down to Mila and possibly more children if they were to have more. Even though he had the construction business with his brothers, he wanted to own something with his wife so that some wealth could always remain within their little family.

When the doorbell rang, Dinero looked at the security surveillance and saw Meesha and Terri standing outside. He'd called them over so he could deliver the news to them in person. He got up and strolled to the front door. When he opened it, Meesha, who was the taller of the two, stood with her hands on her hips. Terri was so engrossed with her phone that she didn't notice that Dinero had opened the door.

"Nigga, why you call us all the way out here to the boondocks? You know my license is suspended," Meesha sassed.

"You act like you drove," Terri chimed in.

Meesha sucked her teeth. "Girl, he doesn't know that."

"Man, bring y'all ugly asses in," Dinero ordered.

The women entered and followed Dinero back to the kitchen.

"Ooh, Meesha, I see you with the fresh feed-in braids. You look fabulous, boo," Asia complimented.

Dinero eyed her hair. "Yeah, but her edges are drifting on a memory, though."

Terri roared with laughter as Meesha cut her eyes at him.

"Shut yo' stupid-ass up," Meesha shot.

Terri leaned over the counter. “Dinero, why did you summon us here? I need to go see my boo, and you're cuttin’ into my plans.”

“You still claiming this imaginary ass nigga, huh?” Dinero chuckled.

Terri rolled her eyes. “He ain't imaginary; I just don't want my business in the streets so we keep it on the low.”

“That means he already got a bitch,” Dinero laughed.

Meesha and Asia snickered as Terri grimaced at him.

“You always got jokes with your ugly ass. Now why are we here?” Terri questioned.

“Listen,” Dinero started, “you know I've been fuckin’ with y’all for the longest because you hoes are loyal to me.”

Asia smacked his arm. “Now why they gotta be hoes?”

“Because he’s a jerk,” Meesha noted.

“They know what they are,” Dinero responded casually. “But like I was saying, y’all been loyal, and I think it’s time to reward y’all.”

Meesha grinned as she clasped her hands together. “So that means a raise, right?”

“Right because I think it’s long overdue,” Terri griped.

“Actually, I'm giving you two edgeless broads my car washes,” he announced with a grin.

The room was quiet as Meesha and Terri stared at him in shock. They then looked at each other and then returned their sight back on Dinero.

"Asia is he serious?" Terri asked.

Asia nodded with a grin. "He is. I thought he was playing, but he's serious. He wants to hand the car washes over to you guys."

Within seconds, Meesha and Terri erupted into celebratory dances. Meesha approached Dinero with her arms opened wide, but his upper body jumped back.

"Back yo' funny looking-ass up. You know I don't like nobody touching me," he snapped.

Meesha scoffed. "Fuck you then. Aye, so the car washes will be completely ours, right?"

"Of course I'm still going to require a small percentage, but they'll be in your name once I sign them over."

"I knew it was a damn catch," Terri hissed.

Dinero waved his hand. "I'm a businessman. I'm always gonna get what the fuck is owed to me, fam."

"Fuck all that. When do we get our shit? I can't believe you're giving us your businesses," Meesha gushed.

"I'll contact y'all later this week. As for now, you and Randy Savage are dismissed," he joked.

"Bye, hoe," Meesha cackled, walking toward the front door.

Terri was showcasing all thirty-two teeth as she approached him. "I really appreciate this Dinero. I'll really be able to feed my family now. Thank you again."

Dinero nodded and watched them leave the house. Even though he talked to them roughly, he wanted to bless them with some property that he knew they would be capable of maintaining.

"Since you're in a giving mood, what are you going to give me?" Asia flirted.

Dinero licked his lips. "You know you can have whatever you want."

"Well," she looked at her Rolex. "We have twenty minutes before the cakes done and Mila's movie goes off. Let's sneak away."

He grinned. "Bet."

NINE

Diar sat uncomfortably as Case's attorney gathered papers for her to look over. The day had finally come for her to sign the prenuptial agreement but the eerie sensation that sat in the pit of her stomach caused her anxiety levels to spike to abnormal levels. Diar felt deep within that this wasn't a good idea, but she had already assured Case that she would sign the document, and she didn't want to go back on her word.

"Okay, Ms. Capers, here are your assets, and these here are Mr. DeMao's assets. What I want you to do is look over everything carefully."

Diar grabbed the sheet and read over the agreement. She noticed that her business was listed as well as Case's tattoo shop and construction business that he shared with his brothers. When she saw a condo listed, she peered over at Case.

"You have a condo?" she quizzed.

He tipped his head. "Yeah, I bought it for my mama last year."

"Oh, I didn't know."

She proceeded to read the rest until she stopped at the house that was listed under his assets.

"Is this the house that we live in now?" she asked no one in particular.

"Well, yes," his attorney smiled. "Since my client purchased the house with cash, this asset will belong to him if you two were to ever divorce."

Diar's jaw clenched immediately as her glower landed on Case. "I thought this was our house?"

"It is."

"Well, why the hell is it listed as *your* asset then?"

Case turned his head toward Diar and returned the same glare she was giving him. "I think he just told you why. I mean, why are you being so extra?"

"Extra? Are you serious right now? So now all of a sudden it's *your* home when you've been telling me all this fucking time that it's our house?" she clipped.

He leaned forward with his face inches away from hers. "I know you're bothered but remember who you talkin' to."

Diar rolled her eyes at his warning and scowled at the attorney. "I'm not feeling this at all."

"Ms. Capers, this is nothing to worry about," the attorney assured. "This is just put in place to protect both parties' financial assets. It's no big deal."

She snorted. "Well, it seems like Mr. DeMao is the main person trying to protect everything from me, which doesn't make sense since I'm set to be his wife in a couple months."

"Doing the most and being dramatic like always," Case muttered.

"I'm not doing anything, but *you* are by springing all this bullshit on me out of nowhere. Did your mother talk you into getting this? I could see Celine putting this in your head."

Case pinched the bridge of his nose before he belted out a loud sigh. "No, Diar this is all my idea. I'm my own man so don't make it seem like she could persuade me to do something I don't want to do. You've never known me to operate like that."

Diar grunted, folding her arms over her busty chest. "Hmmph, this has her name written all over it, but whatever."

"Listen, Diar, I didn't come here to argue with you, especially in front of my attorney. If you don't sign this, I don't see a wedding happening," Case declared with an austere stare.

Diar bore into him, not believing that he'd given her this sudden ultimatum. Surely, she didn't intend for things to get this serious, but it did, and she wasn't sure if she had gone too far, or if she was standing up for what she felt was right. After a few agonizing moments of silence, she peered into his brown eyes.

"Okay," she sighed, "I'll cancel the caterer and the flowers."

Case's brows hiked immediately. "Yo, you serious?"

Diar stood and quickly made her exit out the conference room. She refused to cave in to the demands of Case in an effort to get married. She wasn't pressed for his hand in marriage and since this entire prenuptial agreement didn't sit well with her, she decided it was best to call the wedding off.

What the fuck did I just do?

Of course Diar wasn't one hundred percent confident in her abrupt decision, but she wasn't about to be coerced into something she felt leery about. She stormed out the office and got inside her car. She was so relieved that she'd decided to drive her own car instead of riding with Case because she didn't know what their conversation would consist of after calling off the one occasion she'd dreamt about since she was a little girl. Once she cranked the engine, Diar peeled off and dialed her mother.

"Hello?" Tina answered.

"Ma, I'm just calling to let you know the wedding is off," Diar said quickly.

"Wait, what? What are you talking about?" Tina asked genuinely confused.

"Case wanted me to sign a prenup but I didn't like that he had the house we live in on there. He told me if I didn't sign it, then there was no wedding so I called it off."

I still can't believe I did that.

"Diar, me and your father have made payments on the catering as well as the venue. Now you're telling me that it's canceled. Is this a joke?"

"Listen, I'll refund the money to y'all, but I can't get married right now," she replied unapologetically.

"Y'all young ass kids get on my nerves," Tina ranted. "I gotta go."

Diar sighed when Tina hung up because she felt bad. Tina had been working relentlessly on the wedding, and she hated to disappoint her mother. When she arrived at her boutique, Diar got out the car and walked inside, where she was greeted with her sister, Stefani. She stood behind the counter filling out paperwork as their employee, Malaina, folded some shirts. Stefani glanced up at Diar and beamed brightly. Long gone was her ruby red, short cut. Stefani wore her hair in a black bob with a part down the middle. Her small stature was covered in a denim jacket, white crop top and distressed jeans.

"Ew, what's wrong with you?" Stefani asked, noticing Diar's mean mug.

"I'm not getting married anymore," Diar announced, walking past her and entering the office.

"Um, excuse me," Stefani sassed, following so closely behind Diar that she stepped on the back of her heels. "What the hell do you mean you're not getting married?"

Diar put her purse inside the drawer and took a seat in the chair. She took a deep breath before she looked at her sister, who was anxiously awaiting her reply to her question.

"Case wants me to sign a prenuptial agreement and even though I didn't feel good about it, I agreed. Well, when we got there, his ass had a condo on there that I didn't know about, and then he had the house that we live in right now listed on there. His ass has been telling me all these years that this is our house but now if we were to divorce, it would be his home."

Stefani peered at her with widened eyes. "He really put the house on there? Well, maybe it's because he owned it before y'all got back together."

"I don't care if he owned it before, he stressed that this was *our* house," Diar clipped. "Shit, he even let me redecorate."

"Oh, well, I guess I can understand your frustration."

"Yeah, I'm fucking pissed off by this unnecessary-ass bullshit. So I told Case I wasn't feeling the fucking prenup and his ass presented an ultimatum. He told me if I didn't sign it, then there wouldn't be a wedding, so I told him I'll cancel everything. Fuck getting married."

Diar was consumed with so much anger that she couldn't halt her leg from shaking. She never thought she and Case would be in a position so detrimental that she was unsure of the status of their relationship.

"Girl, mama is about to be so pissed. She has planned everything to a T, and now you've ruined all of her hard work," Stefani joked.

"I told her the news, and she's not happy about it. But I'm not the girl that has to get married. This shit was starting to stress me out too damn bad anyway. I'm good."

"So are you two going to stay together?"

Diar pondered her statement. She couldn't imagine not being with Case. They had been through a turbulent journey just to be together, and she would die if she had to give up their bond.

But getting married seemed to be a task that she didn't have the patience for.

"I didn't necessarily break up with him. I just called off the wedding."

Stefani continued to shake her head. "I can't believe you lil' sister. You have a good man, so why is it so hard to just let go and sign the damn agreement. I'm not dismissing your feelings about it, but if you know you're going to be together for the rest of your lives, why be bothered with a damn prenup."

Diar tilted her head. "Wow, you're so observant Stefani that you've failed to realize that you too have a good man, so why haven't you married Dash yet?"

Stefani waved her hand. "I don't feel like it. I will eventually, I just want us to make sure we develop an air-tight bond before we make that step."

Diar guffawed. "Really Stefani? That's your explanation? You don't feel like getting married?"

Stefani shrugged. "Pretty much."

"Well, I'm not with this marriage shit. I don't have to be his wife if I have to sign all these damn documents to be with him. I mean mama and daddy don't have a prenup and they've been married for what seem like forever."

"Yeah, but they got married back in the day. Things are different nowadays," Stefani pointed out.

"Well, I think I'm cool on getting married."

"If you say so."

Diar tried her best to push thoughts of Case and their issues to the back of her mind. She didn't know where they would go from here now that everything had been canceled. She still wanted to be with him, she just couldn't handle the prenuptial issue.

***

After his disastrous meeting with his attorney and Diar, Case trudged inside his tattoo shop and went straight to his office. He threw his phone on the desk and plopped down in his leather chair.

Case's deep-set eyes traveled over to the window as he aimlessly became submerged in his thoughts. His intentions were always good when it came to Diar. He always aimed to handle her with the best care, but today she had made him beyond furious.

Getting married without a prenup was not an option for Case. He'd seen firsthand how women take everything once a divorce is finalized. While he didn't think Diar would do such a thing, he still couldn't be too sure because when women became mad and bitter, taking everything the man owned seemed like a suitable choice.

"I did not sign up for this shit," he mumbled, grabbing his phone.

Case scrolled to Diar's name and prepared to send her a text before he quickly nixed the idea. He was still vexed, and he didn't want to say something out of anger to her. So he decided he would fall back from speaking to her for the day.

Suddenly, Keece appeared in the doorway, rocking his fitted cap backwards. He was dressed simple in a grey Moncler sweatshirt, grey jeans and Chanel sneakers.

"How'd it go?" Keece asked, taking a seat on the sofa.

Case shook his head, not able to conjure a reply at that very second.

Keece threw his head back, his booming chortling sounding throughout the room. "What the fuck happened?"

Case leaned back in his chair, his face still contorted into a grimace. "The fucking wedding is off."

Keece's thick brows hiked in shock. "On what?"

"Yeah, and you know what? I don't give a fuck at this point."

"So what happened?"

"She got mad about me having the house we live in now under my assets. I know I told her that it's our house, but since I paid for it, it would go back to me. But that shit should've been the least of her worries because I had so many plans for us that she wouldn't even give a fuck about that house."

Keece stroked his chin hair. "So, how did it get to y'all not getting married?"

"I told her if she didn't sign it, then we weren't getting married."

"Yeah, right," Keece challenged.

Case smacked his lips. "Yeah, and guess what her ass said?"

"What?"

"She's about to cancel the caterer and the flowers."

Keece belted out another cackle, causing Case to become more annoyed.

"Aye, Diar is a savage," Keece boasted. "She got your ass with giving her an ultimatum and shit."

"Man, I'm over this shit. Like how is somebody like Dinero married with no problem, but I'm going through all this bullshit with Diar?"

"Man, don't come for my bro," Keece snickered.

"I'm just saying that nigga is the most problematic person I know, and he married with a kid. Shit, Asia actually likes his ass, and I'm over here getting weddings called off and shit," Case grumbled.

"You don't have to get married, bro."

"But I want to marry Diar. I wanted us to get married so we can start a family. I'm trying to have a foundation with her, but she's being stubborn and shit with this fuckin' prenup."

"So you won't marry her without a prenup?" Keece questioned.

"Nah, I can't do. I have too much at stake."

Keece nodded. "I feel you. So what y'all gon' do?"

Case shrugged, unaware of the status of his and Diar's relationship. "Shit, I don't know."

"Y'all will figure that shit out," Keece said confidently as he stood to leave. "I'll holla at you later, bro."

Case bowed his head as he watched Keece exit his office. Diar and their troubles were invading his mind something serious. He didn't have any tricks in his hat. He didn't have any sweet words to convey to her to make her see that this wasn't a bad idea. Case was on empty, and if Diar wanted to call off the wedding for something as trivial as a prenuptial agreement, then he wasn't going to stop her.

***

"Mommy, can you play the Shark song?" Mila requested from the back seat.

Asia groaned. "Honey, we've heard that song three times already. How about we play something new?"

"No, Mommy, I wanna hear the shark song."

Asia begrudgingly turned the radio to Mila's favorite tune and smirked as she watched her bop in her car seat. The two were headed to pick her grandma up from Aimee's house since she had spent a couple of days with her and Big.

"Look, Mommy, its Papa's house." Mila pointed.

Asia chuckled at the fact that Mila knew everyone's house in the family. "Yeah, I see."

"Can we go say hi to him?"

Asia thought for a moment. She didn't like popping up at people's houses, but since it had been a while since they'd visited Dom, she quickly made a U-turn and pulled into his driveway.

"Let's go say hi to your papa," Asia said before unbuckling Mila and pulling her to the front seat.

They got out the car, and Mila ran up to the front door. When Asia approached, she rang the doorbell and looked at the pristine lawn that was embellished with a sculpted water fountain.

"Papa's not home?" Mila asked.

"I don't know. Let's try one more time."

Asia rang the doorbell and waited patiently for someone to answer. After waiting a couple minutes, Asia grabbed Mila's hand.

"Come on, boo. I don't think papa's home. We'll try again some other time."

"Aw man," Mila griped. "I wanted to give him a hug."

"I know, boo, but he's not here."

Just as the two were heading back to the car, Asia saw a white BMW pull into the driveway. Asia was unsure of who it was since the windows were tinted.

"Who's that Mommy?" Mila quizzed.

"I don't know."

When the door opened, Olivia got out the car, carrying her purse. "Hi, are you Asia or Aimee?" she asked, not sure.

"I'm Asia. We were just stopping by since Mila wanted to see Dom, but it seems like he isn't home."

"Yeah that's why I came because I haven't heard from him all day. His friend even called my phone to see where he was because they were supposed to meet this morning."

"Oh, really?"

Olivia nodded. "Yeah, so I came straight home because when I called, he didn't answer."

Asia was now curious and decided to follow Olivia to the front door. She too wanted to make sure everything was okay with Dom. Olivia stuck her key inside the lock and then twisted the knob. The three of them walked into the house where they were greeted with silence.

"Let me go check to see if he's in the bedroom," Olivia muttered.

Olivia hiked upstairs while Asia and Mila stood by the staircase. Asia then turned toward the hallway and strolled into the kitchen, holding Mila's hand.

"There's papa," Mila announced, pointing toward the floor.

Asia gasped as her heart leaped inside her chest. Her eyes had to be deceiving her.

Oh shit.

Asia sprinted over to Dom as he lay on the marble floor face down. His legs were sprawled out with his knees somewhat bent. His exposed arms were positioned in an awkward pose while dribble seeped from his slightly gaping mouth.

"Oh my god, oh my god," Asia chanted, feeling her limbs tremble as she attempted to roll Dom's solid frame over.

"Mommy, what's wrong with papa?" Mila questioned, her tiny voice laced with fear.

Asia ignored her as she grabbed his wrist to check for a pulse. She became frightened when she felt nothing.

"Oh my God!" Olivia bellowed, rushing to Asia's side. "Dom, baby, wake up."

"Go call 911," Asia ordered as she positioned herself on her knees so she could prepare to give him CPR. Before she became a photographer, Asia had been an LPN and she still had a good recollection of what to do when someone was unconscious.

Olivia hopped up, almost falling into the island and ran out the kitchen.

"Mommy, I'm scared," Mila cried.

"Baby, go wait by the door, okay?"

Mila hurried out the kitchen as Asia interlaced her fingers over her left hand and made a fist. She promptly began chest compressions as she counted out loud.

"One…two…three…"

Olivia sprinted back into the kitchen with her phone clutched tightly in her hand. "The ambulance is on their way. I can't believe this," she cried.

Olivia resumed her place next to Asia as she continued to perform CPR. Asia still hadn't seen any sign of a pulse or breathing from Dom, and she was terrified that he may have been dead. She grabbed his head and tilted it back as she performed mouth-to-mouth.

"Is he breathing?" Olivia asked.

Asia was so engrossed with trying to revive Dom that she ignored Olivia's question. She was on a mission to save her father-in-law because if he didn't make it, she knew the family would be in disarray.

"Come on Dom, come on," she whispered, performing chest compressions again.

Minutes later, the doorbell rang. Olivia shot up and dashed to the front door. Asia was still performing CPR as the paramedics rushed inside.

"When did you find him?" a paramedic asked, pulling out equipment from a bag.

"Maybe about five minutes ago." Asia replied, stepping away so that they could take over.

Asia stood, gnawing at her inner cheeks, praying that Dom would gain consciousness. She peered over at Olivia whose face was smeared with tears. Asia wanted to console her, she wanted to assure her that Dom would recover from this, but as she witnessed his lifeless body lying on the floor, Asia wasn't too sure.

TEN

Paris shut down her computer and grabbed her purse from out her drawer. She'd just finished her day at work and was headed to pick her children up from her mother's house. When she exited her office, she stopped at her receptionist, Dasia's, desk.

"Hey, you can clock out if you want. I'm leaving early today."

Dasia's brown eyes seemed to light up. "Oh, great. I can catch the nail shop before it gets busy."

Paris smiled. "Have a good weekend."

"You too."

Paris walked to the elevator but decided she wanted to take the stairs so she could get in some quick cardio. As soon as she reached the first step, her phone rang. She dug inside her purse and pulled out her phone to see that Keece was calling.

"Hey," she answered.

"Where you at?" he asked with a bit of alarm in his tenor.

Paris halted her steps abruptly, her brows displaying the curiosity on her face. "I'm leaving work now and headed to get the kids. Why? What's wrong?"

A penetrating quietness permeated the phone, causing Paris to become on edge.

"Babe, what's wrong?"

"Man…it's pops. Asia and Olivia found him unconscious earlier."

Paris' lids expanded as her lips parted with disbelief. Dom being found unconscious was a shocking blow because he seemed to be a healthy man.

"Oh, wow, is he okay?"

"Shit, we don't know yet, but I need you here with me."

She nodded. "Of course. The kids are with my mom so I'll be right there. What hospital are you at?"

"Froedtert. Call me when you get here."

"Okay, I'm coming now."

She quickly ended the call and hurried down the steps.

Please God, let Dom be okay.

Paris didn't want to think of the damage that would occur if Dom passed away. Keece and his brothers were extremely close to their father. Dom had raised them all and established a bond that seemed to be irreplaceable. If he didn't make it, things would never be the same in the DeMao family.

When Paris reached her car, she jumped inside and quickly peeled off. The Friday traffic was a bit thick but she managed to arrive at the hospital within thirty minutes. When she parked, she sent Keece a text and waited anxiously for his reply. Five minutes flew by, and Paris spotted Keece walking toward her truck.

She got out, met him halfway, and threw her arms around his neck.

"Babe, I'm so sorry," she muttered into his ear.

Keece said nothing as he snuggled her closely to his chest. The couple stood hugged up briefly before he pulled back.

"Let's get in the car. I need to talk to you."

Paris nodded and followed him back to the car. Keece opened the door for her, and she slid inside. He walked around the passenger's side and got in. He sat silently for a while causing, Paris' already rapid heartbeat to shoot through the roof.

"This shit is crazy," he muttered, shaking his head.

Paris grabbed his hand, giving it a gentle squeeze. "I know babe."

"I went to see him a while ago, and his ass was talking about what he wanted to happen when he died."

Paris' eyes narrowed. "Really?"

"Yeah, and I asked him was everything cool, and he was like 'yeah', but now I feel like he knew something was gon' happen. I just hope he ain't hide some shit from us."

Paris remained quiet as she processed what Keece just told her. She prayed that Dom didn't have an illness and concealed it from his family.

"I'm not prepared for this shit, Paris. I ain't ready to live without my pops," he mumbled sadly.

"Baby, don't say that. We don't even know how he's doing at this point."

Keece bore into her with somber eyes. "He's in a coma. The doctors said they're not sure if he will recover because he didn't have any oxygen getting to his brain while he was unconscious. He had a massive heart attack."

"Wait a minute, when did you find this out?"

"Like ten minutes ago."

Paris didn't know how to respond to that news. On the ride to the hospital, she had been hopeful, praying that Dom would be okay, but the gloomy cadence in Keece's tone alerted her that things were far more critical than she had initially thought.

"Pops told me if he was ever in a coma to pull the plug."

"Is that what you're planning on doing?" she asked worriedly.

He nodded. "Yeah, but I know my brothers gon' have a fucking fit. Dinero thinks he's going to pull through, Case does too."

"It may be a fight but maybe if you explain what Dom told you, they would be okay with it."

He sighed deeply before rubbing his hands down his face. "I don't know. I just ain't looking forward to none of this shit. This was unexpected as fuck."

Paris had never seen Keece so dispirited. He was usually the strong one, who handled everything and made sure everyone were okay. Now, he was in a situation that would possibly become permanent. He would soon be losing a parent and while Paris' father had passed away when she was a young child, she still didn't know what to say to Keece who had grown up with his father right by his side.

"You know I'm here for you baby. You're never in this thing alone. Whatever you need from me just let me know."

Keece turned his head toward her. His face showcased how disturbed he was. "I appreciate that. You wanna come in with me. I feel like I should just tell my brothers what's up so we can get this shit over with."

She swallowed hard. "Yes, I'm ready, and I'll be right by your side."

He nodded, opening the car door. Paris did the same and stepped out into the evening air, feeling as if they were both about to walk into a battle zone.

***

Keece sat soundlessly, his hands clasped together covering his mouth. This moment was so surreal to him. The man that had taught him everything about life was laying on his deathbed. He eyed Dom, who was unconscious with a tube going down his throat. His face exhibited a pain Keece had never witnessed. Dom had suffered a massive heart attack that left him comatose. The physicians hadn't given Keece any hope that he would recover to the same person he once was and that devastated him.

Keece's lenses strayed across the room where Dinero and Case were sitting on the other side of Dom's bed. He glanced over at Big and Kiyan, who were seated next to him.

I hate doing this shit…

Although Paris had insisted on being right by his side, Keece demanded that she wait out in the waiting area with the rest of the family. He only wanted his brothers in the room so he could inform them on his plans for their father.

Keece prepared his mouth to spit out the words, but his speech had become unavailable. Something pulled at him, wondering if what he was going to do was the right thing. Sure, he wanted Dom to fight through this physical battle, but he'd left Keece with specific instructions if he were to ever come into this state, and Keece wanted to honor that. He drew in a deep breath, one so deep his lungs visibly inflated. He had done things in his life that were considered strenuous, but this by far had been the toughest dilemma he'd ever encountered.

"I'm pulling the plug," Keece announced, making sure his eye contact was on Dom.

The stillness in the room was piercing. No one said a word and Keece figured they were stunned by his statement.

"What the fuck you mean you pullin' the plug?" Dinero snarled.

Keece looked over at him and sighed. He knew Dinero wouldn't be happy with the news but this was their father's wish.

"You heard me," Keece replied.

"Why would you do that?" Case asked. "I mean it's a chance he could come out of this."

"Did you not hear the doctor say he didn't get any oxygen to his brain while he was unconscious?" Keece quipped.

"Fuck what his ancient ass talking about. He looks like he's one step from falling in the fucking grave. You really gon' listen to his bitch-ass?" Dinero clipped with a glower on his face.

"Man I don't know about y'all, but I'm not trying to have Pops wake up from this shit, and he's not in his right mind. Maybe we should let go," Kiyan advised.

Case waved his hand dismissively. "Y'all niggas trippin'. Y'all act like people don't come out of comas."

"Right," Dinero agreed. "Case was in a coma for weeks and he woke up from that shit."

"It was a medically-induced coma, Dinero. This shit is different," Keece noted.

Dinero snorted. "All that shit is the same. Damn, Keece give Pops a chance to pull through. Why you trying to kill him off?"

Dinero's questioned angered Keece. He would never try to kill his father, but he wasn't going to allow him to suffer.

"I'm not trying to kill him. He told me if he was ever in a coma to pull the fuckin' plug and guess what, I'm going to do exactly what the fuck he told me," Keece revealed, his patience growing thinner by the second.

"When he tell you that?" Case asked with doubt in his tone.

"He told me a while ago."

"Oh so he just told you and not the rest of us?" Dinero challenged. "So now you the only mothafucka he tells shit to?"

"Listen, y'all arguing over the wrong shit," Big interjected. "We need to figure out what we about to do for Pops."

"I'm not trying to argue right now. I'm just trying to tell y'all what he wanted. He wouldn't want to be laid up here like this. Look at him; you think he would want this shit," Keece grimaced.

"I ain't feeling you pulling the plug. At least give him some days," Case reasoned.

"Let's just take a vote because I'm not about to sit here and listen to this shit," Kiyan suggested.

Keece nodded at the idea. "Aight, I vote to pull the plug."

"That's my vote too," Kiyan spoke.

"I'm voting to keep him on life support," Case announced.

"I'm with Case," Dinero added.

Everyone's eyes seem to wander to Big, whose eyes were casted down to the floor. Keece could sense he was in deep thought and he was praying that he made the right choice. Big peered up at Dom, his eyes were filled with what looked to be sadness and regret. After a minute of grueling silence, Big cleared his throat.

"Take him off," he mumbled.

Dinero stood abruptly, throwing his chair against the wall. "So y'all just gon' fuckin' take him off like that?! Y'all not even giving him a chance to recover!"

Keece didn't want to engage in a fight with Dinero, especially inside the hospital room. So he remained quiet as Dinero stared at him with those dangerous, wild eyes.

"Dinero, you want him to lay here suffering like this?" Kiyan seethed.

Dinero scoffed. "He can come out of this shit! You bitch-ass niggas ain't got no fuckin' faith!"

"Why you making this shit harder than what it needs to be?" Keece questioned.

"I'm done with you niggas. We ain't brothers no more," Dinero declared with a certain coldness that rocked Keece to his core.

"Stop overreacting, bro," Kiyan begged with his hands in the air.

"Fuck y'all," Dinero snapped, making his way to the door.

When he stormed out the room, Keece shook his head. This was what he was afraid of. He didn't want to offend any of his brothers but he couldn't watch Dom deteriorate like this.

Case stood up without uttering a single word. He honestly didn't have to because Keece saw the disappointment and devastation etched on his face. He wanted to talk to Case; he wanted to alert him that this was the right thing to do. But when he exited the room in the same fashion as Dinero, Keece brushed the idea off.

"This shit is fucked up," Kiyan groaned, covering his eyes with his hands.

"This is what Pops wanted. Y'all know he hated hospitals, and this is the last thing he would want for himself."

"He really told you to pull the plug if he was in a coma?" Big questioned.

Keece nodded. "Yeah, and the shit don't feel right to me. He just started talking about his death out of nowhere. I wonder if he saw this shit coming."

"We'll never know now," Kiyan noted.

***

Hours later…

Absolute silence pervaded the air as Asia stared at Dinero with empathetic eyes. He looked completely dazed as he sat with his elbows resting on his knees and his head down. When she'd called him earlier to inform him of Dom's condition, she'd witnessed a panic she'd never seen in Dinero. He arrived at the hospital, his nerves in terrible condition as he ordered her to tell him every single detail of what transpired when she found Dom at home.

Now, Dinero was grief-stricken and Asia didn't know what to say to him. Not only was his heart breaking for his father, but Paris had informed her that Keece was deciding to take Dom off life support. Asia wanted to express to Dinero that she thought it would be a better choice than leaving him on the machine, but she didn't want to upset him. With her background of being in the medical field, she knew it was close to impossible with Dom's circumstances for him to recover back to his normal self.

Asia knew all too well the agony of losing a parent. Actually, both of her parents were deceased, but the passing that rocked her being was her mother's death. Still to this very day, Asia had not gotten over losing her mother, and she knew Dinero wouldn't be able to swallow Dom's death either. Her heart broke for him because he hadn't been prepared to say goodbye to his father.

Asia rubbed her hand down Dinero's back in a soothing motion. He was tensed, filled with pain that he wouldn't be able to relieve anytime soon.

I don't even know what to say.

Asia knew Dinero all too well and right now, he wasn't in the mood to speak. In fact, she hadn't heard a word from him since they left the hospital. Their drive home was uncomfortably wordless. Instead of telling Dinero things would be okay, and that she would be there for him, she decided to sit there quietly and allow her presence to show him that she was by his side.

"This shit hurts," Dinero mumbled.

Asia bent her neck just to get a glimpse of his painful countenance. "I know, babe. You know I'm very familiar with this kind of pain."

He turned to her, his eyes filled with heart-rending tears. "Does the pain ever go away?"

Asia shook her head, not willing to give him false hope. The agony of losing a parent is always present. The emptiness of being without the person who raised you and brought you into this world would always exist.

Dinero looked away, hanging his head even lower. "I'm done with my brothers except for Case."

"Why?"

"Because they didn't have no kind of hope for Pops. The first thing they wanna do is listen to the fuckin' doctor and pull the plug. That was some bullshit."

Asia cleared her throat before saying, "Well, maybe they didn't want to see Dom suffer."

Dinero scowled at her, causing her breath to become trapped in her lungs. "So you would've done the same thing? If your mama was on life support, would you have just pulled the fuckin' plug?"

Asia felt like that was a trick question. She didn't want him to feel like she was siding with his brothers so she chose her words carefully.

"I don't know what I would've done, Dinero, but I was only pointing out that your brothers may not have wanted to see Dom in that state. I'm not dismissing your feelings about the situation. I'm just trying to get you to understand how they feel."

"Fuck how they feel," he grumbled. "I knew Kiyan and Big was gone side with Keece. They always have. Now I gotta deal with burying my Pops because they didn't have no fucking faith. I'll never fuck with them again."

Asia's heart ached at his declaration. It wasn't the time for them to be divided. The DeMao brothers needed each other now more than ever, but she knew Dinero was firm about his decision. He had always been stubborn and dismissive at times.

"What do you need from me, baby? I know I can't erase your pain, but I'm here to meet all your needs."

"I just need you to sit here with me."

Asia nodded and intertwined her arm around his. She sat with Dinero in complete stillness and allowed him to wallow in his grief while she prayed that he would get over his differences with his brothers.

***

"Hey, I was just calling you to tell you Dom passed away earlier tonight."

Camara stopped in her tracks, not believing the words that Rochelle had said.

Dom dead? How? What happened?

"How?" Camara asked with shock evident in her voice.

"He had a massive heart attack and the boys decided to take him off life support; well three of them decided. I was wondering if you could please reach out to Kiyan. I know y'all are going through your issues, but he needs you right now."

Camara nodded without a second thought. "Of course. Let me give him a call."

"Thank you. I'm about to reach out to my baby. I heard he stormed out the hospital when they decided to pull the plug, so I need to make sure he's okay."

Camara knew Rochelle was referring to Dinero since he was the youngest of her bunch.

"Okay, I hope everything is okay between the guys."

"It's not, but right now just focus on Kiyan. I'll call you later," Rochelle assured.

"Alright, bye."

Camara ended the call, immediately took Kiyan off the block list and dialed his number. The phone went straight to voicemail, so she decided to call his second phone. When that call rang until the voicemail picked up, she grabbed her keys and headed to the home they used to share. When she arrived, she noticed that there weren't any lights on in the house.

"Hopefully, he's here," she whispered, getting out the car.

Camara walked through the garage and did spot both his cars parked. She entered the house and was welcomed by darkness.

"I can't see shit," she mumbled, taking small steps to ensure she wouldn't fall.

Camara carefully padded into the kitchen and turned the light switch on.

"Shit!" she yelped when Kiyan came into view on the couch in the living room.

His irises were dark as he glared at her. She inhaled a deep breath to settle her pounding heartbeat and slowly trudged to where he was seated. She kneeled down, carefully peering into his saddened expression as he took a swig of the brown liquid in his glass.

"Hey, I just heard the news. I'm sorry about Dom, Kiyan," she murmured softly.

He responded to her with quietness, but his eyes exposed the pain he was currently experiencing.

"What can I do for you?" she asked, not sure of what to say.

He snorted. "Can you bring people back from the dead?"

She swayed her head back and forth.

"Then you can't do shit for me."

Camara released a dense breath, hoping she would be able to be here for Kiyan without him upsetting her.

"Why you here?" he questioned.

"Because I feel like you need someone to be here for you at a time like this."

"How long this shit gon' last?"

Her brows furrowed. "What do you mean?"

"How long you gon' be here for me before you go back to hating me? I don't want this fake-ass concern, Camara."

"It's not fake. My heart is really breaking for you, Kiyan. Please don't turn this into an argument."

His sight remained on her, provoking a nervous sensation to stream through her system.

"I never thought I would lose my family and my father in the same month. I gotta be the unluckiest nigga in the world right now," he chuckled bitterly.

Camara didn't know how to reply to his statement. Their dismantled marriage was something that didn't matter at that moment. She was more concern with the state of his heart regarding Dom's passing.

"You go to the lawyer yet?" he quizzed.

She pinched the inner corners of her eyes. “Kiyan…I don't want to talk about that right now.”

Creases surfaced on his forehead. “Shit, why not? It’s going to happen, right?”

“Your father just died,” she reminded him. “What we’re going through shouldn’t even be on your mind right now?”

Kiyan frowned at her as if she’d sprouted two heads. “Why shouldn’t it be on my mind? You told me you don't love me. You think I haven’t been thinking about that shit since you told me that. My pops dying is just the icing on the fucked-up cake.”

“Listen, I said I wasn't in love with you, Kiyan. If I didn’t love you, I wouldn’t be here trying to make sure you’re okay.”

“Well, I ain't okay,” he grumbled. “I don't have anybody right now. My pops is laying in the morgue. Yo’ ass took my kids and moved out. Two of my brothers ain't fucking with me right now, so I'm not gon’ be okay for a long-ass time.”

Guilt.

Suddenly that feeling enveloped Camara, causing her to feel as if the oxygen in her lungs were escaping her body. Even though Kiyan deserved to be forced with her absence, he still made her feel bad for actually leaving him; especially now that he was suffering from a death in the family.

“I don't know what to say,” she spoke above a whisper.

Kiyan’s pensive stare seemed to cut through Camara.

“Don't say shit. Just walk yo’ ass out of here like you did a week ago.”

Although it was very tempting, Camara decided to stay. She understood his anger was misplaced grief because of the current trials in his life. She lifted from her knees and sat next to him. She wanted to grab his hand but the gesture didn't feel natural for her.

"I know you probably don't want me here, but I'm going to stay. You shouldn't be alone right now, and I wouldn't feel right leaving you. You're hurting and although we aren't together, I still care about your wellbeing."

"But you're not in love with me," he countered.

Camara closed her eyes in an attempt to keep her patience in place. "I'm not, but that doesn't matter right now."

"Right because my pops just died, and you wanna come here and act like you care about how I'm doing," he said sarcastically.

This mothafucka is really trying me.

The tiny voice inside her head told her to leave him be, but her insistence to be here for Kiyan overrode that thought. He needed her, no matter how angry he was with her, and she wanted to at least show him that she still cared.

ELEVEN

Case grabbed his credit card from the front desk clerk and signed the receipt. He dropped the pen and then grabbed the key card.

"Enjoy your stay sir."

Case nodded and slowly trekked to the elevator. After leaving the hospital, Case went straight to a hotel, so he could mourn by himself. His vision was clouded by tears that were waiting to drop at any second. A bothersome ache sat inside his chest, making him feel like his heart would explode at any second.

The only man that had been a constant in his life was gone. Dead. Never coming back, and that reality left Case feeling hollow. He'd been hoping this actuality had been a dream. He'd prayed that he would jolt out of his sleep, wearing a coat of sweat and a rapidly beating heart. But this was real life; no nightmares involved.

Dom was gone forever.

Case was now eternally lost and destroyed by the fact that his father would no longer be with him. He was hoping that Keece, Kiyan, and Big would understand how much he thought Dom could fully recover. Once upon a time, Case had been in a coma, and he'd come out of his state and fully healed from his injuries. It angered him that their first move was to pull the plug without considering that he could possibly survive this.

Why couldn't they wait and see if things would improve?

The internal heartbreak ached more than the two bullets he'd taken years ago. Case had never experienced losing someone of this magnitude. He wished he'd had time to prepare but Dom was taken without notice and that tore him to shreds.

Case approached his assigned hotel door and stuck the keycard inside. He walked into the suite and went straight for the bedroom. He entered and fell face forward onto the plush mattress. Tears he had been holding since he'd left the hospital streamed down from his orbs, instantly dampening his face.

Case's heart broke because he felt like he didn't get enough time in with Dom. He needed more talks of wisdom. He needed Dom to guide him deeper into manhood. He wanted the love and intelligence that only Dom could give but now that wouldn't happen. Case would no longer hear Dom's bass-filled voice. He wouldn't see that smirk Dom held when Case picked his brain about life. He wouldn't hear the special endearment of 'lil' nigga' anymore and that thought alone made him want to fall into a slumber so deep that he would never awake.

Loud ringing startled him out of his crying spell. He pulled his phone out of his hoodie pocket and peered at the screen.

Diar: Asia called and told me about your father. Please answer the phone. I need to make sure you're okay.

Case couldn't talk. He didn't want to be questioned, and he didn't want to confirm his father's death. He only wanted to be by his lonesome so he could pour out as many tears as his body would allow.

Case: Can't talk. I'm fucked up right now. I'll see you in the morning.

Before he could power his phone off, Diar called him. He quickly cleared her call but she called back again. Although he'd just informed her that he couldn't talk, he answered anyway.

"Yeah."

"I'm on my way to you," she insisted.

He groaned, pinching his tears ducts tightly. "Nah, Diar, I don't want to be around nobody right now."

"I can't leave you by yourself. I'll be there in a minute. What's your room number?"

"How you even know where I'm at?"

"What's your room number?" she ignored his questioned.

"413."

"Okay."

Case ended the call without a fight. Diar was adamant about coming and although he didn't want any company, he also didn't want to argue. When his phone rang again, he saw that it was Celine. He had no energy whatsoever for her so he sent her call to voicemail and successfully powered his phone off.

Since he didn't want Diar to see him crying, Case got up and went to wash his face. After that was done, he heard a knock at the door. He took a minute to inhale a deep breath before he went to open the door. Diar stood on the other side, wearing a compassionate expression as she briskly wrapped her arms around his neck and pulled him in for a much-needed embrace.

Case wrapped his arms around her waist and closed his eyes. Despite him requesting to be alone, he didn't realize how much he needed to feel some kind of love. Diar always gave him the best affection, and he relished it while trying to hold back his tears.

She pulled back, peering deeply into his eyes. "I won't say a word. I just want to be here with you."

He nodded, closing the door behind her. The couple then retreated to the bedroom where they lay in silence. Case laid on his side while Diar laid behind him. Her arm was tucked under his as she softly rubbed his chest.

Damn, I needed her here.

Diar's presence somewhat soothed the grief that was fighting to take over. She didn't speak as she promised, but her existence settled the pain that was sitting inside his chest. She graced the back of his neck with a gentle kiss.

"Sorry, baby," she whispered.

Case fought to keep his tears at bay, but he'd lost the bout. He couldn't be strong at a time like this. He was severely fucked up, and he knew he would remain this way for a long time.

***

One week later…

Dinero studied Dom as he lay in his shiny, black casket, wearing an all-black suit. The funeral home had allowed Dinero to come and see him before his funeral was to take place the following day. For most of the week, Dinero had carried on in disbelief. Living without Dom had never crossed his mind. He was aware that death was inevitable, but he didn't think he would be faced with this new reality so soon.

Dinero prayed he would get a call and Dom's booming voice would sound through the phone. He hoped to hear that somehow, his brothers had changed their mind and kept Dom on life support. Unfortunately, his desires had been snatched from him when Rochelle confirmed he had officially passed away.

Dinero bore into Dom's lifeless corpse intensely. The expression on Dom's face disturbed him. He didn't look like he was at peace. He actually appeared to be in pain. His mocha-toned skin seemed to get two shades darker. His round eyes were sunken in and his lips appeared to be bloated.

"Damn, Pops," he whispered, hating that this was it for them.

This would be Dinero's final goodbye, and he still wasn't prepared to let go.

"He was a good man."

Dinero rotated his head at the sound of the voice. "What?"

"I said your father was a good man," the short guy repeated, coming to stand next to him.

He was bald at the top with coarse hair on the sides. His thick mustache hovered over his top lip, and his skin was the shade of copper.

"I'm the owner, Edward," he greeted, extending his hand.

Dinero shook it but didn't respond. He just continued to stare at what was left of his father.

"I remember when I was trying to open this funeral home back in '87, and they wouldn't let me because of some permits I needed. Well, Dom heard about my dilemma and he plugged me with someone who was able to assist me in getting my permits. He was always a pillar in the community even though he did his dirt. But still, he always held his people down."

Dinero lazily glanced at him with a stone face. "You think I wanna hear these old-ass stories?"

Edward's burly chest bounced with laughter. "I apologize. I know this is a difficult time for you."

"You think?" Dinero shot sarcastically.

"I just want you to know that you were raised by a good man. I'm not saying he was perfect, but he was real."

"Who planned the funeral?" Dinero asked, changing the topic.

Dinero had removed himself from everything that had to do with Dom's death. He wasn't even aware of who had finalized everything for his funeral arrangements. Plus, Dinero had made the decision to skip out on the funeral which was why he was saying his final goodbye now.

"Your brothers."

Dinero snorted, returning his sight on Dom. "A'ight, I need some time by myself now."

Edward nodded and turned to leave. Dinero rested his palm over Dom's cold, stiff hand. For the past couple days, he had suppressed his emotions. Numbness spread through his system, prompting him to ignore the burning sensation in his heart. Now the feelings were taking over, causing a lump to surface in his throat.

This was it. The finale. The ending to their journey together.

This would be Dinero's final moments with Dom and it felt so surreal. He couldn't fathom letting go but he had no choice. He just wished the pain wasn't so great. Dinero inhaled a breath so deep it rattled his lungs. His bottom lip tucked between his teeth in an attempt not to cry. Crying was something he couldn't do because it wasn't going to erase the agony of not seeing Dom again.

"Rest easy Pops."

Dinero stole one more look at Dom before he left the funeral home and went home.

***

Big inhaled the contents of his blunt before holding the smoke in his lungs and exhaling. He stood in his garage, watching the heavy rain drops drench the pavement. Today was the day of Dom's funeral, and Big was unprepared. For the past week, he tried busying himself just to take his mind off what was to take place. He'd spent extra time with the kids, his mother, and at his bar just to keep thoughts of Dom being dead from surfacing. Big had been forced to think about his death when he met Keece and Kiyan at the funeral home to make arrangements for his home-going service.

At night was when images of Dom would invade Big's psyche. Memories tormented his mind causing him to lose out on sleep for most of the night. He remembered the day Dom took him in and invited him to be a permanent member of his family.

"Dakaden, I wanna talk to you."

Big turned at the sound of Dom's voice and ran over to him, leaving Keece and Kiyan to play basketball amongst themselves.

"Yes," Big said, looking into Dom's blank face.

"Have a seat," Dom requested.

Big sat on the patio chair with his heart rate accelerating to a rapid tempo. He couldn't quite read Dom's facial expression and that made him nervous. He had been visiting the DeMao household every weekend, becoming accustomed to a certain normalcy he lacked. He was fed generously, played any game system of his choice, and didn't have to worry about taking care of his alcoholic mother, Elle, or his little sister, Danica. Big was able to be a ten-year-old child whenever he visited Keece's home, and he prayed that he hadn't done anything that would halt his weekend visits.

"Do you like visiting us on the weekends?" Dom asked carefully.

Big nodded his head eagerly. "I do…did I do something wrong? If I did, I'm sorry, and I'll never do it again."

Dom chuckled. "No, you didn't do anything wrong. How would you like it if you were to come and live with us?"

Big's chocolate eyes gleamed instantly. "Really?"

"Yes, I would like to invite you to live here with us. You'll never have to worry about where your next meal would come from. I'll make sure you're properly clothed and all of your needs are met. Dakaden, you would be a part of my family. I'll adopt you and give you my last name as well. How does that sound?"

Tears surfaced on the brim of Big's lids. To him, this was an opportunity of a lifetime. His life had been hard, especially with his biological father dying so suddenly. Big had felt a heavy burden ever since then, and he was relieved he would finally gain some solace.

"What about my mom and sister?" Big questioned.

"Your sister will remain with your aunt and your mom will be sent to get help. You can see them whenever you want. You just say the word, and I'll make it happen."

Big nodded, liking the sound of it all. "So I can stay here tonight? I don't have to get dropped off at home."

Dom smiled. "This is your new home, son."

Big jumped into his arms and gave him the biggest hug his small arms could muster up.

"Hey, son," Elle greeted, ambling closer to him.

Big blinked rapidly, coming out of his reverie and looked back at her.

"I just wanted to make sure you're feeling okay before you went to the funeral."

"I'm good," he assured, taking in her appearance.

Since the twins were under the weather, Elle offered to come and babysit while the rest of the family attended the funeral. Since she didn't have dialysis, she seemed to have energy she normally didn't possess.

"I know death is never easy, baby. Sometimes it hits you hard and knocks the wind out your system."

Big nodded because he definitely felt dazed from Dom's untimely passing, but dwelling on it wasn't an option. Dom would never want him to mope around and mourn for him.

"Have you spoken to Case or Dinero?"

He rocked his head back and forth. Ever since their meeting at the hospital, Case and Dinero had been MIA. Keece, Kiyan, and Big were forced to plan the funeral for Dom without the assistance of his youngest brothers. Big understood their anger, so he decided to give them some distance. He did make a mental note to talk to them at the funeral.

"Hopefully they'll come around," Elle offered.

"How're you feeling? You sure you can handle the girls while we're gone?"

Elle waved her hand. “Of course I can. I'm actually feeling great today. Don't worry about me, son, just focus on saying goodbye to Dom.”

Big tipped his head, flicking his blunt into the bushes. “Thanks, Ma,” he said, kissing her cheek.

The two walked back into the house where Aimee was sitting by the door with Zaria and DJ. Big grabbed his black suit jacket and grabbed his keys.

“Let's go,” he ordered.

Aimee stood, grabbing his hand. She had been really supportive and hadn't hounded him with ‘are you okay’ questions and sympathy stares. He figured it was because she'd also experienced losing her parents. Despite him hating that fact, he appreciated having a partner that understood the grief he was feeling.

***

Asia's heels clicked against the marble tile as she opened the door to the basement. She descended the stairs and spotted Dinero leaning over the pool table with the pool stick in position. He knocked the ball into the corner pocket and then stood up straight.

What the fuck?

Asia was puzzled and didn't understand why he wasn't dressed to attend Dom's funeral.

“Dinero, we're about to leave. Why aren't you dressed?”

He ignored her as he made another shot.

"Hello?" she sang.

"I ain't going," he revealed.

Instantly, her heart broke. Yes, Asia knew he was severely affected by Dom's passing, but she never expected him not to pay his final respects.

"Babe, please don't," she begged.

Dinero still didn't give her any eye contact as he continued to play pool. She walked over to him and gently grabbed his elbow. Her turned to her and finally eyed her. Dinero's lenses were vacant, pain evident in his stare.

"I don't want you to regret not saying goodbye to Dom. You'll never get this opportunity ever again, baby. Please reconsider."

"I already said goodbye Asia. I don't have to go to no fuckin' funeral to do that."

She exhaled deeply. "So, what? You're gonna stay here and just play pool all day?"

"Nah, I'll probably go check up on some of my businesses too. Don't worry about me; I'm good."

Asia rolled her eyes, folding her arms over her chest. "You sure, you don't wanna go?"

"I said I ain't goin' Asia," he said with finality.

"You're gonna make me go without you?"

"Shit, you don't even have to go. Stay your ass here." he shrugged.

"I can't do that. I have to pay my respects. He was my father-in-law, you know?"

"Well, go then 'cause you getting on my damn nerves," he ranted.

Asia snorted before turning on her heels and traveling back upstairs. Dinero could be a real asshole, and since Asia didn't want to curse him out at a time like this, she decided to leave him be. She walked into the living room where Lola and Mila were sitting.

"Alright guys, it's time to go."

"Daddy's not coming Mommy?" Mila asked.

"No, he's going to stay home."

Asia glanced at Lola and gave her a shrug. The older woman returned a faint smile and stood from the couch. The trio walked to the garage and got inside the car. Asia didn't feel right about going without Dinero, so she decided another approach. She pulled out her cell phone and dialed Rochelle's number.

"Hello?"

"Hey, it's me, Asia. Did you know your son isn't coming to the funeral?"

"Why not?" Rochelle questioned.

"Do you really think Dinero explained to me why? He's in one of his moods today, and I completely understand. I just don't want him to look back and regret not going to the funeral."

Rochelle sighed. "I'll try to call and talk to him."

"Thank you."

"Alright, I'll see you at the church."

"Bye."

Asia hung up and threw her phone in the middle console. She put her car in drive and prepared to make her way to the church without Dinero.

***

The church was packed to capacity as everyone gathered to say their final goodbyes. Two large photos of Dom were propped on each side of the casket and flowers were aligned on the front of the pulpit. Keece glanced around at the different faces that sat in the pews. Half the people he recognized and half the people he didn't. The only face he didn't spot was Dinero's and that left him extremely bothered.

The DeMao family all sat in the front except for Case. He sat on the other side of the church with Celine and Diar on the side of him. Keece hadn't spoken to him since their spat at the hospital. He'd even tried reaching out to Case but to no avail.

Keece felt like shit. Internally, he was dying, but as the leader of the family, he had to remain strong. Burying Dom was killing him slowly, and it sucked that he had to put on a front like everything would be okay, but he knew it wouldn't. His protector and teacher were no longer in the land of the living. Keece couldn't call Dom when he couldn't figure out one of his life decisions. He couldn't sit and gain any wisdom from conversations with Dom. Keece was on his own, and that truth cut him deeply.

The pastor that was eulogizing the funeral opened up the floor for people who wanted to give some remarks regarding Dom. Keece immediately rolled his eyes when he spotted Celine rising from her seat and grabbing the microphone. She was dressed in a long black dress with a black hat. Celine was teary eyed as she rubbed her lips together and inhaled a deep breath.

"As you know I was Dom's only wife," Celine began.

Paris put her head down to hide her smirk. Keece discreetly shook his head because he knew Celine was about to put on a show.

Celine sniffled. "I just can't believe he's gone. Dominic was a good man and father."

Keece glanced back at Rochelle, who was rolling her eyes with her glossy lips pursed. His mother couldn't stand Celine, and she had good reason to hate her. Celine had created the barrier between Rochelle, Keece, Kiyan, and Dinero, which prevented her from participating in most of their childhood.

"Although I'm going to miss Dominic dearly, he left me the best gift ever, which is my son," Celine cried.

Bitch come on with this extra-ass shit.

Keece had instantly become annoyed with Celine's speech and was praying that the pastor would move on to the next person. He was relieved when Celine passed the mic to the pastor, and he welcomed Olivia up so she could express her time with Dom.

Keece leaned over toward Paris' ear. "You see who ain't here?"

She turned to him and whispered. "Yes, I noticed. Don't make a big deal about it."

"What you mean? How he ain't gon' come to his pop's funeral?"

"I don't know," she whispered harshly. "But don't make a huge scene about it. Maybe Dinero couldn't take seeing Dom like this."

He shook his head, biting his bottom lip. "I swear dude be on bullsh–."

"Church, Keece," Paris scolded.

He rubbed his hand down his face. "My bad."

She nodded, grabbing his hand. "Don't worry about Dinero. Let's focus on laying Dom to rest."

Keece tipped his head but he wasn't going to let Dinero's absence go. He was seething at Dinero's blatant disregard for Dom. He found it fucked up that he didn't have the respect to come to their father's home going. Keece didn't want to be at the funeral just as much as Dinero but he made it happen because it was the right thing to do.

I ain't letting this shit go…

***

Asia gripped Mila's small hand as she placed a single white rose on Dom's casket. They were now at the burial site, and Asia felt sick. The funeral had triggered thoughts about her mother's death. That had been one of the hardest days of her life, especially knowing her father had caused everything. Now that she was sitting at yet another funeral, Asia understood why Dinero opted not to attend.

"Girl, Dom knew every damn body," Aimee muttered, approaching her. "This damn funeral was packed like Michael Jackson's."

Asia smirked at her sister, who wore her hair straight with a side part. "Yeah, it was. Did you catch Celine with that damn performance?"

Aimee rolled her eyes. "Girl, and the award goes to. They should've never passed the mic to her. Rochelle was throwing so much shade behind me."

Asia giggled. "I heard her."

"TT, look, that's where papa is," Mila announced, pointing toward the casket.

Aimee kneeled down and kissed her cheek. "I know, baby."

"Mila use your inside voice," Asia said, looking around at the guests, making sure they didn't hear her.

Aimee stood. "Why didn't Dinero come? Big was hoping to see him so they could talk."

Asia shrugged. "You know he's upset about all this. I thought he was coming until he told me this morning that he wasn't. I tried to talk him into it, but he wouldn't budge. You know he doesn't fold on anything."

"I mean I get it," Aimee nodded, "but I'm just surprised he didn't come."

"Yeah, well, you know when he doesn't want to do something; nobody can talk him into it. Not even me."

Keece advanced toward Asia with his nose crinkled and his eyes narrowed. "Aye, where Dinero at?"

"He didn't want to come," Asia replied.

"Man, I think that's some bullshit," he pointed at her nose. "He could've showed up today. Does he think he's the only mothafucka going through something? We all over here fuckin' grieving."

Asia cocked her head because she didn't appreciate him placing his finger in her face. "Everybody grieves differently Keece. He made a choice so respect it."

"Nah, fuck that. He disrespected Pops by not seeing him off today. And you need to quit making excuses for that nigga."

"Um, Keece, you need to calm down. Asia didn't make him not come, that was Dinero's decision," Aimee reasoned.

"I ain't tryin' to hear that shit," Keece waved his hand. "You should've made his ass come, Asia."

Asia pressed her lips together before she blew out a deep breath. "Listen, Dinero is a grown-ass man, and I can't make him do anything he doesn't want to do. I know you may be bothered by Dinero's absence, but you can stop coming at me crazy."

Keece snorted. "What the fuck you gon' do?"

Asia jerked her head back, not believing Keece was coming at her like this. They'd always gotten along, and she was thoroughly baffled as to why he was taking his anger out on her.

"Aye, nigga, take that shit to Dinero and get out her fucking face with all this bullshit. You out of order for even doing this right now," Case seethed.

Kiyan came over to where they all stood. "Y'all need to chill with this shit. Y'all are making a scene."

Keece smirked, ignoring Kiyan's request. "You tough now lil' brother?"

"Nah, but I'll beat yo' ass though," Case threatened.

Keece brows furrowed. "Nigga, you don't even believe that shit. Don't forget who taught you, mothafucka."

"Not here!" Rochelle gritted through clenched teeth. "Keece you're out of line, and quite frankly all of y'all are doing the most right now. Now break this shit up before I take my shoe off and get to swinging on y'all disrespectful asses."

Case was the first to walk away as Keece gave Asia one more glance before trudging toward the crowd.

"Can you please not mention this to Dinero? I swear I will handle Keece for coming at you like that," Rochelle assured.

Asia nodded. "I won't."

"Thank you. Mila you wanna come with nana," Rochelle offered.

Mila nodded, grabbing Rochelle's hand. "Bye, Mommy."

"Bye, boo."

Asia watched them walk off and catch up to Carlos, who was waiting by the car.

"Keece was on some bullshit," Aimee fussed. "I understand he's going through a lot, but that doesn't give him a right to snap at you."

"Right. He better not say shit else to me again. I'm so tempted to tell Dinero, but I won't break my promise to Rochelle."

"Yeah because Lord knows Dinero would be ready to kill him for that, and we don't need any more family drama."

Asia nodded. "I know. Let me go because Lola is waiting in the car. You know she can't stand too long."

"Okay, I'll see you at the repast."

Asia headed for her car, still bothered by the scene that just took place. She was glad Rochelle had stepped in because she was unsure of what may have transpired if she didn't.

TWELVE

The sun was settling on the horizon, allowing dusk to make its appearance as Dinero sat inside his car. His eyes bounced from the rear-view mirror to the side mirror in anticipation. His face was smoldering with anger as he clenched his defined jawline. When Case called him earlier, informing him on how Keece was disrespecting Asia, Dinero was immediately enraged. Everyone knew Asia was off limits. She was his weakness, the most delicate part of his life, and he couldn't allow anyone to slight her in the least bit, not even his brother.

So now, Dinero sat outside Keece's house, waiting for him to pull up. He could've called, but he preferred to show up in person. Keece had gotten personal coming at Asia, so Dinero had no issues confronting him face-to-face.

When he spotted headlights turning down the street, Dinero bent his head to get a look at the car. Once the vehicle came into view. and he confirmed it was Keece's Maybach, he started his engine and sped in front of the car to prevent it from entering the gate. Dinero hopped out and stalked toward the driver's side. Keece jumped out wearing an identical scowl as Dinero.

"You lost your fucking mind, blocking my gate?" Keece fumed.

Dinero stepped into his personal space. "Let me tell you something, if you ever in your fuckin' life come at my wife crazy, I'ma kill yo' bitch-ass. and that's on Pops, bitch."

Keece grunted, flicking his nose with his thumb. "You threatening me, nigga?"

"Mothafucka, don't act like you brand new to me. I'll murk you for coming at Asia crazy. You must've lost your mind fuckin' with mine."

"So do something about it," Keece challenged.

Paris quickly exited the passenger's seat and wedged herself between the two, who were staring each other down.

"Dinero calm down. My kids are in the car," she pleaded.

Dinero glared at Paris. "You think I give a fuck about that when he was talking stupid to Asia while Mila was there? Don't come at me about no fuckin' kids, Paris."

Keece tried to grab Dinero but Paris blocked him. "Aye, bitch watch your mouth. You fuckin' talkin to the wrong one."

Dinero imitated a gun with his index finger and thumb. "You heard what I said. Talk crazy to my wife again, and you'll be resting right next to Pops."

"You better act on it because I ain't letting this threat go. You gon' have to kill me."

Dinero flashed him a cheeky grin. "You heard what I said."

Dinero turned to walk away and got inside his car. He reversed and swiftly sped away from Keece's gate. He meant every word he'd spewed from his lips. To protect Asia, he would kill anyone, including his own blood.

"Bitch-ass nigga," he spat bitterly.

Dinero grabbed his phone from the cup holder and dialed Asia. He had some choice words for her because he hated finding out about the scene between her and Keece from Case. He wished she would've informed him on Keece's disrespect herself.

"Hello?"

"Aye, what's your problem?" he snarled.

"What are you talking about?" she asked confused.

"Why the fuck you ain't tell me Keece came at you on some rowdy shit today?"

She sighed. "Rochelle asked me not to tell you. She said she would handle Keece."

"So you married to my mama now?"

"No, Dinero. I was only trying to keep the peace. Calm the fuck down."

"I don't care about no fucking peace when a nigga disrespecting you. Fuck what my mama said. You always come to me if a mothafucka ever come at you on some rah-rah type shit. I don't give a fuck who it is, don't keep nothing like that from me again."

"Alright Dinero!" Asia fussed. "I guess this is what I get for trying to be considerate of you since your father was buried. Now bye."

"Bye, Asia."

Dinero disconnected the call and continued to drive aimlessly around the city. This day was bad. He didn't feel well physically or emotionally, and he didn't see his disposition getting any better.

***

"What the fuck, Keece?" Paris grimaced as they entered their home.

Their children ran upstairs as Keece's frown landed on her. She was livid at the way he had just carried on, especially in front of their kids.

"Fuck you talkin' 'bout?" he scoffed.

"Why would you do all of that in front of the kids? Damn, they didn't need to see their father and uncle going at it like that."

He glared at her with expanded eyes. "Are you fuckin' serious right now? So I'm supposed to let that bitch-ass nigga come at me crazy? You must've lost yo' mind or something."

Paris pointed her index finger at him. "No, you lost your damn mind. You started all this bullshit by coming at Asia. I don't know why you even thought that was cool."

Keece bombarded her personal space as he peered at her intensely. "So, you taking they side?"

"This ain't about sides!" she snapped before pacing back and forth. "This is about you creating more drama within the family. Now you're into it with your brother because of your words with his wife."

"Me and Dinero been into it. This shit ain't start with Asia. You think you know every fuckin' thing, but you don't."

"I know you were wrong today."

Keece shook his head and scoffed. "I wasn't shit. If Asia wanna get in her feelings because I was telling her about her dumb ass husband, then that's on her."

"No, Keece, you had no right talking to her like that. That's not even like you to do something like that."

"Paris, shut the fuck up!"

"No, you shut the fuck up!" she bellowed, her arms flailing in anger.

The couple stood, their chests heaving up and down as they exchanged angry stares. Paris and Keece had their share of arguments, but he had never disrespected her by telling her to shut the fuck up. She understood he was fighting through the heartache of losing Dom, but she refused to stand by and allow him to belittle her.

"Fuck this! I don't have to deal with your shit," she hissed, grabbing her purse and keys from the foyer table.

"Where you going?" he questioned.

Paris continued out the door and stormed to her truck. She got inside and cranked the engine. She needed to get away from Keece for a while because he was becoming someone she didn't recognize. He'd always exhibited controlled behavior. He didn't speak recklessly unless he was being violated. But now, his character was slowly altering into something she didn't like.

***

Three months later…

"He needs to bring a pitcher over here because I'm going to be needing a refill all night," Camara declared.

Asia giggled as she sipped on her soda. The women had all gathered at Botana's Mexican Restaurant since they'd been busy with their personal lives. Aimee sat next to Asia as Paris and Camara sat across from her. They were patiently waiting on Diar who was en route to the restaurant.

"I know I shouldn't eat beans, but I need some in my life. I'll just have to suffer being in the bathroom all night," Aimee laughed.

Asia faked a gag. "We didn't need to hear all that, sis."

"Right," Paris added, dipping her chip in some salsa.

Asia looked up and noticed Diar coming through the door. She waved her hand to get Diar's attention. When she spotted Asia, she sauntered over with her long curls bouncing with each step she took.

"Hey, boo," Asia stood to greet her with a hug. "You didn't get lost, did you?"

"No, I didn't. I actually knew where it was because I had drinks here before. Hey, ladies."

Paris, Camara, and Aimee all said, "Hey."

Diar took a seat next to Asia and picked up a menu.

"We didn't order yet because we were waiting on you," Asia informed her.

Diar nodded. "Cool. So how has everyone been? I know I haven't seen you guys since the funeral."

Aimee shrugged. "I've been okay. Big is kind of scaring me though."

"How so?" Paris asked.

Aimee released a sigh. "He's acting like nothing happened. It's as if Dom never died. He carries on like he's not affected when I know he's hurting. Whenever I ask him if he's okay, he assures me that he is, but I don't feel like he is. I think he's just trying to be tough with me so I won't worry."

"Maybe he wants to forget about it and move on," Diar offered.

"You can't forget about your parent dying," Aimee replied. "That void will never go away; trust me, I know. So I'm not buying that he's okay because deep down, I know he's probably sad."

Asia nodded because when their mother passed away, she experienced a vacancy that she couldn't expound upon.

"Be glad that Big is at least pretending to be fine. Keece has been emotionally unavailable since Dom died," Paris revealed.

"That's to be expected since they were so close though," Camara noted.

"So how is he acting?" Asia asked.

Paris rolled her eyes, flicking her jet black tresses over her shoulder. "There's a lot of distance between us. We don't talk that much, and when we're home, we kind of do our own thing. For example, I'll be in the bedroom for most of the time, and he'll be in his man cave. He interacts with the kids but they do notice his gloomy mood. They ask me all the time if he's okay, and I try to assure them that he is, but Keece is deeply affected. Plus, we don't always get along, and that keeps me from being there for him."

"So are you saying his grieving has pushed you away?" Camara asked.

Paris groaned. "That sounds so bad when you say it, but yes. He's mean as hell, and you know I'm not going to tolerate nobody talking crazy to me." she shook her head, visibly stressed by her marital woes.

Asia opted not to respond because she was still bothered by Keece's stunt at Dom's burial site. So she continued to sit quietly and kept her thoughts to herself.

"Just give him some time, Paris. You know Keece always bounces back," Aimee offered.

"We'll see," Paris muttered.

"So, Cam," Aimee sang. "How is it living alone, especially without Kiyan?"

Camara smirked. "It's different. I'm so used to having him next to me that sometimes I have trouble sleeping. But I'm so happy that I don't have to come home stressed and ready to argue with his ass."

"Did you file for divorce yet?" Asia questioned.

Camara swayed her head, her face in a somber expression. “No, I couldn’t do it yet.”

“Did you have a change of heart?” Diar asked excitedly.

“No, it’s not that. I didn’t feel right serving Kiyan with divorce papers when Dom just passed away. I felt like I would be sinking the knife deeper into his heart. I'm not that heartless so I'm holding out for a little while.”

Asia hated to see one of her favorite couples separated. She prayed that they would come to some kind of agreement and reconcile. As a woman, Asia understood that Camara was fed up with Kiyan’s behavior so she couldn’t blame her for leaving. She just hoped Kiyan would see the error in his ways and fight for his wife.

“I understand,” Diar sympathized. “I was secretly hoping you had a change of heart.”

Camara rolled her eyes. “Don't get shit twisted. I'm still not feeling Kiyan like that. I mean, he has improved as far as spending time with the girls. He sees them almost every day now, and he also will keep them while I'm working. But as far as us, there has been no progress.”

“That’s great he is back on his fatherly duties,” Paris gleamed. “I hated to hear how he was slippin’ from his daddy shit.”

“Yeah, that wasn't like Kiyan,” Aimee chimed in. “I'm glad he got his shit together.”

Diar clapped her hands together. “Okay, guys…I think there's a more pressing issue here to discuss.”

“Like why you and Case aren’t married yet?” Paris sassed.

Diar hung her head low and chuckled. “Now why you had to go there?”

Asia grinned. “You know damn well you two are supposed to be married right now. I can’t believe you were being stubborn about that damn prenup.”

“What prenup?” Camara asked confused.

“Case wanted her to sign a prenup so they could protect their businesses. Ms. Diar was acting like he was trying to trap her in a damn contract or something. She called off the wedding because she was being bullheaded,” Asia ranted.

“Well, damn, Asia! Tell all my business why don't you!” Diar yelped.

Asia winked at her. “You're welcome.”

“Girl, you called the wedding off?” Paris asked in incredulity. “I thought y’all postponed it because of Dom’s passing.”

“Me too,” Aimee added.

Diar sighed. “No, it was me, but it was Case a lil’ bit too. But I do regret it immensely.”

Camara poked her bottom lip out. “Aww boo, don't be sad about it.”

“I don't know why you trippin’ Diar. You got the best brother and you over here fussing over a prenup,” Aimee snorted. “You know Case is going to make sure you don't get the short end of the stick.”

"I told her that," Asia laughed.

"I know," Diar whined. "I felt like he was pulling a power move on me so I retorted with my own."

"What kind of power move?" Paris quizzed with narrowed eyes.

"He told me if I didn't sign the prenup, then we weren't going to get married. I felt like he was trying to son me, so I nipped that shit and told him I would cancel the caterer and flowers. I had a lot of confidence when I left the office, but when I got home that night I felt bad but I couldn't take it back. I had to stand on my decision." Diar shrugged with her hands.

"So, technically Case is the one who called it off," Camara pointed out. "So really it's on him, right?"

"Yes and no. Initially, he loaded the gun but Diar pulled the trigger," Asia sassed.

Diar simpered. "Yeah, but I don't know why I feel bad. We haven't discussed anything regarding the wedding, and I'm afraid to even bring up the topic."

"Do you still want to marry him?" Aimee asked.

"Of course I do."

"Well, discuss it with him. Tell him you took the prenup all wrong and that you would consider signing it," Aimee coached.

"Did you sign a prenup?" Diar asked Aimee.

Aimee shook her head. "No, I didn't."

Diar turned to Paris. "What about you?"

"I didn't either." Paris smirked.

Diar cocked her head. "That's not fair that y'all keep saying I got the best guy out of the DeMao crew, and I'm the only one that has to sign a prenup," she quipped.

"I signed one Diar, so you're not alone," Camara announced.

Diar gasped. "Really?"

"Yeah," Camara snorted. "But I didn't care about it and now that I have a business and it's a million-dollar brand, I think I made the right move. When me and Kiyan do go through with the divorce, we'll walk away with our own assets and no one's hand will be in each other's cookie jar."

Asia smirked at the contented expression on Diar's face. She had tried to paint a picture that would get Diar to consider signing the prenup, and she hoped that Camara had gotten through to her.

"You know what? Y'all got me off topic," Diar swiftly shook her head. "I wanted to talk about how Case hasn't had any contact with his brother's except for Dinero. When do you think this drama will end between them?"

Asia exhaled deeply as she pushed her wild mane from her face. It had been three months since Dom's untimely demise and the DeMao brothers were still at odds. Dinero was still angry about them pulling the plug, and he was also still furious at Keece for his scene with her. The only brother Dinero did speak to was Case and that was because they shared the same sentiments over Dom's death.

"I say give it some time," Camara advised.

Aimee stuffed a tortilla chip in her mouth before shaking her head. "I can tell Big misses Dinero and Case. He just won't say it."

"Case has even been working at the second tattoo shop just to avoid Keece. I want to talk to him about it, but at the same time, I want to give him some space. I don't think I should intrude on the feud between him and his bros. I think they should work it out on their own." Diar sighed heavily.

"I just feel like they're grieving right now, and once they accept their new reality, they'll be fine," Asia offered.

"You sure are optimistic," Aimee teased.

"I mean they're brothers and family fight. I'm sure this will blow over soon," Asia assured.

"I hope so, because I don't like seeing them at odds like this. They've never gone this long without speaking to each other," Paris mentioned.

"Well, it's not like they're all not speaking. It's just three brothers versus two," Asia laughed.

"I love how relaxed you are about this. Dinero must not be getting on your nerves too bad," Camara teased.

Asia snickered. "He's been cool. Just working hard to open other businesses."

"That's good. Ladies we have to make a promise that we won't let this rift between our husbands and *boyfriend*," Aimee cut her eyes at Diar, "mess up our shit between each other. Deal?" she raised her drink in the air.

The women all followed and clinked glasses with each other. Asia was happy they'd made time to catch up with each other. She'd missed bonding with her crew.

***

Kiyan peered out the window as the leaves dropped delicately from the trees. Fall had quickly approached, reminding him that the grueling winter would soon be on the way. His eyes roamed across from him as Milan and Kamryn devoured their pancakes. Kiyan had picked them up from school and at their request, taken them to IHOP.

Since the passing of Dom and Camara's departure, Kiyan felt so abandoned on the inside. Waking up in an empty, cold bed had been tortuous. He'd lacked proper sleep and even resorted to trying a sleep aide. Kiyan missed Dom so much, but there was nothing he could do to bring him back. Then, his heart yearned for Camara, but things had been so different between them, and he didn't even know where to start to begin to repair their dismantled marriage.

The only time Kiyan had contact with Camara was when it pertained to the girls. Even then, Camara would only text him, which irritated him because he missed hearing her voice.

Now that Kiyan had been forced to be alone, he regretted the way he'd treated her. She had been everything he needed but because of his selfish and inconsiderate conduct, he pushed her away to the point of not wanting to be with him.

Kiyan didn't have much control on the occurrences in his life, but the one area he wanted to correct was his role as a father. He needed to make sure he spent quality time with his daughters and assure them that they could count on him.

"So, I need y'all help," Kiyan said, grabbing their attention from their plates. "What should I do to get your mama back?"

They blinked at him blankly before breaking out into huge smiles.

"You hurt mommy's feelings Daddy," Kamryn scolded him.

He smirked. "I know, and I need her to know I'm sorry. So what should I do?"

"You can buy her some flowers," Milan suggested.

"Um," he scratched the back of his neck. "I don't think flowers will fix it."

"You can write her a letter and say, 'baby, please, baby, please'" Kamryn playfully begged with her hands clasped together.

Kiyan's head fell back as he broke out in a fit of laughter. Kamryn definitely had his personality and sense of humor.

"You think a letter will get her to come back to me?" he asked sincerely.

Kamryn nodded eagerly. "Yes, and buy her some candy. Mommy likes candy, Daddy."

Yeah Camara's ass stayed having a sweet tooth.

"So, candy and a letter? That's it?"

Milan waved her little finger. "And some diamonds. Girls love diamonds, Daddy."

Kiyan shook his head. "Who taught you that?"

"Mommy and Auntie Paris," she grinned.

Kiyan playfully rolled his eyes. "Yeah, a'ight. So a letter, candy, and diamonds are what I need for mommy to forgive me?"

"Yes, Daddy, and you can't be mean to her no more. You always have to be nice to her," Kamryn scolded.

It stung Kiyan a bit to hear his youngest daughter reprimand him for his treatment of her mother. He never wanted to portray himself as a husband who didn't show love or affection to his wife. Revelations continued to smack Kiyan in his face as he continued to bond with the girls.

"I promise not to be mean to her no more. I also promise to spend more time with y'all too. Daddy hasn't been doing a good job of bonding with y'all, and I'm sorry, a'ight?"

The girls nodded with bright smiles on their faces. Suddenly, a memory of Dom surfaced on his mind.

"You sure you don't want kids?" Dom questioned with his thick brows hiked.

"Hell no," Kiyan scoffed. "I ain't trying to be nobody's daddy. Shit, I don't even think I would be a good one."

Dom smirked. "You don't know what you're capable of until you're in a dilemma that would require you to show what you're made of."

Kiyan sighed dramatically. "Pops, I'm only twenty two years old. I don't need no kids ever. I need to be able to roam freely without having any responsibility."

"I understand," Dom noted, "but down the line, it's possible you may change your mind. Having kids means that you're building a legacy. Besides, the love kids give is endless. Your children will love you forever, no matter what."

"That's cool and all, but I still don't want kids."

Dom laughed. "You lil' niggas gon' be the death of me."

Kiyan smiled as he snapped out of his daydream. He then looked at the two little creatures that had come from his loins. He hadn't done right by them, and that fact pained him immensely.

"So where do y'all wanna go next?" he glanced at his watch. "I have to get y'all back to your mama by seven o'clock, but we can go hang somewhere else."

"Can we go to the movies?" Kamryn asked excitedly.

"I guess we could."

Kiyan allowed them to finish their meals. Once they were done, the trio left the restaurant and went to catch a movie. While the girls got lost in the animated film, Kiyan devised a plan to have Camara back in his life. He knew he needed to act fast before she got a lawyer involved. He thought she would've filed for divorce by now, and the fact that she didn't left him feeling like he still had one last chance to proclaim his love for her and promise her a better husband.

After the movie, Kiyan drove toward the studio and waited patiently for Camara to walk out. Usually, he would drop the girls off at her townhouse, but since he was already on that side of town, he figured he would just drop them off there.

"Daddy, can I get in the front seat next time?" Kamryn whined. "Milan always sits in the front."

"No, I don't," Milan countered.

"Y'all, chill out," Kiyan warned. "You can get in the front next time Kamryn."

After a while, Camara emerged from the studio with a girl behind her. She locked the door and headed across the street. Kiyan blew the horn to get her attention. Startled, Camara looked over and advanced toward the car. Kiyan took a moment to marvel at her beauty as she walked over to them. Her short hair was styled in soft curls. Her milky skin was glowing healthily and her face was lightly made up. He licked his lips at her toned legs that were clad in some skin tight leggings.

Damn, I miss her ass.

Camara opened the passenger door. "Girl, what are you doing in the front seat?" she playfully sassed to Milan.

"Daddy let me ride in the front."

Camara smiled and helped her out the truck. She then opened the back door for Kamryn to get out. Kiyan was hoping she would pay him some form of attention. He needed her to acknowledge him in some kind of way.

"Alright, y'all say bye to your daddy," Camara coached.

"Bye, Daddy," the girls said in unison.

Kiyan tipped his head. "I'll see y'all tomorrow."

Before she closed the door, she peered at him. "Oh, I have to take them to the dentist so you don't need to get them from school."

Kiyan stared into her eyes and then his vision landed at her heart-shaped lips. He'd missed every feature on Camara and wished he could just explain how truly sorry he was for disappointing her.

"Um…a…a'ight," he stammered.

Camara nodded, and then closed the door. Kiyan exhaled as she got in the car with the kids. He was so tired of living with regret, and the only remedy that he needed was *her*…his wife…his best companion.

THIRTEEN

Case rubbed his hand down his wavy fade before pushing out a dense breath. He then held his phone between his ear and shoulder as he listened to Celine ramble about things that had nothing to do with her.

"I don't understand why that woman is still living at Dom's house. She was only his lil' jump off," she fussed, referring to Olivia. "It's time for her to get her own place now that Dom is gone."

"Why you care, Ma?" Case asked calmly.

"Because he was my ex-husband, and I don't think she should be able to live in that house because it wasn't hers. I know Dom left a will, and I'm sure he didn't include her ass in it. She needs to go immediately."

Case grabbed a cleaning cloth and wiped down his chair to prepare for his next session. Celine mentioning Dom's will brought his mind back to the last conversation he'd had with Keece.

"Aye, I know you still got an attitude and shit, but Pops left a will, and we all have to be there in order for his lawyer to read it off."

Case twisted his lips. "According to who?

"According to Pops. He gave ol' boy instructions not to read unless all five of us were there."

"Man, I don't have to be there with y'all. Tell him just to read that shit to y'all, and I'll come in at a different time."

Keece smacked his lips. "Did you not just hear what the fuck I said? If we all ain't there, then we won't know what's in the will."

Case snorted. "Well it looks like it'll remain a mystery my nigga."

"You and yo' brother some lil' bitches. Fuck y'all."

"Case did you hear me?" Celine grumbled.

He shook his head, trying to clear his mind from the daydream. "What you say?"

"I said you guys need to get that woman out of Dom's house. She has no right to be there."

"Ma, why do you care? What do you expect us to do? Kick her out on the street because you don't like that she's there. The house is paid for, and I don't see a problem with her staying there. You need to mind your business."

"Dom is my business," she countered.

"No, he ain't. Y'all have been divorced for years. I don't even know why you trying to play this role. Leave that girl alone."

"You know what? I'll go kick her out myself," Celine declared.

Before Case could respond, Diar walked into his station wearing a timid smile. She was clad in a leather coat with fur around the collar, black jeans and combat boots that he'd gifted her for her birthday. Case remembered them because he had paid a nice penny for the boots. Her weave looked to be freshly done with soft curls framing her face. She bent down to kiss his cheek and took a seat across from him.

"Aye, Ma, I gotta go. I'll talk to you later and don't go messing with that lady," he rushed off the phone before hearing a response.

When Case ended the call, he put his phone back in his pocket and stared at Diar. She tapped her pink nails against her clutch while nibbling on her bottom lip. He could tell she had something on her mind because she rarely visited him while at work.

"You have someone coming in soon?" she asked.

He nodded, still trying to figure out what she'd actually come to the shop for.

"It's a long session?" she probed.

"It's some girl who wants her ass done, so it depends," he said with a straight face, trying his best to keep his snicker from escaping his lips.

Diar cocked her head. "Are you serious?"

He cracked. "Nah, I'm just playing, but what you came up here for? I know it's a reason."

"How come I just can't come see you? Why does it have to be a reason?" she sassed.

Case offered her a knowing look. "Diar you never come up to the shop, so stop frontin'."

"Okay, okay…I did come for a reason."

"What is it?"

Diar inhaled a deep breath and rubbed her peach-toned lips together. "I've been thinking about what could've been, and I feel bad."

Case wasn't following what she was saying, so he asked, "What do you mean?"

"The wedding Case," she said with little patience.

"Oh…what about it?"

"I hate that we didn't get married."

He shrugged. "Well, whose fault is that?"

"Not entirely mine."

His brows wrinkled immediately. "Oh for real, because if my memory serves me correctly, you're the one that said you were canceling the caterer and the flowers."

"Yes, I said that, but after you gave me that ultimatum," she argued.

"Well, that shit still stands Diar. I'm not about to get married without a prenup."

Case hated that they had traveled back to that conversation because he was beyond tired of explaining to Diar how important it was for him. He was a businessman and even though he and Keece weren't on speaking terms, he wasn't about to get his brother caught up in a messy financial situation if Diar and him were to ever get divorced.

"You wanna know what bothered me?"

He sighed. "What?"

"I didn't appreciate you listing the house that we live in under your assets. You stressed to me that it was my house too, and I don't understand how you contradicted yourself like that."

He waved his hand dismissively. "You wouldn't have cared about that house after we got married."

"Why is that?"

"Because I was going to surprise you and have a house built for you. You would've gotten a chance to customize it the way you wanted, and it would've been both of ours. But you fucked that all up so it doesn't matter now."

Diar sat silently with her mouth ajar. Not only did she ruin their upcoming wedding day, she also ruined the surprise of getting her a house built from the ground up. Case had even purchased the land and hired a contractor. Once she called off the wedding, he canceled any plans to continue with the process.

"Why didn't you tell me?" she hissed.

"Why the fuck I gotta tell you about something that's supposed to be a surprise?" he raged. "Why you can't just go with the flow? I've always taken care of you, Diar, so I don't know why you made such a big deal about this prenup. I even had a settlement included into the paperwork because if we were to ever divorce, I would never leave you without making sure you were straight. But like I said, that shit don't matter now."

Case watched Diar intently as she processed what he'd just revealed. He wasn't the type of man to leave a situation and not make sure she was good financially. He would never want to do her like that.

"What do you mean it doesn't matter now?" she asked just above a whisper.

"It means that shit don't matter because we ain't getting married anytime soon."

"Says who?"

"Says me. I'm not in the right mind to take your hand in marriage right now. I still need time to get over my pops not being here."

That wasn't the manner in which Case wanted to inform Diar, but since they'd approached the subject of the canceled wedding, he felt it was necessary to be honest.

"I understand," she swallowed hard.

Case couldn't stand to witness the disheartened expression on Diar's face, so he rose from his seat and stepped in front of her. He grabbed her hands and pulled her up from his seat. Diar attempted to turn her face toward the door, but Case gently grabbed her chin and made her face him.

"I don't want you to think I don't want you, because I do. I just can't be your husband right now, and I need you to give me time for that role. But I'm here Diar. I don't want to be with anybody else except you, so don't think we're breaking up because you're stuck with me. No matter how dramatic and extra yo' ass is."

A small simper surfaced on her face. "Shut up, Case."

He softly pecked her lips while rubbing her ass. Their sex life had been scattered and that was mainly his fault, but tonight, he needed to feel the juiciness between her thighs.

"Aye, tonight though," he whispered. "I really need your help to release this stress I'm carrying."

Diar burst into a loud cackle which caused him to smile.

"Yeah, I bet you got a lot of stress, but I'll handle it for you. I always do."

***

"Wow," Asia whispered as she stared at the positive pregnancy test.

Lately, her body had been off and she couldn't quite grasp why. Things that she usually loved, she no longer could stomach. Coffee was the first thing she'd consumed whenever she would awake, but after one cup, Asia would get nauseous. She also experienced back pain whenever she would lie down at night. It wasn't until she missed her period and began to spot is when she decided to take a pregnancy test.

Asia was thrilled at the news of being with child again. She'd been wanting to have another baby for a while now. Mila was growing up on her, and she yearned to have another baby to hold and dote on. Besides, she never just wanted one kid; she actually wanted a bunch of them. Asia's only fear when it came to this surprise pregnancy was Dinero.

He'd stressed several times that he didn't want more kids. He had been so scared by Mila's shocking arrival and heart surgery that he feared having more children. Dinero didn't want to risk having another child with a health condition, so he decided that one kid was enough. But Asia wasn't being fulfilled with his decision and secretly hoped he would change his mind. Now that she was indeed carrying another one of Dinero's babies, she prayed that he would have a change of heart.

Asia quickly collected the test and wrapped it in tissue. She stuffed it at the bottom of the garbage and then washed her hands. Asia looked at her reflection and inhaled a deep breath. She hated that she had to suppress her excitement for her pregnancy, but until she worked up the courage to tell Dinero about it, she had to keep her joy at bay.

Asia opened the door and jumped at the sight of Dinero standing near the bed.

"Shit, you scared me," she gasped, holding her chest. "I thought you were going out of town for the night."

"I changed my mind. Keece and Kiyan can handle that shit on their own 'cause I ain't fuckin' with them."

Asia shook her head at his stubbornness. "I wish you would just make up with your brothers."

Dinero turned to her, his eyes roaming her frame up and down. "You wanna know what I wish for?"

"No, but I'm sure you're gonna tell me."

"I wish you would come sit on my dick before I take a nap."

"A nap?" she snorted. "Since when does your busy-body ass take naps?"

He shrugged. "I need one before I go back out. Aye, don't worry about that shit. Just drop them panties and come do what I asked."

"Say please, bastard."

"Please," he grinned.

Asia couldn't hide the smile that crept on her lips. She sauntered over to him and grabbed his face. She slid her tongue inside his mouth as his hands squeezed her ass.

Dinero pulled back. "I changed my mind. I want yo' ass in the air."

Asia grinned and slid her pants down. Before she could step out of them, the doorbell rang.

"Who the fuck is that?" Dinero hissed, heading out the room.

Asia pulled her pants up and swiftly followed him downstairs. She stood at the bottom step as Dinero opened the door.

"What you doin' here?" he asked, stepping out of the way so Rochelle could enter.

She rolled her eyes as she passed the foyer. Rochelle held a youthful appearance with toasted toffee skin, shoulder-length black hair and smoldering brown eyes. She took off her tweed pea coat as well as her purse and sat them on the couch.

"Hey, Rochelle," Asia greeted, walking closer to where she stood.

Rochelle pulled her in for a hug. "Hey sweetie. Where is my baby?" she asked, referring to Mila.

"She's at a sleepover."

Dinero narrowed his eyes. "What damn sleepover?"

"Her friend from school invited her over for a slumber party," Asia replied with a shrugged.

"Asia, go get my fuckin' daughter and stop playing with me. You know I don't play that slumber shit," Dinero seethed.

Asia chortled. "I'm just playing, Dinero, damn. She's at my sister's house with Lola."

Rochelle smirked. "I don't know why you even play with this ignorant-ass nut."

"Mama, what you want? Me and Asia was just about to fuck before you came over here unannounced."

Rochelle slapped his arm. "You know what? Don't test me because I should be kicking your ass all over this damn living room."

Dinero chuckled. "What I do?"

"You know what you did. Why the hell haven't you been answering my damn calls?" Rochelle demanded.

"Because."

"Because what?" Rochelle retorted.

"'Cause I ain't trying to hear about how I need to talk to Keece and Kiyan. I don't fuck with them including Big so stop bringing them niggas up to me."

Asia sighed because she was becoming so tired of this charade with Dinero and his brothers.

"But y'all are family Dinero," Rochelle stressed. "You shouldn't be beefin' like this."

He shook his head. "They ain't my family."

Rochelle pinched the bridge of her nose. "So it's gotten that serious now? You don't even want to claim your brothers."

"Fuck them, Mama." Dinero said calmly as he took a seat on the couch.

Rochelle paid Asia a frustrated look before she took a seat as well.

"Dinero, I'm having Sunday dinner in a few weeks, and I would like you to come."

"Who all coming?" he asked.

Asia snickered. "You always wanna know 'who all coming'," she mocked him.

"Because if she says the wrong name, I ain't showing up," Dinero declared.

"I'm inviting my entire family, which means all of your brothers."

Dinero rocked his head back and forth. "Count me out. I told you I don't feel like being bothered with them, and I meant it. And if you think Case coming, he won't."

Rochelle slid her elbows to her knees and stared at him. "Do you think your father would've liked this separation between you all? Because I know he wouldn't have. Why are you so angry Dinero?"

"I'm not angry," he denied. "I'm actually good."

Asia shook her head at his stubborn nature.

"Well, then you can come to Sunday dinner then."

"Nah, I'm not. You'll be good without me. You don't need me there anyway. You'll have your two golden boys there."

"Yes, I do need you there," Rochelle hissed. "I want all my boys to come eat with me, and that includes your silly ass."

"Mama, I ain't coming, so stop talking to me about this shit," Dinero snapped.

Rochelle stood with her hands on her hips. "You better not call me for shit, and I mean that."

Asia watched as she grabbed her coat and purse and exited the house. Her eyes immediately cut at Dinero, who sat as if he didn't have a care in the world.

"That's fucked up Dinero. You shouldn't do your mother like that."

Dinero smacked his lips. "I ain't do her like shit. If I don't want to go eat with them niggas, then I don't have to. Don't come at me trying to make me feel bad 'cause I don't."

"Your mother shouldn't have to beg you to come eat with her. She only wants to spend some time with her family."

"And she will without me," he retorted. "Don't start with me Asia."

"I'ma say this and then I'll leave it alone. Rochelle is your only living parent now and you need to put aside your differences with your brothers and spend some time with her. I wish I could get just one hour with my mom and you're sitting here denying your mother some time. Don't do her like that."

Asia turned to walk away before her tears spilled. Seeing Rochelle ask Dinero to come to dinner had her a little emotional because she wished she could have one last moment with her mother. She hated to witness Dinero deny Rochelle so easily because she didn't deserve that at all.

***

Paris shut the driver's door before opening the back door and grabbing her briefcase and purse. She'd just gotten off from work and was beyond tired. Not to mention, she still had to prepare dinner and get her kids ready for bed, so her resting period wouldn't be for a couple more hours.

Paris opened the door to the house and immediately sat her belongings on the table. She shuffled toward the kitchen and saw Kya and Deuce looking in the fridge.

"What are you guys looking for?" she asked, approaching them.

"A snack," Deuce replied.

"You guys hungry?" Paris asked.

"Yeah, but daddy said he was going to order pizza. So you don't have to cook today," Kya informed her.

Is his ass finally trying to be nice?

Paris nodded. "Okay, well, let me get out of these clothes, and then we'll figure out what kind of pizza daddy ordered. Where is Parker?"

Kya pointed toward the hallway. "She's with daddy in his man cave."

Paris turned and made her way downstairs to Keece's personal palace. The TV was blaring as she landed on the last step. She spotted Keece and Parker engrossed in a sheet of paper as she approached the two.

"What y'all doing?" Paris quizzed with her hands on her hips.

"Daddy's helping me with my homework," Parker beamed.

Keece's vision wandered over to Paris. "I need to talk to you."

"About what?"

"I'll meet you in the bedroom," he said dismissively.

She rolled her eyes. "Yeah, okay."

Paris left the basement and traveled upstairs. She hoped that their conversation wouldn't put her in a dampened mood because she didn't have the energy to fight with Keece. When she entered her closet, Paris changed out of her business suit and threw on some leggings and a T-shirt. When she stepped out the closet, Keece was coming into the bedroom.

"Did you tell Riley that you thought it was a good idea that Kya move with her?" he questioned with narrowed eyes and flared nostrils.

"What?" she asked truly confused.

"You heard me Paris?"

"Yeah, I heard you, but I don't understand where that came from. Don't come in here with a fucking attitude 'cause I'm not in the mood."

"Riley called me and said you told her that. You better not had said that shit," he warned.

Paris' lenses held an instant rage as she stared at Keece. Hearing that Riley had lied on her had her way past furious. Without saying a word to Keece, she walked back into the closet and grabbed her phone. She quickly dialed Riley's number and waited impatiently for her to answer.

"Hey, Paris?" Riley answered in a giddy tone.

"What the fuck did you tell Keece?" Paris demanded, avoiding pleasantries.

"Huh…what do you mean?"

"You know what the fuck I mean," Paris gritted, "why would you tell Keece that I told you moving Kya to Atlanta was a good idea?"

"I didn't say it in those words Par—"

"Bullshit!" Paris cut her off, "you think lying on me is going to get you what you want. Why are you trying to cause trouble in my fucking marriage?"

"I'm not Paris; I just thought Keece would consider it if I told him that you thought it was cool. I'm only trying to get my daughter to be with me, Paris. I thought you would understand."

Paris was appalled at Riley's reasoning for lying on her. She didn't understand how Riley thought that using her in a ploy to move Kya away would work in her favor.

"Bitch, you had to have lost your mind, and because you thought that shit was cool, you ain't taking Kya no fucking where."

"What!? You can't do that Paris! You're not her mother!" Riley bellowed.

"Newsflash, Riley; I am her mother, I take care of her every day while you come on whichever weekend you choose and keep her for two days at the most. Bitch, you ain't shit but a babysitter."

"How dare you say I'm a babysitter? Bitch, I pushed that little girl out; not your uppity ass. You can't tell me I can't take my daughter."

"Let me remind you that you don't have full custody; Keece does. What that means is she ain't going no fuckin' where. Now get off my line and don't ever in your life dial my number again."

"Bit–"

Paris disconnected the call before Riley could get the word out. She sat her phone on the island in the closet and stormed back into the room where Keece was sitting at the foot of the bed.

"I just want you to know that you better not say shit else to me."

"Why?" he questioned.

"Because you should know me better than to believe I would even tell Riley something like that."

"Didn't I ask your ass if you said it?" he argued.

"No, your ass believed it. I could tell by the tone of your voice that you believed her. Why would I tell her something like that Keece? Me and Riley ain't even that cool for me to say I think she should take Kya to Atlanta. Did that thought ever cross your fucked-up mind?"

Keece jumped up and bombarded her personal space. "You act like I accused you. I asked yo' ass if you said it or not so you better calm down with all that shit you talkin'."

"No," Paris pushed him. "Your tone was accusatory as fuck. Don't try to switch up now. I'm so sick of your ass, I swear."

"What the fuck you mean you sick of me? I ain't did shit to you, Paris!"

She jerked her head back. "Oh you haven't? Well, let's see, you're introverted as hell now. You barely talk to me and when you do, it's only a couple words. You spend your time away from the house and when you're home, you go straight to the basement. So yeah, I'm sick of your ass being a jerk to me."

Keece chuckled. "Aye, you a trip for real. I just buried my pops three months ago. You expect me to bounce back like nothing happened? Stop being selfish."

"No, I don't expect you to go back to your usual self, but I also don't expect you to just shut me out like this!" she screeched with tears in her eyes.

The distance that was brewing between the couple left Paris feeling inadequate. She wanted to be the person to help during his grievance process. She yearned to be there for him the way he'd always been for her. If he needed to cry, she wanted to be the person to wipe his tears. If he needed to vent and reveal his true emotions, Paris wanted to be the person to hold on to every word that left his lips.

But Keece had pushed her away.

His actions had made it very clear that he didn't want to be bothered with her. Keece spent most of his time either by himself or away from the house. At first, Paris gave him space to mourn Dom's death, but after the third month passed, she felt slighted that he was still distant from her.

Paris shook her head. "I'm done arguing and for your information, I would never tell Riley something like that. I thought you would know me better than that."

Keece didn't reply. Instead, he turned to walk out, leaving her standing in the middle of their bedroom. Paris snorted, frustrated by yet another night of arguing with her husband. A bit of fear crept in her psyche because she didn't see how long they would survive in this state. Paris wasn't used to fighting with Keece like this. They always had an understanding with one another, but now it seemed they had lost focus on what truly mattered.

FOURTEEN

Big stepped into his bedroom and gently shut the door. The room was dimly lit from the TV as Aimee laid diagonally across the bed. Big shook his head because he hated when she did that. He took off his bomber jacket and crawled into bed. His toned arms made dips in the mattress as he hovered over Aimee. His lips met her cheek repeatedly until she woke up. Aimee's eyes fluttered opened as he kissed her lips.

"I need you to get up," he ordered in his deep baritone.

"Why?" she rasped.

"'Cause I need to get away, and I need you with me."

Her forehead creased immediately. "Get away where? What time is it? What about the kids?"

"It's ten after eleven and the kids is straight, baby. Just get up and put some clothes on."

Big stepped down from the bed and pulled Aimee up with him. He could tell she was still confused by the perplexed expression on her face. He went to sit in the lounge area of their room as she took a shower and got dressed. Once Aimee was ready, she stepped over to where he rested.

"I'm ready. You sure the kids are good? I don't want to be worried Big."

He stood, kissing her forehead. "I promise they are. Now let's go."

Big grabbed her small hand and led her out the room and downstairs. When they got outside, the car service he had ordered was parked in front of the house. The driver opened the door for the couple so they could slide in the backseat.

"Big, where are we going?" Aimee asked with narrowed eyes as she buckled her seat belt.

"I told you," he smirked, "on a getaway."

"For how long?"

"Just three days and don't worry, my mama got the kids and Asia gon' come over and help her out. I just really needed some time away with you. Is that cool?"

She grinned. "Of course it is. How long you've been planning this?"

"For a week."

Aimee playfully rolled her eyes. "Sneaky ass."

Big shrugged and held her hand. He'd been stressed but he managed to hide it well. He didn't want to alarm Aimee or his kids so he did his best at moving through life as if nothing happened. But recently, Big felt like he was having an emotional breakdown. He'd become intensely sad which threw his emotions off. Trying to bottle the feelings of Dom no longer being here had taken a toll on Big mentally, and that was the reason for this unexpected getaway.

When they arrived at the airport, Big grabbed their luggage that had already been in the truck. He and Aimee then boarded the private jet and settled into their seats.

"Hello, my name is Charlotte, and I'll be your flight attendant for your flight to Puerto Rico. Can I get you something to drink?"

"I'll take a bottle of water," Big replied.

"I'm fine. Thank you." Aimee smiled.

Charlotte walked away as Aimee smiled at Big.

"Puerto Rico, huh? You better have a bomb-ass bathing suit packed for me too," she teased.

"I had Asia pack you something so if it's not to your standards, then blame her ass."

Aimee nodded. "Oh, I'm sure my sister gon' have me lookin' right then. She knows what I like."

The couple sat in silence as they prepared for takeoff. Big couldn't wait to be surrounded by beautiful, clear waters and a tropical sunset. Once they were clear to roam freely in the aircraft, Aimee unbuckled her seat belt and stood. She sat on Big's lap and wrapped her arms around his neck.

"Are you okay?" she asked softly.

For months, whenever she would ask that question, Big would assure her that he was fine. But he could no longer keep up this façade of being all right. He had to be honest with Aimee, or he was going to go crazy.

"Nah, I'm not," he revealed, feeling like he'd released a burden off his shoulder.

"I could tell, but I didn't want to press the issue. You know I fully understand what you're going through."

He peered into her angular eyes. “I just…I didn’t want you to worry, but I'm fucked up. I keep wanting to call pops but shit…”

Big’s sentence trailed off as he became lost in the thoughts of Dom being dead. He’d had a hard time accepting his reality, especially now that Dom’s presence was absent.

“Well, you know I've felt the emotions you're currently feeling. I still haven’t gotten over my mom’s death. There is no timetable that says you're supposed to get over a parent’s death so if you want to be sad or down, you can do that. Babe, you don't have to be superman all the time. It’s okay to have some days where you just want to break down.”

Big rubbed his hand down his face. “I know, but I feel like that ain't gon’ bring pops back so I don't even bother. I ain't never been a nigga to cry about shit.”

“But you can’t keep your feelings bottled up because it’s not healthy,” she reminded him.

“Do you still cry about your mama?”

Her eyes turned somber. “All the time. I just don't do it in front of everybody. I have moments when something will remind me of her, and I’ll just cry. Or it’ll be her birthday or a special day that makes me think of her, and I’ll break down. ”

Big pulled her closer and graced her neck with a kiss. Aimee had been the light of his life. When their relationship first began, he didn’t always handle her with care. His decision to cheat on her almost cost him his life as well as his relationship with her. After he was given a second chance by God and Aimee, he made a vow to do right by her. Now they had years under their belt with four kids and a tight bond. He was grateful that he had her to hold him down because if he wasn't with Aimee, he was sure to be a depressed mess.

"You promise to always be with me?"

She looked at him. "Always babe."

"Even if I start crying like a lil' bitch?"

She threw her head back, chortling. "Yes, boy. I'll probably love you even more because you're showing me your vulnerable side. If you're going to cry, I would rather you do it in front of me so I can be there to console you."

Big said nothing as he held her tighter. He peered out the window as the clouds skated through the sky. He hadn't cried once since Dom died but he felt like it was time to release his pain. He couldn't keep holding on to the grief because it was tearing him down mentally.

***

Camara sat at her desk and looked over her sale numbers for the day. Her jewelry business had been booming so much lately that she was thinking about adding other accessories such as, designer sunglasses and vintage clothing pieces. Camara had been doing really good at marketing her business with campaign ads that Asia would shoot and also purchasing ad space from popular Instagram personalities. Ever since her split from Kiyan, she had focused solely on her work, and it had shown to truly pay off.

"Cam, you have a delivery," said Tae.

Camara turned around and noticed Tae carrying a huge basket full of candy. The treats ranged from Skittles, Sour Patch Kids, M&M's, and Laffy Taffys.

With her perfectly arched brows furrowed, Camara said asked, "What the hell? Who sent this?"

Tae shrugged as she sat the basket on the desk. "I don't know. The delivery guy just gave it to me."

Camara rummaged through the basket in search of a card. When she found it, she quickly tore the small envelope open and pulled it out.

Enjoy Camara.

"Who the hell sent this?" she whispered.

"Did you get a new boo or something?" Tae quizzed.

"Shit, I wish," Camara snorted. "I could use some…never mind."

Tae giggled. "Girl, I heard that."

Camara snickered. "I didn't say anything."

"Umm hmm. Maybe it was your husband," Tae suggested.

Camara sucked her teeth. "That nigga ain't got a romantic bone in his body. He would be the last person to send me something like this. It definitely ain't him."

Tae snickered. "Well, I guess you have a secret admirer then."

"Whatever."

Camara was perplexed but she didn't have time to dwell on the surprising delivery. She did however grab the box of Sour Patch Kids for a snack. She continued on with her day until nightfall. Camara glanced at her phone and noticed it was past seven o'clock. Her employees had already clocked out so it was just her at the studio.

"It's time to take my ass home," she mumbled.

Camara shut down her computer and grabbed her purse and phone. She exited the studio, making sure to lock the doors. She thought about calling one of the girls to get drinks but her fatigued body made her reconsider. She was tired and in need of a bath and her bed. Kiyan had agreed to keep the girls overnight so she decided to enjoy a quiet evening at home.

When Camara arrived at her townhouse, she went straight for the bathroom to take a bath. After soaking for over an hour, she got out and put on a cropped t-shirt and boy shorts.

Wine would be nice right now.

Camara quickly padded into the kitchen and poured herself a glass of wine. She then went back to her bedroom and settled into her bed. She browsed Netflix in search of something to watch. Interrupting her quest was her phone ringing on the nightstand.

It's him.

Kiyan never called Camara, only texted her. She reluctantly picked up the phone and swiped her thumb across the screen.

"Hello?" she answered.

Silence pervaded the other end of the phone.

"Hello?" Camara hissed with a little more bite to her tone.

"It's me," Kiyan muttered.

Okay… what the fuck do you want?

Instead of expressing what was on her mind, Camara chose her words carefully. "Did you need something? Are the girls okay?"

"Nah, they're good. I was just…I needed somebody to talk to."

She sighed, grabbing her wine glass. After taking a huge gulp, she asked, "And you decided to dial my number?"

"What? Am I not supposed to do that?" he shot with sarcasm.

"I mean," she shrugged, "we haven't been on the best terms, so I didn't think I would be your first choice to call when you needed somebody to talk to."

"I know, and it's all my fault for us being in this situation…but shit…I can't tell the way I'm feeling to nobody else."

Wow is he really accepting responsibility for our marriage ending?

For all the years Camara had known Kiyan, she never witnessed him hold himself accountable for his actions. He'd always blamed her for everything, and it was refreshing to see him take accountability for once.

"You're still battling your feelings regarding Dom's death?" she questioned.

"Yeah," he sighed, "and I don't know how to get over it."

"Kiyan, you may not ever get over your father dying, especially after only three months."

He exhaled heavily. "This humbled me."

Camara pursed her lips. "How so?"

"It made me realize that I don't have time to waste. Even though I grew up with my pops, I feel like I didn't get enough time with him. Shit, I didn't even have a chance to say goodbye to him. That's why I'm trying to do better with Milan and Kamryn. I feel like I need to spend as much time with them as I can. I don't know when it'll be my last day on earth, and I don't want them feeling like I wasn't shit."

Camara closed her eyes, pondering Kiyan's words in her mind. She was relieved that he had finally put his fatherly duties on his priority list because it broke her heart when he would carry on as if he didn't have children.

"I'm glad you realized that Kiyan. Our daughters love you, and sometimes they would ask why you didn't like being with them."

"Don't tell me that," he groaned.

"It's the truth," she shrugged. "I used to have to come up with a story about you working hard because I couldn't tell them that you were just living in your own world, forgetting about your family."

The other end of the phone became silent. Camara didn't bring that up to hurt his feelings. She just wanted to stress how much his absence not only affected her but the kids as well.

"I was fucking up, Cam. I'm man enough to admit that. That's why I'm trying to do shit differently now."

She sighed. "I appreciate that. You had me out here like I was a single mother."

"Yeah, I know...how's the business doing?" he changed the subject.

She perked up at that mention. "It's doing great. I surpassed my million dollar mark already."

"Word? That's what's up. When am I getting back my investment?" he cracked.

Kiyan gave Camara startup money for her jewelry business. He'd stressed that it was an investment and often joked about wanting his money back.

She smirked. "You can charge it to the game, fam."

He cackled heartily. "Damn, it's like that? That ain't how you do business, Cam."

"Well, you invested in me when you were my husband, so you shouldn't expect anything in return."

"I'm still your husband, Cam," he reminded.

"Yeah, but not for long."

Kiyan was quiet as he processed her statement.

"How come you haven't file for divorce yet?" he asked.

She shrugged. "Because I didn't want to send papers while you were grieving. I do have a heart Kiyan."

"I don't see my grieving process ending anytime soon. You should just file and get it over with."

Camara's eyes rolled harder than they ever had. She knew Kiyan didn't care about her divorcing him. He never fought for her and that always frustrated her. How could he be so content with their family breaking up when it was killing her having to send her kids with Kiyan while she stayed at her home? This new setup for them was foreign, and no matter how much she tried to assure herself that this was for the better, Camara still felt like shit.

"It's just like you to tell me to file," she clipped.

"What am I supposed to tell you?" he retorted. "You got your mind made up already. I'm just picking my battles."

"Picking your battles?!" she belted. "How Kiyan? How are you picking your battles by telling me to file for divorce? Make me understand."

"Didn't you tell me you don't love me anymore? As far as I'm concerned, this marriage is over. You don't even love me so why wouldn't I tell you to let go of this marriage and file for divorce?"

"I said I wasn't *in love* Kiyan," she griped. "I'll always love you, but you made me fall out of love with you."

"You need to tell me how you really feel, Cam. I just told you to file because I thought that's what you were going to do anyway, and you snappin' on me and shit. What do you want from me?"

Camara parted her lips to speak but her voice was missing. Kiyan's question had posed a bundle of thoughts to form in her psyche. She honestly didn't know what she wanted from him. Some days, she didn't want him in her presence and then some days she missed him terribly.

Being a fucking woman with all of these conflicting ass emotions is a bitch.

"I don't know what *I* want from you. The main thing I need you to do is continue building your relationship with Milan and Kamryn."

"And I'll do that, but I need you to be clear with me."

"I am being clear," she countered.

"No, you ain't."

"Whatever Kiyan. Is this conversation over or what?"

"Damn, you don't wanna talk to me no more?" he chuckled.

A small simpered graced her face. "You ain't talking about shit."

"Well, I guess our marriage ain't shit now is it. I'm sorry for disappointing you, Cam. I hope you find somebody to treat you way better than I did, because you deserve it. The girls getting hungry so I gotta go."

When Kiyan ended the call, salty droplets suddenly spilled from Camara's eyes. Her chin trembled as an array of emotions ransacked her body. She was so disappointed in Kiyan as well as herself. She hated Kiyan for ruining something that could've been so beautiful. She was also frustrated with herself for secretly wanting them to work things out. But with the type of man Kiyan was, she knew he wouldn't put up a fight for her. He'd even encouraged her to file for divorce which let her know that it was maybe time to let go.

***

Asia pulled into the parking lot and placed her car in park. She turned around and grabbed her bag and mat before getting out the car. A smile spread across her face as she entered the building that smelled like warm vanilla.

"Welcome to Sky's Place. Which class are you here for?" asked the receptionist.

"I'm here for the six o'clock class."

The woman nodded. "Okay, great. The class will take place in studio C."

Asia tipped her head before walking down to the appointed studio. When she stepped in, she noticed that everyone were positioned Indian style on their yoga mats.

Shit, I'm late.

Asia's friend, Sky, who was the yoga instructor, turned her head and beamed brightly at her. Sky waved happily as Asia returned the same gesture while making her way toward the back of the room. She kicked off her shoes, unrolled her mat, and sat down on her bottom. Yoga had been Asia's stress reliever ever since one of her clients recommended it to her. It calmed her in such a way that left her peaceful internally and physically fit. She figured since things had been tensed, especially in the family, she wanted to release some of her stress.

"Alright everyone, we're going to begin in a cross-legged position and inhale deeply," Sky instructed in a soothing tone.

Asia crossed her legs and did as she was ordered. For the next hour, she contorted her body into different positions as she performed special breathing exercises. Once the class ended, Asia felt more de-stressed and calmer as she gathered her mat. She slipped on her shoes and strolled toward Sky, who was bidding the other students goodnight.

"Hi, Asia," she sang, wrapping her arms around her shoulders. "I've missed you."

Asia smiled as she hugged her back. "I've missed you too. I've been so swamped with work and family that I haven't had time to come to class."

Sky waved her hand. "That's okay. Let's go catch up in my office."

Asia nodded, following her out of the studio and into Sky's cozy office. The two women sat on the sofa while Sky turned on the TV.

"So, what's been up? How are Mila and your husband doing?" Sky questioned happily.

"Mila is doing great. My father-in-law passed away three months ago so my husband is trying to bounce back from that."

Sky's face softened immediately. "Oh my. I'm sorry to hear that."

"Yeah," Asia sighed, "it was so unexpected and sad. I'm also the one that found him. Well, me, his girlfriend, and Mila."

"Oh my God," Sky gasped. "Mila was there too?"

"Yes, girl, and she was so scared. Sometimes, she still asks me about that day. The whole family is in disarray, so this yoga class came right on time for me."

"I bet it did. I'm glad I could help you," Sky smiled sweetly.

"Me too, but enough about my life. What's going on with you? How's the baby and your husband doing?"

Sky's dimples sunk into her cheeks. "They're great. We're planning for another baby; preferably a boy because my Ryker needs a son."

"Aww that's so sweet," Asia cooed, thinking of her bundle of joy that was cooking in her belly. "What about your sisters? Oh and your dad too. He's out of jail, right?"

Sky nodded. "Yes, he's been out for an entire year and he's doing amazing. He flips houses for a living and he's been extremely successful. Let's see, Mafia had a little girl with her husband, and Finesse is adjusting to being a wife."

"Finesse is your wild sister, right?" Asia quizzed.

"Yes, but she slowed down a lot. She's been busy with her barbershops and her husband keeps her on her toes. I'm so glad Cannon came around because I don't know what kind of path Finesse would be on if he didn't."

"That's great because I know you used to worry about her a lot."

Sky sighed dramatically. "Did I? She used to stress the entire family out."

Asia giggled. "I remember those days."

When Asia's phone vibrated inside her bag, she took it out and noticed Dinero calling her.

"This is my husband. Give me a second."

Sky tipped her head. "Sure."

"Hello?" Asia answered.

"Where the hell you at?" he barked.

Asia's face instantly contorted into a scowl. "I went to yoga class. Why?"

"Well, yoga yo' ass home and come get this dog-ass nigga."

"Who?" she asked genuinely confused.

"Nero's ass. He just pissed on the kitchen floor."

"Well, did you let him out?"

"Hell nah, this ain't my fuckin' dog," he ranted.

Asia exhaled deeply before rolling her eyes. "What the hell did you expect to happen if you didn't let him out?"

"I ain't tryin' to hear that shit. Come get his ass before I drop him off at the Humane Society."

"You ain't shit. I swear when I get home, I'm going to make him bite the shit out of you," Asia threatened.

"And I'ma shoot his ass…aye, while you out, bring me something to eat."

"Boy fuck you," she snapped and ended the call.

Asia looked up to see Sky giggling with her hand over her mouth.

"Sky please don't laugh at my life. My husband is a real fucking jerk at times," Asia laughed.

"I'm sorry, I couldn't help it. Hey, I'm doing a couples yoga night. You should come with your husband," Sky suggested.

Asia shook her head. "Girl this is my escape from my husband and his ass is too damn embarrassing. He would be acting a fool in here."

"Aww, he can't be that bad."

Asia twisted her lips. "You don't know how ignorant he is. No thanks, boo. I'll pass."

"Okay, well, hopefully I'll see you next week."

"For sure."

Asia stood, throwing her bag over her shoulder. "Let me go because I need to go make sure my dog is safe. Thanks for the talk boo. You know I always enjoy our time together."

Sky stood, wrapping her arms arounds Asia's shoulders. "You're welcome, my dear. Call me."

"I will."

Sky walked Asia to the door. "Have a goodnight sweetie."

"You too," Asia shot over her shoulder as she walked outside.

On the way to the car, Asia's phone signaled she had a text message, so she looked at the screen.

Dinero: If you don't bring me something to eat, I'ma do Nero how Frankie Lymon did in that movie. LMAO!

Asia chuckled as she shook her head. Dinero was always sending her threats whenever she didn't do what he wanted. She knew he would never harm Nero and was trying to get a reaction. Because she wasn't in the mood to deal with his antics, Asia reluctantly agreed to his request.

Asia: OK bastard. I'll bring something but it'll be straight off the dollar menu.

***

Big wiped his eyes with the pads of his fingers and sniffled. He sat quietly on the edge of the jet tub, releasing all the pain of not having Dom around. He'd finally cried. He'd finally showed how saddened he was by Dom's passing. When he felt an ache appear in his throat, Big rushed to the bathroom so he could cry by himself. He was still too alpha to allow Aimee to see him cry. Showing his emotions, in that manner, in front of her was something he wasn't ready to do.

I can't believe he's gone...

Once Big felt like he'd released all his tears, he stood and splashed his face with some water. He grabbed a towel and patted his skin dry. He noticed his eyes were red and a little puffy as he stared at his reflection in the mirror.

I gotta get my mind right…

This trip was strictly for him to clear his mind of his grieving thoughts, and spend some alone time with Aimee. So he got himself together so they could enjoy the island together.

Big walked out of the en suite and spotted Aimee leaning over the balcony as her wild hair blew in the wind. The beaming sun glistened on her skin, providing a sun-kissed glow. She was clad in a teal bathing suit that hugged her curvy physique. The bottom was a thong which showcased her ample ass. Immediately, the member in Big's shorts sprung to attention. His mood had changed instantly and at that very second, he craved some pussy; Aimee's pussy.

Big walked up behind her and fisted her hair. He tilted her neck to the side and kissed her skin hungrily.

"Oh, I see what you're on," she purred.

Big's hand trailed down to her bikini and slid inside. His fingers found her moist clitoris and immediately began to rub it in a circular motion.

"Can I have your pussy?" he grumbled deeply in her ear.

"You know you can," she grinned.

"No, I want it forever. Is it mine, Aimee?"

She turned her neck and kissed his lips. "Yes, baby, it's yours."

Big's digit voyaged to Aimee's sweltering honey pot. He dipped his index finger inside causing her back to arch.

This is why I keep getting her pregnant.

Aimee was Big's addiction. He desired everything about his wife and couldn't keep his hands off her. She carried the best pussy he'd ever sampled, and he couldn't bear going without it.

"Turn," he ordered.

Aimee did as she was instructed with her bottom lip tucked between her teeth. In one sudden motion, Big picked her up. Her thick legs wrapped around his defined waist as he strategically pushed her bikini bottom to the side. Aimee bore into his eyes, wrapping her forearms around his neck.

"You okay?" she asked.

He nodded. "I'ma be even better when I get inside your walls."

She chuckled before throwing her head back. Big slid his shorts down and released his stiffened dick that had been fighting to get out. He positioned the head at her opening before plunging deep inside her soaking center.

"Oh," she moaned breathlessly.

Big slowly slid in and out of her tunnel, trying to keep himself from screaming out. His feet and hands tingled as Aimee's wetness put him under a spell. The same spell that married her, impregnated her, and gave her just about anything her heart desired.

"Fuck," he groaned.

Aimee grabbed his face and brought his lips to hers. He devoured her mouth loving the sweet taste of her fleshy tongue.

His hips moved at a steady pace before he began to rotate them. With each stroke, her center seemed to get wetter and wetter.

Aimee began to counter his movements with her own hip thrusts. The couple moved in sync, becoming lost in the pleasure their bodies were providing.

"The best dick ever," Aimee whispered, clawing her nails into his mocha-toned skin.

Big tucked his hands under her arms and gripped her shoulders. He picked up the rhythm of his pelvis, hammering her sex with such precision. He looked down at his dick disappearing into her wet pussy. Within seconds, the white cream Big loved so much covered his penis as Aimee's legs quivered around his waist.

He glanced up and noticed her face was contorted into a pretty scowl. Aimee's breast had popped out of her top, so Big leaned over and sucked on her chocolate nipple as an orgasm rippled through her system. His speed had picked up. His balls tightened as a chill ran down his spine. Big was near his peak and after four more thunderous strokes, his teeth clamped down on Aimee's nipple and exploded inside of her.

Big held her body tightly as he released everything from his sack. He looked up at the contented smile on her face and burst into laughter.

"Why you grinning?" he asked amused.

"You know why," she giggled. "I really needed you."

Big stood straight and pulled out of her. He helped her down to her feet and pulled her bikini top over her nipple.

"Shit, I needed it more than you."

She peered up at him. "Are you sure you're good?"

He gripped her ass, kissing her forehead. "After the nut I just bust, I feel *sensational*."

Aimee doubled over in laughter, causing him to chuckle. "Okay, Future. Let's take a shower together so we can eat and fuck all over again. We only have two days left."

FIFTEEN

Paris sat in her truck and dialed Camara's number. She'd just left the office and wanted to go out for a drink. Since she hadn't seen her bestie for a week, and her kids were hanging out at Rochelle's, Paris decided to invite her out.

"What's up, heffa?" Camara answered.

"What're you doing, suga?"

"I just got done organizing the new inventory. I'm about to leave in a minute."

"Where are the kids?"

"With their daddy. Don't that sound weird?" Camara joked.

Paris snickered. "Stop shading Kiyan. He's trying."

"Yeah, thank God for that, huh?"

"Look, I called to see if you wanted to get a drink. I need a lil' alcohol in my life before I take my kids on this weekend trip."

"Where y'all going?"

"Well, Parker's birthday is tomorrow, and she wants to go to the National Civil Rights Museum in Memphis. She has this obsession with black history. You know that's my lil scholar," Paris laughed.

"Aww she is so special and such an easy kid. My girls be wanting sweet sixteen parties and shit. Is Keece going?"

"I told him about it a couple weeks ago. If not, I'll just take them by myself. I can use some time away from him."

"Y'all still not getting along?"

"No, but I'm not trying to dwell on it. Do you wanna get drinks though?"

"Sure. Big's bar, right?"

"Yes, so we can get discounted drinks," Paris snickered.

"Yo' cheap ass. I'll meet you there in a minute."

"Okay, bye."

Paris ended the call and made her way to Big's bar. She arrived after thirty minutes due to the after work traffic. Clad in her houndstooth suit and black stilettos, Paris strutted inside. Sounds of Kodak Black's "ZEZE" blared through the speakers as she found an empty stool at the bar.

"Hey, what can I get for you?" asked the bartender.

Paris tapped her nails on the wooden surface. "I need something real nice. How about an Incredible Hulk?"

"Sure. Coming right up."

Paris pulled her phone out her purse and surfed through Instagram. After waiting fifteen minutes, Camara finally arrived.

"Hey girl. I had to make a stop at the UPS store."

"Damn, I ordered a bracelet yesterday. I should've told you to bring it to me," Paris griped.

"Oh, well, the shop is closed for the night," Camara hissed playfully.

"You heffa."

The bartender came back with Paris' drink. "Here you are sweetie."

Paris quickly grabbed the glass and took a sip. Her head fell back as the strong liquor rushed down her esophagus.

"Damn, is it good?" Camara joked.

"Girl, it's more than good. What are you getting?"

"I just want a beer."

"Eww," Paris scowled. "That shit is disgusting. I don't see how you drink it."

Camara shook her head. "A cold brew is good. Just mind yo' business, bish."

"Girl, bye."

The two friends enjoyed idle conversations until Camara confided in Paris about her scrambled feelings about Kiyan.

"So, you don't know if you want to be with him or go through with the divorce?" Paris asked.

"Let me be clear, I don't want to be with him right now. I needed to free myself from his disrespectful ass, but when I think about filing for divorce, I freeze up. It's weird."

"No, it's just that you still love him and don't want to make a permanent decision based on your emotions."

"I'm not in love with him though," Camara corrected.

"But you still love him Cam. Why don't you guys just remain separated until you figure out what you wanna do?"

"Yeah, I guess," Camara muttered. "We'll see."

Paris looked around at the other patrons, before turning forward. Her lenses doubled back when she spotted someone familiar posted in the back near the pool tables.

I didn't even know he was here.

Keece sat in the back with a fitted cap sitting low on his head. She could barely see his eyes but his small nose and bushy facial hair was in plain sight. A diamond necklace adorned his neck, creating the perfect twinkle against his black Off-White sweater.

"I didn't know Keece's ugly ass was here," Paris snorted.

Camara followed her line of sight and giggled. "You know Keece is anything but ugly. Who's that chick at the table with him and Big?"

Paris shrugged, taking in the girl's appearance. She was fair skinned with a thirty-inch weave and long eyelashes that looked as if she was prepared to fly away.

"I don't know who that manufactured-ass bitch is."

Camara chortled. "Now why she gotta be all that?"

"Because she is."

Paris watched with envy as Keece smiled at the woman. She giggled loudly with her hand planted on her busty chest. Paris couldn't stand to see Keece entertaining another woman. Even though Big was at the table, she still felt like Keece was being inappropriate.

It had been months since she'd seen his enticing smile or that deep dimple that sat on his right cheek. They hadn't even shared a composed conversation with each other, and it bothered her tremendously that he was sharing one with someone other than her.

“Are you going over there?” Camara asked.

“No, I'm going to sit back and peep this shit for a moment.”

And that, Paris did. She watched for twenty minutes straight as Keece interacted with the unknown woman and Big. When Keece and the girl pulled out their phones, Paris stood abruptly and strutted toward the back of the bar. When she approached Keece, he stared at her with eyes that didn’t express he was shocked by her presence. Paris quietly took a seat next to him as she glared at the woman sitting across from him.

“What's up, Paris?” Big greeted with a sneaky smirk.

Her eyes cut at Big then landed on Keece who was still a little too calm for her liking. She leaned over to his ear so that her words couldn’t be heard. His masculine cologne hit her senses instantly.

“It’s funny you're over here sniggling and giggling when I haven’t seen you smile in months. What you call yourself doing Keece? You flirtin’?”

He smacked his lips. “Man, gone. We talking about the tattoo that she wanted. That’s it.”

Paris glowered at the girl who offered her a smug-ass smirk.

“Don't worry, boo. I don't want your man,” she giggled.

“Bitch, does it look like I'm worried about your mediocre ass?” Paris quipped. “Don't get ahead of yourself.”

“Stop,” Keece gritted with darkened eyes.

“Stop, my ass,” Paris retorted.

Paris looked at his phone screen and noticed his Instagram app was opened. But something else immediately caught her attention. When she looked down at his left hand, his ring finger was empty.

"Where's your ring?" she quizzed with narrowed eyes.

Keece glanced at his finger. "I forgot it at home."

She chuckled. "Yeah, okay."

Paris stood abruptly and stormed away. Witnessing Keece out and about without his wedding ring caused a sharp pain to shoot through her heart. They always wore their rings and seeing him without his was sending a clear message to her. Paris didn't want to believe their marriage was on the rocks, but what was she to think when he wasn't even wearing the jewelry that represented their union.

"I'm about to leave before I start swinging on his ass," she seethed, approaching Camara.

"What happened?" Camara asked, standing from the stool.

"Aye, come here," Keece commanded, walking up to Paris.

Paris opened her purse, threw some bills on the bar and proceeded out the door. She could feel Keece's presence behind her as she stomped toward her truck.

"You don't hear me talking to you?" he growled.

"Take yo' ass back in there, and finish flirting without your wedding ring," she shot over her shoulder.

"I told you I forgot it at home. Why you trippin'?"

Paris stopped in her tracks and briskly spun on her heels. She cocked her head to see if Keece was serious when he posed that question. Without giving it much thought, she slid her wedding ring off and threw it in the street.

"How did that feel?" her brow was arched with a smug expression on her face.

A menacing scowl surfaced on Keece's face as he stared at Paris in disbelief. His eyes were so black she thought he was possessed by a demonic spirit.

Damn, maybe I shouldn't have done that.

"I should beat your fuckin' ass for that! Did you lose you fuckin' mind?!" he exploded, advancing toward her.

Paris turned around at lightning speed, attempting to go toward her car, but Keece grabbed her and spun her around. He gripped her cheeks between his fingers as his jaw clenched tightly.

"Why the fuck would you do that?" he demanded, inches away from her face.

She snatched her face out of his grip only for him to grab her elbow. "Why shouldn't I? That ring hasn't meant a lot lately so why not throw it away."

Keece roughly released her from his hold and jogged toward the street. He pulled out his phone and turned his flashlight on. He bent down in search of her ring while Paris quietly tiptoed toward her truck and slipped inside. She started the engine without looking back at Keece and peeled off.

Paris knew she had gone too far, but she didn't care. As far as she was concerned, Keece had taken things to a new height when he left the house without his wedding ring. It hurt her, and as immature as it was to throw her ring away, she felt like he needed to be taught a lesson.

Fuck him.

***

Keece was fuming as he angrily got inside his car. Paris had showed her entire ass tonight, and he was going to make sure to finish it. He couldn't believe she had thrown her ring in the middle of the street like it was a piece of garbage.

She lost her fuckin' mind.

Keece understood that she was bothered that he wasn't wearing his ring, but she had no right to disrespect him like that. He honestly forgot to put his ring back on after he got out the shower. He didn't notice that it was missing until he was halfway to Big's bar, and he refused to turn around just to get his ring.

When Keece pulled up to his house, he spotted Paris' G Wagon in the designated spot. He parked his car and got out. Once he got inside the house, he hiked up the stairs two at a time and went straight for his bedroom. When he didn't see Paris, he traveled down the hall to where he heard music playing in one of the guest rooms. He tried to turn the knob but noticed it was locked. Keece forcefully banged on the door almost knocking it off the hinges.

"Open this fuckin' door!" he yelled.

When he didn't hear the response he was looking for, Keece turned his shoulder toward the door and rammed his body into it. Within seconds the door was open with pieces of wood hanging from the frame. Paris was lying back in the bed with her ankles crossed. Keece turned the music off that was playing from the Bluetooth speaker on the dresser.

"Don't come in here fucking with me!" she hollered.

"Fuckin with you? You came at me all crazy at the bar, and then your childish ass gon' throw your fuckin' ring in the street. I couldn't find that bitch either so you assed out. And I ain't buying you another one."

"So what?" she shrugged casually. "I don't even want to wear a ring."

Keece looked at her with so much disdain. He couldn't understand why she was stressing him out, when she knew his mind wasn't clear. Not only was he dealing with his father's death, but he was fucked up about not speaking to two of his brothers. He'd made a promise to Dom that he would always look out for Case and Dinero, and now Keece felt like a failure because they hadn't had contact in months.

"You wanna end up like Cam and Kiyan?" he seethed.

Paris gave him eye contact, and he swore he saw a bit of fear in her orbs.

"Why are you mentioning them?" she quipped.

"Because you creating more problems for me, and I don't like that shit. Stop trying to sabotage our fuckin' marriage, Paris! Damn, you gettin' on my got-damn nerves!"

Her upper body rose immediately. "How am I trying to sabotage our marriage?"

"Because you didn't even have to put on a scene like you just did. And then you throw your wedding ring in the street like it wasn't shit. I honestly forgot to grab mine after I got out the shower, but you just took shit way too far."

"You're a fucking lie!" she raged. "You don't ever forget your ring, but now that we're going through shit, you wanna say you forgot it. Keece, I ain't stupid so run that game on somebody else."

He flicked his nose with his thumb. "You got it, Paris."

"What the hell is that supposed to mean?"

"It means do you. I'm done arguing with you. You can have that shit. I'm already stressed enough."

Keece turned and exited the room. He refused to keep going back and forth with Paris, who didn't seem to understand how broken he truly was. He needed time to get his mind together, and she wasn't helping him cope with any of his dilemmas. He chose to leave her be and try to figure his problems out without her.

***

The next morning…

Keece's eyes fluttered open as he stretched his limbs. The bright sunshine beamed through his ceiling-to-floor windows causing him to squint a bit. He smacked his pasty mouth as his upper body rose up and looked around the bedroom.

"Damn," he muttered, when he realized he had fallen asleep in his clothes.

Keece reached for his phone and noticed it was ten o'clock in the morning. After checking several messages, he slowly lifted himself from the mattress and entered the bathroom. He peeled his clothes off and stepped into the shower.

The argument between him and Paris surfaced on his mind as he hung his head under the showerhead. Last night, he declared he was done with her. Paris' actions had caused him to become consumed with so much anger that he didn't want to speak to her. But now that Keece had cooled off, he wanted them to come to an agreement because he hated being at odds with her.

Paris was typically his safe haven, his peace, and he couldn't fathom spending another day being mad at her. Keece was already in conflict with Case and Dinero, and he refuse to put his wife on that list.

Let me swallow my pride and make this shit right…

Once his shower was complete, Keece got out, dried his body with a towel, and threw on a pair of boxers. He then walked out the bedroom and traveled to the room where Paris was sleeping. He stood in the doorway and found it empty.

"Fuck she go?" he whispered.

Keece strolled out the room and voyaged downstairs to the kitchen. He searched the entire lower level but didn't find her. When it was determined he was home alone, Keece went back upstairs and grabbed his phone. He quickly dialed Paris number only to be greeted with her voicemail. Keece disconnected the call and dialed Rochelle's number.

"Hello?"

"What's up, Mama? Are the kids still there with you?"

"No, Paris came to get them early so they could catch their flight. I thought you went with them."

He pinched his chin patch. "Nah, where they go?"

"Keece, it's Parker's birthday so they went to Memphis, so she could visit the museum there. Don't tell me you forgot?" Rochelle quipped.

Shit!

Keece had indeed forgotten that it was Parker's birthday. He'd also forgotten that Paris told him about this trip a couple weeks ago.

"Nah, I didn't forget," he lied. "Let me call Kya's phone."

"Yeah, okay," Rochelle replied with doubt in her tone. "I'll talk to you later."

Keece ended the call with Rochelle and immediately FaceTimed Kya. After two rings, her cute face came through the screen.

"Hey Daddy."

Keece smiled. “What you doin’?”

“Me and Parker are watching videos on YouTube and Deuce is playing on his tablet. Mommy is taking a nap before we go to the museum. Why didn’t you come with us, Daddy?”

“I’ll be there,” he assured. “Let me speak to Parker.”

Kya passed the phone and Parker appeared. She greeted him with a bright smile.

“Happy birthday, baby.”

She giggled. “Thanks, Daddy.”

“What kind of gift do you want?”

“Uh,” she pondered with her index finger on her chin. “I don't know.”

“You sure?”

She shrugged coyly. “I can’t think of nothing.”

“Okay, I’ll figure it out for you. Do you know what hotel y’all staying at?”

Parker looked at Kya, who then took the phone. “I don't know, but it’s fancy and pretty.”

“Can you share your location with me?”

Keece often did this with Kya when she was away with Riley. He didn’t completely trust Riley so he made sure to be aware of Kya’s whereabouts at all times.

“Yeah, I can.”

He nodded. “A’ight, do it as soon as we get off the phone, and I’ll be there in a couple hours, okay?”

“Okay.”

"And don't tell your mama I'm coming. I wanna surprise her."

Kya grinned. "Okay."

"Bye."

Keece sat his phone down, walked into his closet to pack a bag so he could go spend time with his family and try to repair the breakdown in his marriage.

***

Hours later…

Keece walked into the hotel and went straight for the elevator. He'd texted Kya earlier to see what the room number was to their suite. He rode the elevator in silence as he glanced at the time on his phone. It had taken him three hours to pull off a private flight, and he was relieved that Paris and the kids hadn't left the hotel yet.

Once Keece arrived to his desired floor, he stepped off the elevator and strolled to the suite. He knocked twice and waited patiently for someone to answer the door. Seconds later, the door slowly swung open and Paris appeared. She looked angelic with soft makeup enhancing her exotic features. Her black tresses were styled in waves with a tribal headband wrapped around her head. She wore a graffiti-print denim jacket, white T-shirt, and dark jeans with fringed boots.

Paris' glared at him before her eyes suddenly softened. "What are you doing here?"

"I don't get a 'Hi husband, I'm sorry for acting a fool last night'," he smirked.

She sucked her teeth. "No, you don't," she then stepped to the side to allow him access to the room.

Keece entered and sat the gift bag he was carrying next to the sofa. He turned to Paris, who was still paying him skeptical glares.

"Why are you trying to do family shit without me?" he questioned calmly.

Her arms folded over her heavy breasts. "I distinctly remember telling you about this trip a couple weeks ago. I guess you were too caught up in being an asshole to remember."

He grinned at her dig but before he could respond, he heard little voices yelling, "Daddy."

Keece turned around to see his kids rushing him with their arms in the air. Keece bent down and wrapped his arms around the kids the best he could.

"Y'all missed me?" he asked them.

Their happy faces nodded eagerly.

"Daddy, why didn't you take the plane ride with us?" Parker asked.

"'Cause your mama didn't want me to travel with y'all." he simpered.

"Stop, Keece," Paris barked behind him.

"A'ight, I'm just playing. I overslept, and that's why I came late. Here, Parker." He reached for the gift bag and passed it to her.

Her doll-like eyes beamed as she rummaged through the bag. A gasp escaped her lips when she pulled out a pair of hot pink rollerblades with her face painted on the side of them.

"Thank you, Daddy," she gushed, dropping the skates on the floor and wrapping her arms around his neck.

Keece hugged her tightly. "You're welcome."

"Okay, guys let's get going. We have a fun day planned ahead," Paris announced.

Keece stood and held Parker's hand as Deuce held his other one. They all exited the suite and hopped on the elevator. Keece stole glances at Paris as she tried her best to ignore him.

Childish ass.

Keece rented a truck for them to get around in, so they piled inside as he got in the driver's seat. He cranked the engine and made his way toward the National Civil Rights Museum. Their visit was very interesting as the family browsed through the different eras of the civil rights movement. Keece smiled at Parker who took pictures and schooled them on events she had learned about. He couldn't believe how smart she was at only six years old. Her fascination had come from when she and Paris sat and watched the movie *My Friend Martin.* Since then, Parker had been so into the injustice of black people.

"Look Daddy, that's the bus, Rosa Parks, was told to give up her seat," Parker said excitedly.

Keece smirked. "I see."

He glanced over at Paris, who seemed to be engaged in what was on her phone. The grin on her face instantly irritated him as he stepped over to where she stood.

"Why you keep smiling and shit every time your phone go off?" he hissed quietly.

She rolled her eyes. "Um, do you pay my phone bill?"

"Yeah, I do."

She smirked. "So, what? It's still my phone."

"Me and you gon' have to talk for real tonight. I don't like all this shit between us."

Paris pursed her lips. "Yeah, okay."

Keece chose not to engage in that conversation at the moment. He wanted to enjoy Parker's birthday before he tackled his issues with Paris. After enjoying the museum, they all went to The Hard Rock Café. Keece and Paris played nice for the sake of the kids while they ate. Once Parker was satisfied with her birthday activities, the family traveled back to the hotel where the kids watched TV and Keece and Paris retreated to the bedroom.

He sat at the foot of the bed, picking at his fingernails while Paris leaned on the wall with her arms folded.

"Listen, I know I've been kinda off and shit and you know the reason for that," Keece began, "I'm trying to cope with my loss and sometimes I wanna be by myself to do that. I don't mean to shut you out but I need time alone."

"Why not allow me to help you mourn though?" she asked.

"It's not intentional, Paris. I just wanna grieve by myself."

"Well, it feels like it's intentional. You've been treating me like shit."

His brows wrinkled. "How?"

"By acting like I'm a nobody. Not speaking to me and withdrawing yourself from me. You make me feel like I don't matter."

Keece rolled his eyes at her response because he couldn't understand why she was taking things so personal when he was only trying to figure out how to move on with Dom not being here anymore.

"It's not about you, Paris. Stop being in your feelings."

Her mouth descended in shock. "How can I not be in my feelings when you won't let me in? You need to think before you say shit."

Keece rubbed his hands down his face. "I didn't start this conversation so we can start arguing. Don't start that slick talk with me."

"Don't tell me what to start. I don't know who you think you are, but you're not about to keep shittin' on me. I will leave your ass."

Fury was smoldering in Keece's eyes as he frowned at Paris. She had been reckless with her mouth as well as her actions lately. Her throwing her ring away was the ultimate disrespect, but saying she would leave him felt like a gunshot to his heart. It was imperative that he check her because she'd seemed to forgotten who she was married to.

Keece stood, stepping into Paris' face. He was so close he could smell her cool breath. A bit of nervousness flashed through Paris' peepers as he bore deeply into them.

"You said you gon' do what?" he questioned in a relaxed manner.

Paris swallowed hard. "You heard me."

"Nah, I didn't. Why don't you repeat it," he urged.

She stood in silence, peering into Keece's pensive stare.

"That's what I thought," he spat arrogantly. "I've invested too much into you just to let you walk away. I married you for a reason, Paris, so don't go thinking you can just leave because it will *never* happen. Okay?"

With a bitter nod, she concurred.

"Now, apologize to me," he ordered.

Small folds appeared between her brows. "For what?"

"For throwing your wedding ring in the street. That was immature and uncalled for, and you owe me an apology for disrespecting me like that."

A deep sigh flowed from her lips. "You owe me one too."

"Give me my apology, Paris," he commanded with a little more bass in his tone.

"Alright," she griped. "I'm sorry for throwing my ring in the street. I was mad, but that gave me no right to do that, and I apologize."

He grinned, showcasing a beautiful set of teeth. "Good. I'm sorry for making you feel like you don't matter, because you know you're my greatest blessing. Now here," he pulled her ring out of his pocket. "Put this back on, and never take it off."

Paris smirked as she did what he'd ordered. "Thanks, but don't try to be my friend now. I'm still not feeling you like that."

"I see, but I had to nip this shit between us. Now that I somewhat got you out of the way, I gotta make shit right with Asia because I feel bad for coming at her the way that I did."

Paris cocked her head. "Yeah, you were wrong. Buy her some flowers and make sure your apology is sincere 'cause you took your anger for Dinero out on Asia and that wasn't cool."

Keece smirked before wrapping his hands around her waist and cupping her ass. He kissed her lips softly, provoking a moan to escape her lips. The couple hadn't shared any affection recently and that was Keece's blame. He couldn't deny the feeling he was receiving, and he was ready to show Paris just how much he missed her.

Keece began to pull at the waistband of her pants, but Paris stopped him.

"I can't babe. I'm on my period."

He threw his hand back and groaned. "I don't care. I still want some pussy."

She giggled. “No, Keece. I would feel so uncomfortable.”

“Girl, I don't care about that shit. I wanna feel your walls. Just lay a towel down.”

“No. How about we try in the shower? At least I would feel a little more comfortable in the water.”

“I don't care what we do. I just wanna fuck you real good.”

Paris playfully rolled her eyes. “Meet me in the bathroom while I check and make sure the kids are good.”

Keece nodded before kissing her lips and making his way into the en suite. He was relieved to be on the same page as Paris because he couldn’t take arguing with her another day. He needed them to always be on good terms because if they weren't, his spirit just didn’t sit well.

SIXTEEN

Dinero pulled up to a stop light and looked over to his left. He rolled his window down and gestured for Case to do the same. When Case rolled his window down, he asked, "What?"

"Aye lets race," Dinero suggested excitedly.

"Nigga, I ain't about to race you with this Audi. You know you would win in that punk-ass Challenger."

"Come on, man," Dinero laughed. "Why you won't race me? You scared?"

"Scared of what? You would be cheating because you know you got a fuckin' Hemi."

Dinero waved his hand. "You a bitch, and yo' ass starting to drive like Miss Daisy anyway."

Case laughed. "Fuck you."

When the light turned green, Dinero peeled off swiftly in an attempt to stunt on Case. The two had just come from the barbershop and were headed home. Dinero was anticipating hearing Asia's mouth since both of his phones were dead, and he didn't have his car charger.

Dinero bumped Lil Wayne's "Magnolia" on his way home. When he turned into his subdivision, he turned the music down and slowly drove down the street. He noticed a woman walking down the street wearing a muumuu with bare feet.

"Fuck wrong with her?" he murmured.

When Dinero got a clear vision of her face, he slammed on his brakes and quickly put his car in reverse.

"What the fuck she doing out here?" he mumbled, throwing his car in park and opening the door.

He jumped out the car and looked around. "Grandma Fossil, what the fuck you doing out here with no shoes?"

"Kailangan ko upang makakuha ng bahay," she rattled off.

"I don't understand that Spanish shit you talkin'. Get yo' ass in the car."

Dinero grabbed her elbow and ushered her inside the passenger's seat. He closed the door and jogged to the other side of the car and got in. He couldn't believe Asia's grandma was roaming the neighborhood at night with no shoes on.

"I can't believe you out here trick or treatin' and shit with no shoes on. Asia know you out here?" he ranted, driving toward his house.

She said something in her native language that immediately intensified his irritation.

"Damn, man, somebody could've snatched yo' old ass up. You know that human trafficking shit is real. They don't discriminate and yo' elderly ass would've been the first person on the bus."

It took Dinero five minutes to arrive at his home. When he pulled into the driveway, he spotted a police car parked near his garage.

His auburn skin instantly turned red. “I know Asia ain't got the fuckin’ law at my crib.”

Dinero hopped out the car and helped grandma out of the passenger seat. His keys jingled in his hand as he inserted one into his lock. Once he opened the door, Asia and Aimee were talking to the cops until they spotted Dinero and grandma passing the threshold.

“Lola,” they both cried in unison as they ran to hug her.

Dinero wasn't concerned with their reunion. The only thing on his mind is getting the police out of his house.

“I've been calling you, Dinero,” Asia fussed. “Where did you find her? We've been looking all over for her.”

Dinero cut his eyes at Asia. “Get these mothafuckas out my house. You know I don't fuck with the police.”

“Well, your ass wasn't answering. What the fuck was I supposed to do?” she hissed quietly.

“Dinero, we looked for Lola for almost two hours. That was our only option,” Aimee offered.

“I don't care. Get them the fuck up outta here,” he demanded.

Asia sighed. “Officers, thank you, but my husband found her.”

The two cops nodded and proceeded toward the door.

One of the officers stopped near Asia. “Is she fine? Do you think she needs to get medical attention?”

“She’s a’ight,” Dinero interjected.

The officer tipped his head and proceeded out the door. When the door shut, Dinero turned to Asia.

"Why the fuck I found her walking down the street looking like a damn homeless person? How you let her just walk out the house? You know her mind is old as hell."

Asia smacked her lips. "Mila came up to me and said she just walked out the house. I didn't know what the hell was going on, so I came down stairs and noticed the back door wide open. I walked around the neighborhood to look for her. Then I called Aimee and we both got in our cars and tried to find her. You weren't answering, and I was scared so I called the police," she explained.

Dinero sighed and shuffled into the kitchen but stopped when he noticed Big sitting at his island.

"Who the fuck invited Black Panther to my shit?" Dinero quipped.

Big shook his head chuckling. "You childish as fuck."

"He came to help since your ass was MIA. Why was both of your phones going to voicemail Dinero?" Asia snapped.

"'Cause they were dead, and I ain't have my car charger. Asia you know I don't fuck with Big, so I don't know why you got him in my house."

"Dinero shut up, and talk to your brother. You're acting like a damn kid with all this immature shit," Aimee hissed, guiding grandma to take a seat on the couch.

"Both of y'all gotta go, and take your roaming ass grandma with you," Dinero pointed toward the door.

"Aye nigga, I ain't leaving until you holla at me," Big threatened.

"I bet you my .45 will get yo' ass out of here," Dinero challenged.

"And I bet mine will keep me here. Now, what's up?" Big retorted.

"Babe, please," Asia begged. "Just talk to him."

Dinero gazed at her for a moment before he sighed. He hated being so soft for Asia, but because she had begged him to, he agreed.

"Come on with yo' crispy ass," he huffed to Big, walking toward the garage.

The brothers silently walked into the three-car garage. Dinero turned to Big with his arms folded against his chest and his jaw clenched. His posture was defensive because he was ready to fight at the thought of Big voting that their father be taken off life support.

"We gotta let go of this shit between us. Pops wouldn't like it," Big mentioned.

Dinero scoffed. "Well, we'll never know what he wouldn't like, now would we? Y'all mothafuckas took him off the machine like he didn't mean shit. Didn't even give his ass a chance."

"Pops didn't want to be hooked up to no machines. He gave instructions for us to pull the plug."

"You runnin' with that shit Keece told you? Get the fuck outta here," Dinero waved his hand.

"When have you known Keece to be a liar?" Big questioned. "Shit, all you gotta do is think about what kind of man Pops was, and you would have your answer. You know he didn't fuck with doctors at all. Come on, bro."

Dinero contemplated his words. Dom had always been anti doctor for as long as he could remember.

Dinero shook his head. "I still don't give a fuck. He would've pulled through."

Big exhaled heavily, pinching his inner tear ducts. "A'ight bro. You got it. Now I need us to get over this shit. I don't feel right not interacting with you and Case."

"You miss me gay-ass nigga?" Dinero shot.

Big chuckled. "Why you be on that gay shit?"

"I'm just saying. It sounds like you missin' a nigga." Dinero shrugged.

"You know what? Yeah, I miss my brothers," Big admitted. "Shit don't seem right if we're not all on the same page, especially with Pops being gone, we need to stick together."

Dinero tried to be logical at the moment and get out of his feelings. Yes, he was hurting tremendously without Dom, but he did miss talking to Big.

"A'ight, I'll let it go with you, but I don't fuck with Keece. That nigga gon' have to catch this fade for talking crazy to Asia."

"I feel you, but y'all gotta work it out too. We all need to be on one accord."

"I ain't gotta work shit out. Now take yo' chinky-eyed ass wife and her crazy-ass grandma and get the fuck on. Y'all done stressed me out tonight."

Big jerked his head. "Nigga, I ain't did shit to your funny looking ass. And grandma staying here. She ain't about to have my twins walking down around the neighborhood."

Dinero chortled. "I can see those Bebe's kids running down the street too."

Big punched his arm. "Get off my kids bro. I'm 'bout to bounce. Stop by the bar later."

Dinero sucked his teeth. "Man, I've been gone all day. You think Asia gon' let me out her sight?"

"I mean you figure it out any other time, so get creative."

"We'll see."

The two walked back in the house where Asia was checking her grandma's feet. Mila ran up to Dinero, and he picked her up.

"Daddy, grandma got lost," she informed him excitedly.

"She ain't get lost. Her mind just gone."

"Dinero don't say that," Asia hissed. "I think she stepped on a piece of glass. Lola said she was trying to tell you her feet hurt."

"You think I understood what the fuck she was saying?" Dinero clipped.

"You ain't shit," Asia huffed.

"As a matter of fact, go pack her shit because she going to Big and Aimee's. I'm not about to be pulling up and watching her play ding dong ditch every damn night."

Aimee laughed loudly. "You're so damn ignorant."

"No, I want her here. I'm going to take her to the doctor tomorrow," Asia assured.

"You better do something 'cause next time I'm locking her ass out."

***

"Kamryn and Milan, do you want me to pick out your clothes, or are you guys gonna do it?" Camara asked.

"I wanna dress myself, Mommy," Kamryn begged,

"Me too," Milan added.

"Okay, well, go pick you out something to wear. If I don't like it, I will pick out an outfit," Camara warned.

The girls nodded and ran out of the bedroom. It was a Saturday afternoon and Camara had decided to take the day off and take the girls toy shopping. Since their report cards had come back with straight A's, Camara thought it was appropriate to reward them.

Just as she was about to walk into her closet, she heard the doorbell ring. She shuffled to the door and looked out the peephole. She saw a white man dressed in what looked to be a black uniform.

What the hell he want?

Camara opened the door with a perplexed expression. "Can I help you?"

"Are you Camara DeMao?"

"I am."

"I have a delivery here for you. If you could sign here, I would appreciate it."

Camara grabbed the hand held monitor and signed her name on the line. The delivery guy then passed her a red heart-shaped box.

"You have a good day."

"You too," Camara replied absently as she studied the box and shut the door with her foot. She ambled over to the peninsula and opened the box.

Oh my God!

Camara gasped before she covered her mouth with her hands. A diamond necklace along with a matching tennis bracelet glistened so brightly it almost caused her to lose her vision for a moment.

"This is gorgeous," she whispered.

She looked at the message that was on the back of the box.

I hope to see you soon Camara.

"Now this is getting too creepy," she mumbled, gliding the pads of her fingers over the diamonds. "Who sent this shit?"

"Ooh Mommy, let me see," Milan requested.

Camara held the box up to show her the jewelry.

"Daddy sent this."

Camara smacked her lips. "I'm sure he didn't send this boo. He doesn't do this type of stuff."

"He did though," Milan insisted.

"How do you know?"

"Because he asked me and Kamryn how to get you back, and we told him to send you candy, some diamonds, and a letter."

The candy.

Camara had dismissed any thoughts of Kiyan sending her the candy because he was never the type of man to surprise her with many things. The only surprise he had given her throughout their relationship was a house and that was years ago.

"So you sure this was sent by your dad?" Camara asked once more.

Milan nodded. "Yes, mommy, we told him to."

Camara was somewhat warmed by Kiyan's gesture, but then, she was still apprehensive. Sending gifts weren't going to solve the issues within their marriage. Yes, he was doing something out of the ordinary, but Camara refused to be sucked back in only to be disappointed in the end.

Camara sat the box down and went back to her bedroom. She picked up her phone and dialed Kiyan's number.

"Hello?" he answered after two rings.

"You know sending candy and jewelry won't fix anything between us, right?"

"What are you talking about?"

"You know, Kiyan. The candy and now diamonds you just had delivered to the house. It's a nice gesture but you still aren't a good husband to me, and no amount of material shit is going to change how fucked up you really are."

Kiyan scoffed. "I didn't send you shit, so calm down."

"Bullshit! Milan already told me it was you because you asked them what to send me."

"And you believe her? Why would I send you anything when you left me? That doesn't make sense."

"Maybe because you want me back," she countered.

"Remember Cam, I'm the one that told you to file for divorce. I'm not trying to hold on to you or get you back."

Kiyan's words felt like bee stings against her skin.

Why won't he fight for me? Why is he content with our family being apart?

"Goodbye, Kiyan."

Camara angrily hung up, hating that she had even reached out to him. He always frustrated her with every conversation they'd had. She knew he was lying about sending the gifts but she couldn't understand why. Why couldn't he be open and reveal that he wanted his family back? Why did he have to send gifts when Camara didn't want that? She only wanted him to be a better man for her and their daughters, but per usual, Kiyan seemed to take the immature approach and not be frank about his true intentions or his fuck ups.

***

Asia turned on her right side in an attempt to get comfortable. It was after midnight and she was having trouble falling asleep due to the many things that were settled on her mind. She was still very concerned about her grandma, who was showing early signs of dementia. Before she became a full-time photographer, Asia had worked at a nursing home. She'd experience patients with Alzheimer's and Dementia, so she knew the symptoms, and her grandma seem to be showcasing the same signs.

Asia was also stressed about revealing her pregnancy to Dinero. Hiding her nausea and excessive fatigue was becoming overwhelming. Not to mention, Dinero had begun vomiting throughout the day.

The door to the en suite opened and Dinero stepped out wearing his boxers and holding his stomach. He walked to his side of the bed and fell into the mattress.

"You okay?" Asia asked.

"Hell nah," he grumbled. "That nasty-ass food at Big's bar got me throwing up. I should call the health department on his ass."

I should just tell him…

Asia exhaled deeply before she said, "I have to tell you something."

Dinero said nothing, so she tapped his shoulder.

"Did you hear me?"

"Yeah, I was waiting on you to finish."

"Okay…um…I've been keeping a secret from you."

"Asia don't tell me nothing crazy," he warned. "I ain't in the mood to fight you right now."

Her heart rate seemed to accelerate at his caution.

"I'm pregnant," she blurted out, holding her breath at his response.

Dinero was silent again.

"Did you hear me?"

"Yeah…I thought you were on birth control."

"I was but…I didn't like the way my body felt so I stopped taking it."

"And you couldn't let me know that?"

Asia rubbed her eyes in frustration because she didn't want this to cause any problems in their marriage.

"I mean, I didn't think you would care that much."

"Why wouldn't I?"

"I just didn't think you would."

He groaned. "How far along are you?"

"I don't know yet. My appointment is next week. Are you mad?"

He released a sigh. "I'm mad you ain't tell me you got off birth control, but I'm not mad about you being pregnant."

Asia raised her head to look at him, although they were laying in the dark. "You for real?"

"I can't really be mad. It ain't like I got a hoe pregnant. I just don't want nothing to be wrong with this baby. I really don't have time for that kind of shit."

Asia's face softened. She knew that would be his biggest concern and despite her secretly feeling the same way, she wanted to remain optimistic. She grabbed Dinero's hand and squeezed it gently.

"You shouldn't think like that, baby. I really think this pregnancy and baby will be a lot different than Mila's. Besides I now know that I'm pregnant so I can take the necessary precautions to ensure a healthy baby. I also feel like this'll be a do-over since we didn't get to experience Mila's pregnancy together. I'm looking forward to you rubbing my belly and having a baby shower with the family. I feel like it's my first pregnancy I can really enjoy with you."

"I feel you 'cause we both know you can be real slow at times. I never knew a woman to walk around nine months pregnant and not know it. You gotta be the slowest chick I've ever met."

Asia slapped his bare pec. "I ain't slow."

"Shiiitt, who walks around not knowing they're pregnant? You at the top of my slow list," he cracked.

Asia chuckled. "You know what? Fuck you."

"You know it's true."

"Whatever." she leaned over and softly pecked his lips. "I hope we have a son. I need a little mama's boy who will love me."

"Nah, I'm good on a boy. Give me another girl."

Asia was surprised by his declaration. She thought every man wanted a son to carry on their legacy.

"Why you don't want a son."

"Because I don't need no lil' boy trying to come in my house and take over. I need to be the only nigga in here."

Asia rolled her eyes. "Who says stuff like that? You need help."

"Nah, you need to let this be your last pregnancy. You tryin' to be like your sister and Big? They got Tha Dogg Pound and shit with all those kids."

"Stop talking about my nieces and nephew. I actually want three kids, Dinero, so you're gonna have to give me another baby after this," she whined.

"Nah, Asia, I don't want three kids. Respect my wishes."

"I need one more, and you're gonna give it to me."

"I'll go get snipped behind your back. Don't play with me."

Asia hollered with laughter. "You would do something like that too."

"Yeah, I would, so stop playing with me."

Asia snuggled closer to him. She pecked his lips with a soft kiss. She had been so worried about revealing her pregnancy to Dinero and she was relieved that he had taken the news far better than she had expected.

"Even though you're a pain in my ass, you're *my* pain in the ass. I love you baby." she smirked.

"You think you a joy to be around?" he retorted.

"Yes, I do."

"You a fuckin' lie, but I deal with you because I kinda love your beggin' ass."

"Kinda?"

He chuckled. "I'm just fucking with you. You know I love your Chinaman lookin ass."

***

Diar sat nervously in her seat as she watched Case tattoo. Not only was she in awe by his skills, but the person he was tattooing was one of her favorite rap artists.

"You checkin' out my homie?" Case asked her.

Diar blinked rapidly. "Huh?"

"You feeling Fabian or something?" Case smirked.

Diar smacked her lips. "No, I'm just admiring your work. Don't front me off."

Fabian laughed. "Don't be putting me in your shit either, bruh."

"Nah, she's playing a role. She don't never come with me to tattoo, now all of a sudden she wanna come because it's you."

"Not true," Diar giggled. "Sometimes I do travel with you."

"Yeah, okay," Case spat sarcastically.

She smirked. "You're such a jerk."

The three of them were posted in Fabian's basement that resembled another luxury apartment while Case completed the tattoo on his back. It was true that when Diar heard Case was going to tattoo Fabian, she begged him to come. She had met Fabian before, but she didn't want to pass up another opportunity to be around her favorite rapper.

"Aye, when is your mixtape coming?" Case asked. "You usually put out one for the holiday season."

"It's coming on Thanksgiving. I'm just waiting on the feature from Carti," Fabian replied.

"Carti," Diar interrupted excitedly. "You two on a track is going to be bomb as hell."

Fabian smirked.

"Yeah that's a good look for the Mil," Case added.

"I know. We were supposed to work together earlier this year, but our schedules wouldn't let it happen. But I sent him the record so I'm just waiting on him to send it back."

"That's what's up," Case praised and then glanced over to Diar. "You up next, baby?"

"Who me?" she pointed toward her chest. "You know I can't take that pain."

"Aye, Fabe, you know the way she got with me?" Case smirked.

"How?" Fabian asked.

"She came to the shop to get two tattoos when her ass don't even like needles. Her cry baby ass was acting like she was getting a huge piece, when I only tatted a small ass symbol."

Diar laughed because she remembered making a big deal over the small tattoo that Case had done for her.

"Damn," Fabian sang. "That's love right there."

"Stop telling our business, Case," she joked. "Besides, I had to do what I had to do."

"Yeah, you a real one for that," Fabian teased. "Most girls would think they're too good to go after the man they want."

"So you next, right?" Case asked her again.

Diar shook her head. "No, Case, I don't want any more tattoos. You know that."

"Come on. Just one more," Case urged.

"I don't have anything to get," she argued.

"Let me tat you with something I want you to have. It'll be a surprise for you."

"Hell no!" she bellowed, causing Fabian and Case to laugh. "You're not about to tattoo your name on my skin. I'm not falling for that trick."

"I'm not gon' tat my name," Case assured.

"Diar don't fall for that shit," Fabian instigated.

Case chuckled. "Come on, baby. You know I wouldn't do you like that. You don't trust me?"

She cocked her head. "I do, but I don't like not knowing what you're branding my skin with."

"I got you, Diar. I'm not going to put nothing crazy on you; not even my name. So what's up? You gon' let me do it?"

Diar sighed heavily, considering his request. She didn't like needles and barely wanted to get the tattoos he had previously done for her. But the sneaky smirk on Case's face pushed her to throw caution to the wind and reluctantly agree.

"Okay," she groaned, "but if you put your name on me, I'll never talk to you again."

"Yeah right," he quipped. "But I'm a man of my word. I won't tattoo my name on you."

Once Case completed Fabian's tattoo, he wrapped up his back and then ushered Diar to the chair. Fabian walked upstairs, leaving the couple alone. Slowly, she stepped toward him and took a seat. Case peered at her with lustful eyes as they roamed all over her voluptuous body.

"I'm tryin' to figure out where I want it," he mumbled, grabbing her leg.

"Don't put it nowhere crazy like my neck or face," she warned.

Case smacked his lips. "What kind of man do you think I am, huh?"

Diar chuckled. "You sure you want me to answer that?"

"You sure you wanna talk shit when I'm about to tattoo your skin?" he retorted.

Diar rolled her eyes but didn't respond to his threat. Case pulled her boot off and then pulled her sock down exposing her ankle.

"I'ma do it here," he announced, getting his tools ready.

"It's not going to be big, right?" she queried worriedly.

"Nah, its gon' be small. Now sit back and don't look down, a'ight?"

Diar nodded and did what was instructed. She closed her eyes as she attempted to block out the oncoming pain that was about to take place. When the tattoo gun was powered on, her heart galloped inside her chest.

"Ow," she whined, feeling the stabbing pain.

Case shook his head and continued to tattoo her ankle. Diar winced as he hit sensitive areas on her skin. Within twenty minutes, she was relieved to hear Case shut the gun off.

"You're done?" she asked with her head still tipped backwards.

"Hold on. Let me wipe it off."

Diar waited impatiently before Case said, "Okay, now, look."

She excitedly looked down at her new artwork and saw that it read *C&DD.*

Case rolled his eyes at her silence. "You need me to tell you it's our initials?"

Diar looked at the ink again and a smile spread on her face. "Aww that's sweet, but last time I checked, my last name was Capers."

"It's going to be DeMao though," he assure with an authoritative tone. "Look, I got the same tat."

Her cheeks ached as she looked at the same ink that was on his wrist. “That so sweet, but did I hear you say my last name is going to be DeMao?”

“Yeah.”

“When?” she quipped, her lips pursed.

“When I get my mind right for you, and you sign the prenup.”

“You're still on that, huh?”

He nodded. “Yeah, I am. I need that to happen so we can move on with our lives.”

At this point, Diar didn’t care about the prenup. Case had proven to be a stand-up guy, and she knew he wouldn’t do her dirty if they were to ever get a divorce. She just didn’t want it to curse their upcoming marriage because she planned to be with Case for an eternity.

“Okay, I’ll sign it, but you still have to get me a house built,” she spat playfully.

Case licked his lips. “We’ll talk about that after you sign the agreement. I need to make sure you sign it this time.”

“I will for real,” she affirmed truthfully. “Just make sure we never have to visit the prenuptial agreement or a divorce ever.”

Case leaned in and pressed his lips against her. Diar swirled her tongue inside his mouth, provoking a puddle to appear in the seat of her panties. He pulled back, licking the remnants of Diar’s flavor.

"I swear you'll always be mine, and I'm always yours. We belong to each other so I know divorce will never be a part of our journey."

SEVENTEEN

Camara looked at the address on the invitation to make sure she had arrived at the correct place. She huffed and threw the piece of paper in her front seat.

"Milan, you know I'm irritated with you. I did not have plans in my schedule to attend a birthday party you told me about at the last minute," Camara complained.

"But Mommy it's my best friend. I can't miss her party."

Camara sucked her teeth as she pulled into Butler's Skateland. She parked right near the entrance and inspected the parking lot.

"Why it ain't no cars here? You sure this is where the party is?" Camara questioned skeptically.

"She told me at school that the party's at Skateland."

"Yeah, okay. Let's go in."

Camara, Milan, and Kamryn got out the car with Milan holding a gift bag. They all walked in and stopped at the front to pay for access inside. Once that transaction was completed, Camara and the girls entered the area where the skating rink was but she didn't see anyone there.

"Girl, ain't no damn party here," Camara groused. "Where the people at?"

"Mommy, look," Kamryn pointed. "There's Daddy."

Camara followed her finger and spotted Kiyan sitting on a bench with his phone in his hand.

"What the hell?" she mumbled, advancing toward him.

Kiyan looked up from his phone and smiled. His warm gesture instantly irritated her because she didn't have time for his games.

"What are you doing here?" she hissed.

Instead of answering her, Kiyan landed his attention on Milan. "Thank you, baby girl. You really are down for your daddy."

Milan ran up to him and hugged him tightly.

"And me too, Daddy?" Kamryn asked.

"Yeah, you too," he assured, pulling her into a hug as well.

Camara impatiently folded her arms over her chest. "Kiyan, you better not tell me this was a set up."

He stood, trying to hold his smile. "It was."

"You know what? I don't have time for this. I have more productive things I can be doing than playing with your ass."

Camara turned to leave but Kiyan grabbed her by the elbow. "Don't leave, Cam. Just chill with me and the girls for a minute. I promise I won't get on yo' nerves."

Camara snatched out of his grip with a piercing glower on her face. Kiyan's eyes were hopeful which was something she hadn't seen in months. After a couple deep breaths, her scowl softened.

"Only for a little while," she reluctantly agreed.

"Bet," he grinned, "What size you wear in skates?"

"An eight. It's a shame you don't know my shoe size," she shot in a nasty tone.

"I do know your size, but I also know you wear different sizes in different shoes," he explained. "Why you gotta be so mean?"

She smacked her lips. "Man, please."

Kiyan chuckled as he walked away with the girls following after him. She plopped down on the bench wondering if staying was a good idea. Their last conversation didn't go so well, and she didn't want Kiyan to drain her of the good energy she had left.

After a while, Kiyan and the girls returned, carrying skates. Kiyan passed her a pair while he help the girls put their skates on.

"Mommy, are you going to skate with us?" Kamryn asked.

Camara nodded as she secured her feet inside her skates. "Yes."

Camara stood and skated on the rink. The DJ began to play Cardi B's "Money" as Camara glided around the floor. Eventually the girls along with Kiyan joined her. Kiyan passed her up leaving a whiff of his rousing cologne.

Don't fall for that shit.

It had been a while since Camara had received some sexual attention, and she was on the verge of exploding. Her trusted battery operated toy hadn't been enough for her; she needed the real deal.

Camara shook off her horniness and continued to skate with the girls. Kiyan passed her again but this time he turned to skate backwards as he stared at her. His bedroom eyes caused her heart to palpitate as he grinned at her. Unwillingly, her mouth formed into a curve at his blatant flirting.

"Can I skate with you?"

"Why?" she countered.

"Because…I want to."

"No, go skate with your daughters."

"Nah, I wanna skate with their mama."

Kiyan grabbed Camara's hand and pulled her along as they circled the rink. When his hand slipped on the small of her back and slithered around her waist, a heap of butterflies danced in her stomach.

"I'm glad you came. I really needed to see you," he whispered in her ear.

"You needed to see me? Why Kiyan?"

"'Cause I missed you."

Camara didn't respond to his revelation right away. She was trying to determine how she felt because she had so many mixed emotions when it came to Kiyan.

"I asked the girls to help me get you back, and that's where the basket of candy and jewelry came in at."

She shook her head. "I already knew it was you. Why did you lie?"

He shrugged before positioning himself in front of her and skating backwards. "I needed to soften you up because I wanted to have a discussion with you."

"When?"

"Now, if we can."

Camara checked on the girls, who were having fun amongst themselves, before she reluctantly nodded. Kiyan guided them off the floor and into the area with the benches. The couple sat as Camara tried not to become lost in his hunky visage.

"Listen," he began," I know shit between us is fucked up, and I'll admit that it's all my fault. I didn't handle you the way that I should've cared for you, and I actually don't blame you for leaving my ass."

Camara tipped her head, but didn't reply.

"So...I'm aware that I don't deserve you. I wasn't supportive, and I didn't help take the load off you. I was too stuck in my own agenda that I neglected what was really important and that's you and my kids. The girls actually told me to write you a love letter," he chuckled. "But I thought it would be better to talk to you face-to-face.

"Two things happened to me that made me get my shit together. The first one was when you told me that you wasn't in love with me. That shit hurt worse than a gut punch. I never thought I had pushed you to the point where you stopped being in love with me, but I had to accept that shit, even though it was the most difficult shit I have ever done."

"Kiyan you have to realize that you haven't been good to me for quite some time. Your behavior made it easy for me to fall out of love with you."

"I know," he murmured. "I don't blame you for that cause I was wildin' out. But like I was saying, that shit rocked me but when my pops died, that almost took me out. After he died, I went home and realized I didn't have my family there anymore. Cam that shit stung like a mothafucka. I broke down not only for my pops but for you too. I wasn't shit, and I don't deserve a woman like you after how I was acting, but I do want to ask you for a favor."

Her brow arched. "What's that?"

"Can you please hold off on the divorce? I'm not asking you to move back in, or I'm not asking for you to give me a second chance. I am asking that you not go file for divorce and give me time to prepare myself to be a better man for you and my girls. I know you're probably thinking that I have a lot of nerve, and maybe I do, but I wanna get this shit right because it took me losing my father to realize that nothing matters except my family."

Camara peered at him, admiring the sincerity in his eyes. She hadn't seen this Kiyan in years. The man who was vulnerable when need be, would confess his wrong doings, and pledge to make things better when they weren't right.

"I just want the chance to say I at least fought for my family. I can't let you walk away without giving my all to get you to fall back in love with me. I know I haven't told you this in a while, but I love the fuck outta of you, even though I wasn't showing you through my actions. Just please hold off on the divorce. Give me a chance to be the man you fell in love with."

Camara swiped away a tear that dropped from the brim of her eye. This was what she had wanted from Kiyan, to show some kind of urgency to put their marriage back together. His efforts had been admirable, but she needed him to show her that there was going to be a permanent change to him.

"I don't know Kiyan—"

"You don't have to answer right now," he cut her off. "Just sleep on it and let me know. It's not fair to demand an answer from you now because I know it's a lot to consider, especially when it comes to me."

Her chest swelled with anxiety because getting back with Kiyan was a risk she didn't think she wanted to take. But then again, she still held feelings for him that she couldn't quite expound upon.

"I'll sleep on it," she promised.

He grinned. "A'ight cool. Can we go back and skate now?"

She nodded with a faint smile. "Sure."

Kiyan grabbed Camara's hand and helped her to her feet. The couple got back on the skate floor and continued to enjoy their time with Milan and Kamryn. So much was on Camara's mind that she wasn't really enjoying the outing. Kiyan and his talk had invaded her thoughts, and now she felt more conflicted than she did before.

***

Asia wiped down the white vanity at her studio with a wet cloth. She was scheduled to shoot a campaign within the next hour and wanted to make sure the glam team had a clean space to work from. When she was done prepping the area, Asia walked toward her back drops and pulled the white one down. She was in the middle of straightening it out when she heard the door chime.

Asia looked up and noticed Keece strolling inside carrying a bouquet of flowers. She tried to halt the smirk that was forming on her face but failed miserably.

"What the hell do you want?" she quipped teasingly.

He smiled. "I wanna call a truce."

"Nah, we still ain't cool."

Keece advanced toward Asia and bear hugged her. "I'm sorry, sis. I was wrong as fuck," he laughed.

Asia giggled, trying to squirm out of his embrace. "Nah, you really hurt my feelings Keece."

"I know," he stepped back, handing her the flowers. "Here, I thought this would be a nice start."

Asia grabbed the white tulips, inhaling their scent. "Thanks, but you know I'm not walking into my house with these, right? You ain't about to have Dinero interrogating me tonight."

Keece shrugged. "Yeah, I wouldn't do that either, but I'm sorry though. I was wrong for coming at you crazy. You forgive me?"

"I don't know," she side eyed him. "You were a lil' harsh."

He chuckled, pulling on his chin patch. "Yeah, and I apologize. You know you've always been my favorite sister."

"Bullshit. You told Aimee that same shit; and Camara."

He burst out laughing. “Damn, I forgot about that, but for real you know you my girl. On the real, if you had a twin, I would still choose you.”

Asia chortled, holding her stomach. “You’re so full of shit Keece, but I forgive you.”

“Good looking out,” he smiled. “What's been up with you though? How’s my niece doing?”

“Mila is fine. I've been doing a lot of shoots lately and trying to keep from being overwhelmed by my busy schedule. I also found out,” she paused with a smile, “that I'm pregnant again, but don't tell nobody.”

“Word? That’s what's up. What Dinero say?”

“Surprisingly, he took it better than I thought he would. I guess he’s cool, but never mind that. I need you and your brothers to stop with this bullshit Keece.”

He exhaled a dense breath, rubbing his hand over his low curly cut. “I know, man. My pops would be so disappointed too.”

“Yeah, you know Dom didn’t play this beefin’ with family shit,” Asia noted.

“You know before he died, he asked me to always look out for Case and Dinero. He said because Case was the youngest and Dinero was the wildest,” he chuckled.

“My baby calmed down a lot. He’s not as wild as he used to be.”

“Yeah, but still, I feel like I'm letting my pops down by not looking out for them.”

"Well, why don't you talk to them?"

Keece smacked his lips. "They both stubborn as fuck. If it was that simple, I would've been did that shit."

"Yeah, you're right," Asia agreed.

"You wanna know how pops used to make us settle shit?"

"How?"

He used to make us fight in the backyard when we was growing up. If we were arguing, he would make us square up and settle the shit afterwards."

Asia shook her head. "Most parents don't like for their kids to fight, and your father actually made y'all fight?"

"Yeah," Keece snickered. "My pops was a different kind of father, plus that shit taught us all how to fight."

"So you brought that up to say what?"

Keece pondered her question. "I need your help with something."

Asia's eyes narrowed. "Like what?"

"Bring Dinero and Case to one of our warehouses, and I'll handle the rest."

"You really think Dinero is going to let me bring him to meet you?" Asia quipped.

"Nah, you can't say you're meeting me. Just make up something to get them to the warehouse."

Asia thought for a moment, trying to come up with something that Dinero and Case would believe.

"I don't know what I could say though."

Keece pinched his bottom lip. "Tell them you need an opinion on a building for a bigger studio."

"That might work, but then it might not because Dinero is going to think I don't appreciate this building since he got it for me."

"Man get creative Asia. You know how to shut that nigga up," he cracked.

She rolled her eyes. "Whatever, Keece. When do you want this to happen?"

"Let's do it Friday. I need to settle this shit so we can see what's in pop's will."

"Why haven't you guys already handled that?" she queried.

"Because all five of us have to be there in order for the lawyer to read the will. I tried to tell those niggas that, but they wasn't fuckin' with me."

"Hmmph," Asia nodded. "I'll help you out Keece, but you better always be nice to me from now on."

He grinned. "I'll never disrespect you again."

***

Dinero rested his head on the passenger's side window feeling the nauseous sensation take over his upper body. His sickness had traveled well into the afternoon, and he was already over it.

"This why I didn't want to get you pregnant again," he complained.

Asia glanced at him before returning her sight on the road. "Because you're sick?"

"Hell yeah. Why the fuck do I get sick when yo' ass is the one pregnant? This is the most stupidest shit I ever been through."

Asia snickered. "I'm sorry, baby. I have no control over that."

He cut his eyes at her. "Where the fuck we going anyway? I got shit to do."

"I told you I wanted to show you this building for my second studio."

"What's wrong with the one I bought you?" he quipped, his eyes searing into her.

"There's nothing wrong, baby. I actually love that space. I was looking into this one to possibly do some sets for photoshoots and videos. I would never get rid of the studio you bought me."

Dinero didn't respond to her right away. After moments of silence, he said, "You better had said the right thing."

"Whatever."

"Aye, what the doctor said when you took Grandma Fossil?"

Asia smacked her lips, making a left turn. "Can you stop calling her that?"

"What's wrong with the name? She looks like one of those dinosaur fossils on the discovery channel."

"No the fuck she doesn't. For your information, the doctor is going to perform some tests because I'm concerned she entering into the early stages of dementia. She's extremely forgetful and doesn't remember simple tasks. Also, the wandering has me concerned because she never did that before."

"Yeah, and don't let her ass babysit Mila either. Shit, she'll be all on Center Street with my damn baby walking around like a fuckin' hobo."

Asia tried to keep her laughter in but failed miserably, causing Dinero to smirk. "You're such an asshole."

"You know I'm speaking the truth."

Dinero and Asia continued their idle chat until she pulled up to what looked to be a warehouse. He glanced to the right of him and noticed Case parked inside his car.

"Why Case here?" he questioned immediately.

"Because I asked him to come," she replied, taking off her seatbelt.

Dinero's antennas were up and he automatically knew Asia was up to something. "Why you asked him to come?"

"Dinero, can you just get out the car please?" she hissed, opening the door and stepping out the car.

Dinero grumbled obscenities as he opened the door. When he stepped out the car, Case did the same and strolled over to them.

"I didn't know you were coming," Case mentioned.

"I ain't know either. Asia on some funny shit, and I'ma smack her ass if she don't tell me what's up."

Asia grinned sneakily. "Dinero, just trust me. Now let me show you two the property."

Dinero and Case reluctantly followed Asia to the door. Dinero opened the door first and stopped in his tracks when he noticed Keece, Kiyan, and Big sitting at a brown wooden table. Dinero immediately turned to Asia.

"You set me up?" he quizzed with narrowed eyes.

She chuckled nervously. "I wouldn't say that but Keece did ask me to get you two here so you can resolve your issues."

Case smacked his lips.

"Remind me when I get home to slap the shit outta you. You know I don't fuck with him," Dinero gritted, returning his glare on Keece.

"Boy you ain't gon' do shit. Now make up with your brothers, and I'll make sure," she leaned toward his ear, "to have something real slippery for you tonight," she whispered.

Dinero's manhood seemed to twitch at her promise. "Yeah, and I want that mouth too."

Case snickered, shaking his head.

"Okay. I'll wait for you in the car."

"Nah, go home," Dinero ordered. "I'll have Case drop me off."

Asia nodded, kissed his lips, and exited the warehouse. Dinero and Case slowly advanced toward the table and took a seat. The space was silent as Dinero attempted to control the anger brewing inside him.

"We gotta end this shit," Keece stated.

Dinero glanced at Kiyan, who was slouched in the chair. "Kiy, I heard Cam left yo' ass," he smirked. "Good for her."

Case chuckled lightly as Big shook his head.

"Don't worry about my marriage, fuck boy," Kiyan retorted.

Dinero's cold stare returned on Keece. "I ain't tryin' to hear that shit you spittin'. You crossed the line when you came at my wife crazy."

"I already apologized to Asia," Keece spoke coolly.

"Nigga, you ain't apologize to me," Dinero seethed.

Keece sat up straight, his hand resting in front of him on the table. "Is that what you want? An apology?"

"I think we both deserve an apology," Case spoke up.

Keece quickly peered at Case. "For what?"

Case leaned on the table with his elbows. "For being so fucking dismissive to us the night pops passed. I hated that you made a decision and wouldn't consider me and Dinero. There was no compromise with you and that shit was fucked up. Me and Dinero weren't ready to let go, and instead of you trying to meet us in the middle, you made a decision without trying to understand our grief. Yeah y'all took that punk-ass vote but you already had your mind made up to take him off."

Everyone was quiet, awaiting Keece's response. Dinero was glad Case told Keece about his shit because he didn't like the way he handled them at the hospital. Granted, Dinero would've told Keece off in a much graphic way, but nonetheless, he was glad Case told him.

"You're right," Keece agreed, "I should've been more opened to how y'all was feeling at the time. I apologize."

"Did you know pops was going to die?" Dinero quizzed.

Keece began to speak but he stopped. Dinero's anxiety skyrocketed as he awaited Keece's reply.

"I didn't know he was going to die, but weeks before he did, I went to see him, and he was talking different," Keece revealed.

"Like what?" Case asked.

Keece shook his head visibly confused by the memory. "He asked me to look out for you and Dinero whenever he dies. And then he told me if he was ever in a coma to pull the plug. That shit was weird."

Dinero's brows furrowed. "You ain't ask him why he said that?"

Keece nodded. "Yeah, I did, but he told me he was good. Even though I thought that shit was crazy, I took his word and dropped the issue."

"You see, Dinero and Case, pops didn't want to be on no fuckin' life support," Kiyan shot.

"Why because Keece said so?" Case quipped.

"You think I would lie about that?" Keece challenged.

"We don't give a fuck," Dinero interjected. "You could've kept him on for a couple days before y'all niggas just killed him."

Big groaned. “Come on y’all, this shit don't even matter right now. What's done is done.”

“Dinero, we can square up if that would make you feel better,” Keece offered.

Dinero chuckled. “Square up? Nigga we ain't teenagers no more. I’ll pop the fuck outta you. Besides, I might throw up on yo’ bitch-ass right now.”

Case guffawed as Keece smirked.

“You'll shoot me? Your brother?” Keece asked in disbelief.

“Yep,” Dinero confirmed, “and go home, eat a nice meal, and fuck Asia like I ain't did shit.”

“Silly ass nigga,” Big mumbled.

Keece released a deep breath. “A’ight, I'm not in the mood to fight with y’all no more. Pops would be pissed if he knew we ain't spoken in four months. Let’s end this shit, so we can mourn together.”

Keece held his hand out for a shake. Case and Dinero looked at each other briefly before Case reached his hand out and shook his brother’s hand. Keece then extended his hand toward Dinero.

Dinero leaned back, interlocking his fingers behind his head. With a smirk gracing his face, he said, “I don't shake hands.”

Keece burst out laughing while rolling his eyes. “Fuckin’ bitch.”

“So this beef shit over right?” Big asked.

Case nodded while Dinero shrugged. “Once I get over this sick shit, I'm beating yo’ ass Keece.”

“I’ll be waiting,” Keece assured.

“Now that this shit is out the way, I need y’all niggas to help me get my wife back home,” Kiyan expressed.

“Tell us what made her leave,” Case commanded.

“A’ight, so, I was on some bullshit…”

The brothers began to listen to Kiyan pour his heart out about Camara leaving him. Dinero didn’t feel sorry because Kiyan had treated her like shit, but he too was in the dog house once before so he decided not to be too hard on him. Although he would never admit this publicly, he felt good being back in the presence of all of his brothers. Deep down, Dinero knew Dom would be disappointed with their behavior, and he didn’t want to live knowing his father was looking down on him not pleased with his behavior.

EIGHTEEN

TWO WEEKS LATER...

Keece glanced at the time on his phone screen and then relaxed in his seat. He'd finally gathered all of his brothers for the reading of Dom's will. He had been anxiously thinking about what Dom had left to them. He also wondered if Dom provided any clues to his untimely demise. Every night when he laid down, Keece often replayed the last conversation he'd had between him and Dom, and a part of him felt like he knew his time was coming to an end.

"Where the fuck ol' boy at? Fuck, I got shit to do," Dinero complained.

They had been waiting for over thirty minutes and Keece was even becoming quite impatient.

"He said our appointment was at 11:30," Big noted, glancing at his Audemar Piguet.

"So dude was pop's lawyer?" Kiyan asked Keece.

Keece tipped his head. "Yeah at the funeral he introduced himself and told me about the will."

Seconds later, a man with mahogany-toned skin, a bald head and full beard entered the office. He was decked out in a cool grey suit and shiny black shoes.

"Good morning, gentlemen. My name is Evan, and I apologize for my tardiness. I had a meeting that ran a little late," he expressed before sitting behind an oak desk.

“Damn,” Dinero huffed. “You had us waiting like we ain't got shit to do. Coming in here with that big ass Bernie Mac suit on.”

Case snickered as Big and Kiyan shook their heads with grins on their faces.

Keece covered his eyes as he chuckled. “Bro, chill.”

Dinero cut his eyes at Keece before waving his hand dismissively.

“Again, I apologize. Shall we start?” Evan asked.

Keece bowed his head.

“Okay, let me first say that Dominic was a brilliant man, and I had the pleasure of being his attorney for almost twelve years. Normally, we don't read off a will in such dramatic fashion, but Dom wanted me to handle his last wishes and also instructed me to read it to you guys. He’d prepared this will over a year ago before he was diagnosed with heart disease.”

Keece’s eyes quickly fell on Big’s and then trailed over to Dinero who held the same perplexed expression as him.

“He had heart disease?” Case asked with a pained tone.

“Yes, you guys didn’t know?” Evan questioned.

“Nah, we didn’t,” Keece uttered.

“He didn’t say shit about being diagnosed with anything. This is fucked up,” Kiyan scoffed.

“Well, I'm sorry to hear that gentlemen. I'm sure he had his reasons from keeping his diagnosis from you all.”

The room was so quiet you could hear a mouse tiptoe. Keece was bothered that Dom had withheld the status of his health. He knew his father was a man that didn't believe in doctors, but he wished he had attempted to establish some kind of care so that he could still be with them.

"Okay, let's begin. Which one of you guys is Kiyan?" Evan asked.

Kiyan raised his hand.

"Okay, Dom wants you to have his summer lake house as well as five million dollars. Out of that five million dollars, you must open a trust fund for your two children in the amount of one million each."

"Damn," Kiyan uttered.

"Okay next is Keece. Your father wants you to continue as leader of the construction company. He leaves his house in The Hamptons and he also left you six million dollars. Just like Kiyan, you have to establish a trust fund for your three children in the amount of one million dollars each."

Keece's chest swelled with a feeling he couldn't quite grasp. He was overjoyed that Dom had thought about his children and wanted them to have money for their future.

Evan glanced down at the paper. "Which one of you is Dakaden?"

"That's me," Big spoke up.

"Okay, your father wants you to take over his tow trucking business. He also left the sum of seven million dollars. You must open a trust fund for your four children in the amount of one million each."

"Damn, how Big get all that damn money?" Dinero fussed.

"Obviously, he got the most kids," Keece pointed.

"That's bullshit," Dinero retorted.

"Stop hating," Big laughed. "I'm still left with the same amount as Keece and Kiyan."

"Okay, let's move on to Dinero which must be you," Evan said with a smile.

Dinero said nothing as he folded his arms over his chest.

"Okay, Dinero, your father leaves behind his '69 Chevelle and '84 Monte Carlo. You will be awarded the sum of five million dollars and you're also instructed to establish a trust fund for your daughter in the amount of one million dollars."

Keece rolled his eyes as Dinero smiled. "Yo' lucky ass. He really left you the MC."

Dinero grinned. "Yeah, pops loved me the most."

The room was filled with grunts and lip smacking as Dinero gloated.

Evan smiled. "Okay and that leaves Case. Dom wants you to obtain ownership to his property in Hawaii, and he also left you five million dollars. He wants you to establish a trust fund whenever you decide to have children in the amount of one million dollars."

Dinero smacked his lips. "So he get a whole five milli to himself?!"

Case snickered. "Looks like pops loved me the most."

Keece and Kiyan laughed at Dinero's expense.

"Watch this nigga not have kids on purpose and shit," Dinero cracked, causing the room to erupt in laughter."

"I have more," Evan added. "To Olivia, he leaves behind his main property here in Milwaukee and also two hundred and fifty thousand dollars. He wants you all to have equal shares in the construction company also, Dom listed for a woman named, Rochelle, to obtain one million dollars."

Keece's eyebrows rose in disbelief. "Rochelle? Are you sure it says that?"

Evan looked at the paper before nodding. "Yes, it states the name Rochelle."

"Damn, pops looked out for mama," Kiyan noted.

"She ain't gon' take it though," Dinero chimed in.

Keece shrugged "Probably not. Is that it?"

"Yes," Evan smiled. "That concludes the reading of the will. Do you have any questions?"

"Yeah, um, I gotta baby on the way. Can you edit that shit and add another million?" Dinero asked.

"Nah, nigga, used the other four million you got left," Kiyan shot.

Dinero smacked his lips. "Mind yo' damn business Kiyan."

Keece shook his head and extended his hand. "Thanks for your time." he shook Evan's hand.

"No problem. I wish you all good luck in your future endeavors." Evan spoke genuinely.

The DeMao crew stood and shook Evan's hand before filing out of the office. Keece had been filled with anxiety over the reading of Dom's will, but now the relieving sensation that was coursing through his body felt good.

"Aye, I'm about to call mama and tell her about the money," Dinero said, pulling out his phone.

The men stopped in the middle of the hallway as Dinero put the call on speaker phone. After three rings, Rochelle answered.

"What the hell you want?" she quipped.

"Mama, you still mad at me?" Dinero laughed.

"I don't deal with sons like you. Now what do you want?"

"What you do to mama?" Kiyan asked.

Dinero snorted. "I ain't do shit. Aye, mama I got three things that'll make you happy with me."

"Mmh hmm," she grunted. "What is it?"

"Well, for one, I'm still fine than a mothafucka," Dinero bragged.

Keece smacked his lips. "You ugly as fuck."

"Quit hatin'," Dinero retorted.

"Boy that ain't gon' cheer me up. Now what's next with your funky ass?" Rochelle hissed.

"A'ight, but for real. Asia is pregnant again."

"Aww, really," Rochelle gushed, "I'm so happy because I didn't want Mila to be the only child."

"Damn, I thought you ain't want no more kids?" Case asked.

"Asia trapped me," Dinero replied.

"Asia ain't trapped shit," Rochelle laughed. "Stop lying on my girl."

"Man, she did, but check this out. We just left from reading pop's will and guess what?"

"What?" Rochelle quizzed.

"He left you a million dollars."

The phone was quiet, prompting everyone to look at the screen to make sure she was still on the line."

"Mama, you heard me?" Dinero asked.

"Are you lying to me?" she questioned skeptically.

"Nah, Mama, he really left you a million dollars," Keece reiterated.

"Why? Is this a joke?" she asked still unsure.

"Nah, it ain't no joke," Dinero snorted. "Listen, I know you ain't gon' accept it so send it my way and I'll make good use of it."

"You must be crazy. His evil ass owes me so please believe that money will be mine. Shit, Dom owes me more than that if you ask me."

Keece and Big chuckled at her response. Keece thought his mother would be crazy to turn down a million dollars; even if it was from Dom.

"Well, a'ight, Mama, I was just letting you know what was up. I'll hit you later," Dinero assured.

"So that means you'll be here on Sunday for dinner?" she questioned.

"Yeah, I got you," Dinero assured.

"Okay, cool. Bye, baby."

Dinero ended the call and looked at everybody before he said, "A'ight, lunch on Case since he got the most money out of all us."

Case snorted. "I ain't paying for y'all big grown asses."

"Yes, the fuck you are or we gon' jump yo' bitch-ass," Keece threatened.

Case smirked. "Fuck y'all," he spat, and broke out running toward the door with the stairs.

All the brothers ran after him, chasing him all the way to the lobby and catching him in the parking lot.

EPILOGUE

SIX MONTHS LATER...

Loud banter and joyful chatter filled the room as family gathered to celebrate Case and Diar's upcoming nuptials. Their wedding was scheduled to take place the following day and since the couple had opted out of having a wedding party, they gathered their families for an intimate dinner.

Diar smiled at Stefani and her long-time boyfriend, Dash, as they flirted with each other. She cleared her throat to get the two's attention.

"Dash, how you gon' let me get married before my big sister?" Diar teased.

He smiled brightly, showcasing the most perfect set of teeth she'd ever seen. He stroked his full beard as he glanced at Stefani. "That's a question you need to ask your sister, Diar."

Diar quickly looked at Stefani who was gulping down a glass of wine.

"I'm waiting, sis," Diar sassed.

"Yeah me too," Kayla chimed in, seated next to Dash.

"Don't worry about what I do within my relationship. The end," Stefani quipped.

Diar twisted her lips. "'You're lucky I'm preoccupied with my own nuptials because I would hound you for more."

"Whatever."

On the other side of the room, Kiyan stared at Camara as she placed a wine glass to her shiny lips, and softly sipped on the alcoholic beverage.

He leaned in closer to her ear. "You look really pretty, Cam," he whispered.

She smiled bashfully. "Thanks, Kiyan."

"Aye, I was wondering if... I can come in when I drop you off tonight?"

She shot him a side eye. "Why?"

"Because I wanna spend some time with you by myself. I ain't on no funny shit if that's what you're thinking."

Camara rolled her eyes. "I don't know Kiyan. You know me and you are just friends right now."

Kiyan grinned. "Married friends, but I understand. Just think about it."

Camara nodded and took a sip of her wine.

Paris leaned over toward Camara's ear. "Stop trying to play hard to get."

"I'm not playing. Kiyan is gonna have to work for me. Do you not remember how much of a bitch-ass nigga he was? Paris don't get soft on me now."

Paris cocked her head. "I know, Cam, he was terrible but he's been working six hard months, and it's time to pay up."

"Pay up what?" Camara quipped.

"Some of that cat. You know you need some dick," Paris accused.

Camara snickered. “I do, but I gotta make sure he stays this nice sweet man he’s transformed into. He’s not going to get me with the okie doke again. I deserve better.”

“I feel you, but it wouldn’t hurt to let him put an arch in your back,” Paris laughed.

Camara chortled. “I hate you. Worry about Daddy Keece putting it down, and stay out my business.”

“Oh you know my honey leaves me satisfied. Now it’s time to let Kiyan do his job.”

“Whatever you say Paris.”

***

“Sister, you're about to pop soon,” Aimee gushed. “I can’t wait to meet my new niece. It’s amazing to see your belly this big but when you were pregnant with Mila, your stomach was flat as hell.”

Asia rubbed her protruding belly. “I know girl. I'm counting down the next four weeks until my lil’ pumpkin arrives.”

Aimee rubbed her stomach but Dinero smacked her hand away.

“What the fuck?” Aimee quipped.

“Don't touch her,” Dinero commanded. “I don't want you passing those annoying ass spirits to my damn baby.”

“Boy, this is my fuckin’ sister. I can touch her when I feel like it,” Aimee retorted. “If you keep fuckin’ with me, I’m going to pull my taser out on your ass.”

"Nigga, don't smack my wife's hand no more either," Big threatened.

Dinero sucked his teeth before looking at Keece. "Aye, bro, handle my light work for me," he joked, pointing toward Big.

"I ain't in that shit," Keece laughed.

"I knew you was a bitch," Dinero scoffed.

Asia laughed. "Dinero, don't start showing out. Diar's family is going to think you're crazy in this restaurant."

Dinero snorted. "Fuck them. Miss Daisy's people look slow, just like her ass."

"Stop," she whispered harshly. "Don't be rude."

He glanced down at her and sighed. "A'ight, I'll try to be chill tonight."

She kissed his lips. "Thank you."

A glass chiming interrupted the chitchat in the room. Case stood, wearing a black dress shirt, Tom Ford printed jacket, and black slacks. He looked quite debonair as he licked his lips and inserted his right hand in his pocket.

"I just wanted to thank you all for coming out to celebrate me and Diar's union. This has been a long journey for us, and I'm glad we've finally made it to the finish line."

A couple people oohed and awed as Diar blushed.

"It was a rough year for me because of the passing of my father, but Diar held me down as well as my other family members, and I'll always appreciate you all for that." He looked over at Diar. "I love this girl with all my heart, and even though she made things a little difficult for me with this wedding situation, I still wouldn't want to be in this thing called life without her. So I want to dedicate this toast to my future wife."

Everyone raised their glasses and clinked them with one another. Case bent down and kissed Diar's lips passionately.

"You know you're stuck, right?" he whispered.

Diar giggled, holding the sides of his face. "Is that so?"

"Yeah, now that you signed the prenup, I ain't never letting you go anywhere," he chuckled.

Diar smiled. "I didn't plan to baby. I'm yours forever."

The end.

CPSIA information can be obtained
at www.ICGtesting.com
Printed in the USA
LVHW052200060219
606615LV00017B/314/P

9 781791 779801